When a Brown Girl Flees

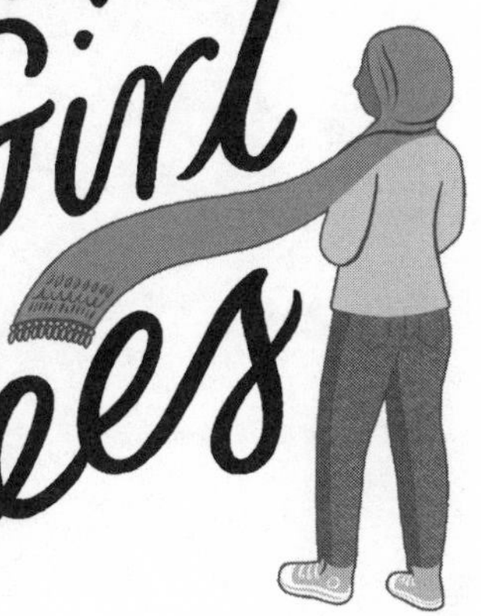

Aamna Qureshi

When a Brown Girl Flees

Tu Books
An imprint of LEE & LOW BOOKS INC.
New York

TU BOOKS, *an imprint of* LEE & LOW BOOKS INC.
95 Madison Avenue, New York, NY 10016
leeandlow.com

Manufactured in the United States of America
Printed on paper from responsible sources

SUSTAINABLE FORESTRY INITIATIVE   Certified Sourcing
www.sfiprogram.org
SFI-01681

The text paper is SFI certified.

Edited by Elise McMullen-Ciotti and Stacy Whitman
Book design and spot art by Sheila Smallwood
Typesetting by ElfElm Publishing
Book production by The Kids at Our House
The text is set in Adobe Caslon Pro
10 9 8 7 6 5 4 3 2 1
First Edition

Library of Congress Cataloging-in-Publication Data
Names: Qureshi, Aamna, 1999– author.
Title: When a brown girl flees / Aamna Qureshi.
Description: First edition. | New York : Tu Books, an imprint of Lee & Low Books
   Inc., 2023. | Audience: Ages 14–18. | Summary: Eighteen-year-old Pakistani
   American Zahra makes an impulsive decision to run away from home and move to
   New York in an attempt to heal, learn to love herself, and renew her faith in family
   while navigating mental health and religious guilt.
Identifiers: LCCN 2023019615 | ISBN 9781643795058 (hardcover) |
   ISBN 9781643795065 (ebk)
Subjects: CYAC: Self-actualization—Fiction. | Family life—Fiction. | Muslims—
   Fiction. | Pakistani Americans—Fiction. | Long Island (N.Y.)—Fiction.
Classification: LCC PZ7.1.Q74 Wh 2023 | DDC [Fic]—dc23
LC record available at https://lccn.loc.gov/2023019615

For my sister, Zaineb,
who I can't live without.

Trigger Warnings

depression, anxiety, emotional abuse, physical abuse,
self-harm, suicidal ideation, slut-shaming, PTSD

If you are struggling or in crisis, help is available.
Call or text 988 or visit 988lifeline.org for
support and resources.

Author's Note

I first wrote this book in the spring of 2016, when I was a senior in high school and going through a lot of the aches and pains Zahra is going through. I was dealing with a lot of the same confusions and discomforts that accompany growing up. Everything seemed like a question mark. Everything hurt.

I didn't know how to navigate this world as a teenage girl, as a Muslim, as a Pakistani American, as a hijabi, as a daughter . . . as anything. I felt so pressured—as teens on the precipice of adulthood often do—to *know* everything. Thus the not-knowing, wretched enough, was made twice so by everyone's expectations and my inability to fulfill them.

When I started writing this book, I truly had no idea how it would end. I didn't know what answers to give my main character because I didn't have the answers myself. But somehow, during the process of writing, the answers came to me, and I was able to grow alongside my characters. I hope, too, that this book gives you answers.

This story is a love letter to oneself. It's the type of book I wish I could have read when I was growing up, and it's the type of book I hope brings healing and clarity to whoever reads it.

While I took great care in crafting this story and hope that I handled the sensitive topics therein with delicacy, please forgive me if you feel I mishandled any aspect of this book. The last thing in the world I want to do is cause anyone pain, especially with my words.

All my love,

Aamna

Chapter 1

It was an ordinary Monday when I left.

June 27, two days after graduation—twelve days before the wedding.

I was driving past the train station on my way home from my tutoring job, my mouth cold from an iced caramel latte, my hands sticky with sweat, music playing on the radio. It was summer music, easygoing and upbeat, coaxing listeners to move with the rhythm. The weather was blazing, the sun scorching, and I saw shirtless boys riding bicycles, their laughter carefree in the wind.

An ordinary summer day.

The summer after senior year was meant for relaxation, to find myself before college. It was meant for all the mental sorting I needed to do before stepping on the path toward a new life. I was supposed to form healthy habits, watch the sun rise, drink good coffee, spend time with friends. I was meant to garden and read and cook and breathe and live. No internships, no summer job, no homework. Freedom.

But I would experience none of these things.

The thought of leaving came to me while I was stopped at a red light. I had another five minutes before Ammi would call, wondering precisely how far from home I was. Five more before she called again to double-check. Then ten before I was grounded.

I turned to look out the window. There it was—the train station I passed every day. I had only ever been on the train once before, on a school-chaperoned trip to San Francisco from where we lived in Sunnyvale.

What if ...

But my thoughts were elusive, and I gave no words to them in my mind. I simply turned on my blinker and switched into the empty lane beside me in a daze. Faintly, I told myself, *You'd never dare.* Faintly, I thought I'd turn back the instant I entered the parking lot.

Brown kids didn't just run away.

But I found myself parking, then pulling the key out of the ignition. Thoughts swarmed my mind, incoherent buzzing turning into pro-con lists and consequences.

I closed the door to my thoughts and opened the door to the car.

It didn't seem real, like when you know you're mucking

up a drawing, but you keep scribbling anyway, knowing full well you could toss it and start again. I grabbed my bag and stepped out of my car.

My phone rang. *Ammi*, the screen read, vibrating in my hand as I held it. My finger hovered over the Accept button. Then the ringing ceased. My body was fluid, dreamlike.

I felt nothing.

I turned my phone off and dropped it onto the seat, then slipped my keys into the sunglasses holder.

Nothing.

I went to the kiosk and bought a train ticket. I got on the train, my bag bumping against my leg as I walked down the aisles.

Nothing.

I sat.

Still nothing.

Then the train began to move.

My breath was sucked out of me in a clean swoop, anxiety filling my lungs. I suddenly stood up. Blood pounded in my ears, too loud and too fast. I curled my toes, fighting against the anxiety, holding it back.

Breathe, I thought.

Breathe. I forced myself to take a breath. *Get it together, what the hell?*

I loosened the stiff muscles of my fingers, spread my toes flat, and straightened my back from its crumpled state. *Inhale for seven, hold for six. Exhale for eight. Inhale for seven, hold for six. Exhale for eight.*

Kya hua? What's wrong? My thoughts alternated between Urdu and English. *Kya hua?*

Nothing. Nothing was wrong, but everything was. The realization of what was happening hit me suddenly—that this was real, not a dream, that this was life, not a piece of paper I could toss.

I argued with myself. *Get off the train. Say it's an emergency.* There had to be an emergency brake somewhere, like in the movies.

No. You are not getting off this train. You are leaving. Bhaago! Run, run, run!

But I didn't want to go. I wanted to go home, curl up in my lavender-scented sheets, listen to the sound of Geo News coming from Baba's office, and smell roti cooking downstairs. I wanted to wonder when my older brother, Ahsen, would come home, knock at my bedroom door to see if I was asleep, then come in to talk when he saw that I wasn't.

But I couldn't go home. Not to have Ammi yell at me the instant I walk through the door, not to have to stand there silently and take it, not to have Baba come in asking, "Kya shor mach raha hai?" *"What is this noise?"* I couldn't watch Ahsen come home smelling like weed, eyes red-rimmed and face dazed.

I couldn't go home, but I wanted to. I needed to go home, but I didn't want to.

All these thoughts whirled in my mind, splitting me in half to argue each side, as if I were two people, debating my fate. It was a civil war, and all the casualties were mine: I lost both ways. I won both ways.

I wished for time to stop, to still, for the world to go frozen. I closed my eyes, pushing away the feeling of the train moving beneath me, the smell of public transportation. My senses stripped away, layer by layer, until there was silence, until there was nothing.

And then—all I could hear was Ammi's voice, broken and raw, yelling, *How could you? How could you?* over and over, and it made me want to rip my heart out of my chest, knowing I caused her that pain, knowing those tears were because of me, knowing that anger in her eyes was directed at me.

If only I could take it back. If only I could rewind.

I opened my eyes.

It didn't matter. I couldn't hurt her anymore. And she couldn't hurt me. No more would we be each other's misery. I was leaving. *Main bhaag rahi hoon.* And that was it.

Everything will be better, I told myself. *You couldn't stay*, I reminded myself. *Yaad nahi hai kya hone wala tha? Don't you remember what was going to happen?*

Months after winter break, I was given two options.

"Zahra, idhar ao," Ammi had called me to her room one day. It was her serious voice, which meant, *don't speak, not until I am through, and even then, at your own caution.* It meant, *I am angry.* It meant, *your feelings do not matter.* It meant, *you will obey.*

I always did. Always.

"Ji, Ammi?" Hands tucked behind my back, teeth nibbling on my lip, eyes empty.

"Dekho," she said, sitting down in front of me. "I am giving you two options. Ya, toh main tumhara rishta dhundun, aur tumhari shaadi ho eesi summer main. Ya, tum doctor ban jao. It's your choice."

"Ammi, kya matlab shaadi ya doctor?" I asked, but it was futile. *What do you mean I get married or become a doctor?* We Parachas were a stubborn lot, and once a decision was made, it was written in stone. No erasures.

Ammi smiled then, her lips twisted in disgust, eyes hard. Words were poised in her defiant eyes, and I knew what she would say. Ashamed, I interjected before she could.

"Acha, teek hai." I nodded. "Can I have some time to decide, please?"

"Graduation tak."

Two months.

Ammi always won.

No matter how soft she seemed on the exterior, her interior was solid, yet to thaw. It was frozen still from January, frozen still from the catalyst that divided my life into Before and After.

I needed time. Time to think. Time to breathe. Time to be. Without her watching my every move, without her eyes following me wherever I went, like she had been the past few months. I wanted to take a deep breath after months of quiet breathing, after tiptoeing and counting each word, ensuring each was not another spark to ignite my mother's rage.

I was so tired. I was so, *so* tired.

On the train, I watched the sun set, orange and pink paint spilling across the horizon, God's brushstrokes. In my heart, I said subhanAllah, God is magnificent. I said alhamdulillah, all praise is due to God. I said Allah hu Akbar, God is great.

But it felt like Allah wasn't there.

I closed my eyes, and in the darkness I reached for the light. I reached for the future I had always dreamed of.

Chapter 2

$\mathcal{I}$ opened my eyes after a while of just being blank: no thoughts, no sleep.

Outside the train window, sunset signaled the time for Maghrib, and I knew I should pray, but I wondered if God would even listen after what I had done, what I was doing still. All I felt was a thick fog of melancholy filling my lungs with each breath I took. I was too empty to make dua, to cry to God and plead for forgiveness. I simply sat and nibbled my lower lip, eyes traveling.

Two seats down sat a man in a suit, not old but not young, and our eyes met. He smiled at me and no matter how benign the gesture, fear burned through my veins. I smiled back to let him know I was not a Terrorist, but he quickly averted his gaze. I thought I saw him watching, eyeing this solitary young girl with no father or brother to protect her.

The sky swirled into a deep navy blue. It was past dark, and I wasn't home. Guilty tension twisted my stomach. *Ammi will be livid*. With the anxiety came fear, as if any moment now, I would be caught and yelled at and broken again.

But Ammi wasn't here. I was on the train—*the train*—miles and miles away from home, going even farther, and there was nothing she could do.

I felt so worthless. Always screwing up, always falling short.

At least I wouldn't disappoint them anymore, and I knew deep down, Ammi would be happy. She would be sad, no doubt, but there would be relief there as well. No more roller coaster of emotions, no more hopes turning to disappointment, no more love, and no more anger. In grief, she would venerate her memory of me, and in those memories, she would live forever content, even with the undercurrent of melancholy.

Toh acha hai, I told myself. *Then it's good.*

I was going to make a new life and do what I wanted to do. Nobody could stop me. *No one, no one, no one.*

But I still looked over my shoulder, still felt a phantom hand roughly grabbing my arm and pulling me back, nails digging into my skin.

I tried to concentrate on my next move. There was some time until the train reached the city from the suburbs. Where would I go?

I could go . . . anywhere.

The realization struck me suddenly. My horizons widened, the world suddenly seemed accessible to me, within my grasp. No longer did other countries seem eternities away. Distant continents beckoned me forward, arms open.

As swiftly as it came, the excitement dimmed. I usually had everything planned out—suitcases packed for weeks, carry-on ready with essentials, two books to read if I got bored, and my journal to write in if I needed it—but now, I had nothing. Not even my phone.

At the very least, I had my wallet, my laptop, and a comfortable outfit on, but it wasn't my favorite, nor my comfiest. I couldn't help but think about all the things I was leaving behind, all my clothes, all my books and trinkets, my jewelry, the comfiest pair of flats, and a bag in the most gorgeous shade of teal. My medals, my vitamins, my deodorant, my hoodies . . .

But—*no.*

That was the past and this was the beginning of a new future, a rebirth. Those mementos would simply remind me of the circumstances, and in the end, the guilt of my past life.

Let Ammi pass my bedroom every night on the way to hers, I thought bitterly. *Let her remember me, smell my perfume, try to catch the ghost of me. Let her miss me, let her hurt, let her suffer.*

How awful I was, to think such things. I wanted to hurt myself for thinking them, but I thought them anyway. I wanted her to hurt as much as I hurt, to miss me as much as I would miss her. I knew not from where this cruelty came, but it was inside me, nestled in my heart.

It knocked against my ribs, loud even over the screeching of a halting train, even over the clamor of business calls, laughter, and chatter as I exited onto the platform an hour and a half later. San Francisco was the heart of the West Coast, from which all other blood flowed. There was a bus, a train, and just a few miles away, a plane. I could go anywhere—just a swipe of my card and I could hop on, no baggage, nothing.

Only me.

But who was she?

I'll go to Boston. I adored it there whenever we visited, but—

No, I can't.

Ahsen went to school in Boston. Ammi had friends there. Baba had colleagues and workmates. Word would get back to Ammi before I even had the chance to breathe deeply. And where would I stay? What would I do? Did I even know how much an apartment in Boston cost?

Maybe I could go to New York. I'd always loved New York. The gorgeous brownstones, the canopied streets, the towering buildings. Four months ago, I got into New York University, but Ammi refused to send me. I had to stay home and attend the university fifteen minutes away for easy access and a monopoly over my weekends.

Meanwhile, my older brother, Ahsen, was finishing university in Boston, visiting only in the summers and between semesters, if that. But he was a boy. He was allowed to do such things.

What the hell am I doing? Sitting in a train station well after dark, wondering where to go? Ammi would have already sent Baba out to look for me by now, and it wouldn't take them long to find my car in the train station and put the pieces together. They would find me. I could already feel it, the sting of Ammi's hand on my cheek.

The air was too hot, too humid, too thick. I couldn't breathe. I had to keep running. I couldn't go back, not now. I grabbed a map from a newsstand. *How do I get to the airport?*

It all looked too complicated. Whenever we came to San Francisco, Baba drove, and we'd arrive in a little over an hour. I had never done anything of this caliber by myself. I looked for somebody to ask for help, but all I saw were busy people, quickly walking.

"Excuse me," I whispered, trying to grab somebody's attention. But they didn't notice. I felt my voice shrink further.

I was on my own. I was alone. I had to figure this out.

What if I can't? My vision fogged, and I began hyperventilating. I desperately wished there were somebody to calm me down, somebody to hold my hand. But there was nobody.

Inhale for seven, hold for six. Exhale for eight.

Somebody help. Somebody . . .

Inhale for seven, hold for six. Exhale for eight.

Please—somebody, please help me, please.

Nobody came. I stood in the center of the sea, waves crashing over me, pulling me under, vomiting me out only to take me back down again.

Inhale for seven, hold for six. Exhale for eight.

I focused on the map and searched for a plausible route. In the end, it was simple. *No big deal.*

It took forty minutes of stress to get to the airport—some walking and a bus and the hyperawareness that I was a little over five feet tall and alone. And a girl. If I had been a boy, perhaps I wouldn't have been afraid. What made them so fearless?

From birth, boys were cultivated to take on the world, while girls were taught to hold somebody's hand. When Ahsen was ten, he was allowed to walk half a mile to the park close by, even though he had to cross a main road. When I was ten, I couldn't walk two streets down to a school friend's house without Ahsen by my side. One example of thousands.

Since childhood I had never gone anywhere alone, never dreamed of crossing the street unless I was holding Baba's hand, while Ahsen would run across the street, arms wide open. I grew up with protective figures in my peripheral and direct lines of sight constantly. Ahsen galloped freely.

Did they love me more, and that's why they were more protective? *Impossible.*

It didn't matter. Now, I was determined to run free, eyes forward, hands caressing the wind.

Chapter 3

*U*ntil I arrived at the airport, and I had no idea where to go. This was why brown girls don't just run away.

How falsely advertised running away was—there were so many technicalities that it gave me a headache. I couldn't simply hop onto a plane, I had to *find the right terminal.*

Weary, I sat down at the coffee shop and pulled out my laptop. I deleted all my social media, already ringing with notifications—goodbye Facebook, Twitter, Instagram. Then I checked my bank account.

I had a decent amount of money saved up from tutoring and graduation gifts and Eidi.

But where to? I couldn't come up with any destination. I'd never even thought of where I would go if I could—what was the point of imagining my life in Florence, a city I'd always wanted to visit, if I could never end up there anyway? My future was entirely dependent upon whomever I married and where he lived and worked.

Like a wave that followed the tide, I had always listened to the ocean of my mother's words, letting them flow through me, never letting my own thoughts stream in their own direction.

But if I was doing this, I would do it properly.

Maybe I *would* go to New York.

It was the farthest away I could go without leaving the country. One foot in, one foot out. I couldn't bring myself to leave the country. It felt . . . too much. Too scary. And logistically, it would be more complicated.

So, I would go to New York.

There was nothing stopping me, no current pulling me in a different direction. It was practical.

Still, I was afraid.

Ahsen had traveled across Europe one semester, all alone, and he wasn't perturbed. He went city to city, staying in hostels, roaming the streets, thinking and living. But I could not do that.

Tum ladki ho, I heard Ammi say in my head, as if being a girl was reason enough.

I felt the need to be taken care of, for somebody to hold my hand, somebody to guide and protect me as they had been doing my whole life through. I was eighteen years old and still couldn't handle being alone.

But there was nobody here.

I kept checking behind me, half waiting for Ammi to be here, half expecting somebody to catch up with me and ask why I was alone.

I was solitary, sticking out like a sore thumb, but nobody noticed. I was just another person, blending into the background of thousands of people going about their lives.

I took a steadying breath. I looked up which airline sold tickets to New York, then went to the kiosk with the nicest-looking woman working there.

"Hi, welcome to Delta. How can I help you?" she asked.

"Can I buy a ticket?" I asked, voice sugary, smile toothy and dimpled. It was my white people voice, extra sweet to come across as nonthreatening as possible.

"Of course," the woman said, smiling politely. "Where to?"

"New York," I said. I pulled out my wallet and my debit card, grateful I had a separate bank account from my parents.

"JFK or LaGuardia?" the woman asked. I bit my lip. *What was the difference?*

"Um. JFK."

"Would you like nonstop or are layovers okay?"

"Uh . . . nonstop, please."

"When would you like to depart?"

"When's the next flight?"

"Unfortunately, there's no more for tonight. The earliest would be tomorrow morning at 11:15 a.m.—nonstop."

"Okay, that's good."

"Would you like a roundtrip ticket or one-way, miss?"

My smile faltered. *Am I coming back?* Tears pricked my eyes, my lower lip trembling.

"One-way is fine," I said, voice thick. The woman's face

softened with concern. Blinking fast, I offered her an encouraging smile.

"That will be $472. Arrival at 8:00 p.m. Credit or debit?"

"Debit."

"Enjoy your flight."

"You too—I mean, thank you . . . have a good night!"

Luckily, I was in the right terminal for my flight. All I had to do was go through security, then wait for the gate to open. Then, hop on a plane.

Since it was a Monday night, the security line wasn't too bad. Luckily, I had an enhanced license, so I could travel domestically without my passport.

A few minutes later I was pulled aside for a "random security check."

I sighed, adjusting my hijab.

A man called two women over, and I was escorted to a separate area behind a curtain. I lifted my arms, and the woman patted me down, hands traveling into each groove to ensure there was nothing hidden. Then began the inquisition. I already had the answers ready, so familiar with them as I was.

"Where are you going?"

"New York."

"For how long?"

"A few weeks."

"Are you traveling alone?"

"Yes."

"Purpose of travel?"

"My . . . friend is getting married."

"What do you have in your bag?"

My voice was sweet, smile sure, but my heart ricocheted between my ribs. I expected her to ask me where my parents were or how old I was. Did I look legal? With my chubby cheeks and no makeup on, I knew I didn't.

She reached for my bag, and it took her five minutes to empty it completely, check for hidden compartments, then nod to herself. She wrote something incomprehensible on my boarding pass, then nodded again.

The curtain opened.

As I stepped out, I felt the stares of children, adults deliberately looking anywhere but at me. Inside me, I let go of the emotions of excitement and fear and anger and guilt and despair and irritation, stripping them off like layers of clothing after a tiring day.

I walked to the right gate, eyes blank, jaw tense. The air conditioning was on too high; my skin was drying.

I should have eaten because I hadn't had anything since lunch, but I didn't have the energy or the appetite. I bought a coffee and sipped on it sporadically, slowly, until it got cold and disgusting, but I kept drinking anyway.

I usually loved the airport, loved seeing hundreds of families from across the globe in one place, dozens of cultures and sizes and colors and beauty. Some tired, some hopeful, some ecstatic, some melancholy. This was humanity—messy and gorgeous.

For a moment, I almost began thinking of family trips to the airport—seeing cousins off, receiving grandparents, traveling ourselves. Apathy nudged the thoughts away, however, telling them not to bother me, telling them to hush.

Afraid to get robbed, I held my bag in my lap, hugging it, pulling my legs up to encapsulate it. Uncomfortable but tired, I closed my eyes.

Flashes of the past few months flitted through my mind like photographs flying in the wind: my nails digging into my skin; choosing an engagement dress; not speaking for days; fake smiles; nodding, *ji, Ammi, okay, Ammi*; a ring being slid onto my finger; crying myself to sleep.

Slowly, everything faded away, until there was nothing left but an empty shell of a girl with no voice, no heart, no soul, no mind—*nothing, nothing, nothing.*

Sleep came quickly, despite the early hour in the evening.

That night, I did not dream.

Chapter 4

One moment I was asleep, the next jerked awake by an announcement.

"Flight DL182 to JFK, now boarding."

Sleep damp in my mouth, I rubbed my eyes, stretching my back. There were some people already in line to board my flight, mostly men in suits or mothers with babies. I saw an old Indian woman and her husband in the back, and they reminded me of Nana Abu and Nano.

Surprisingly, I wasn't disoriented to wake up in the airport. My back just hurt, a physical feeling I could not ignore. I focused on it. Everything else was surreal. I looked at the time on the screen for the gate and saw it was ten in the morning. I had slept almost fourteen hours, which should have been alarming, but I didn't think about it.

I went and stood in line to board. It felt like watching a movie, like I was standing outside my body, watching everything occur. I saw myself hand the attendant my boarding pass and smile as he told me to enjoy my flight. Loneliness lodged in my larynx, an unavoidable lump, rendering me voiceless.

I walked through the tunnel, and the blasting air conditioning and the distinct smell of travel brought back memories of every plane ride I could remember. The last one to Turkey for vacation, and before that, Pakistan, and before that, Morocco, and Pakistan again.

Before my failure, when I was the perfect daughter, my life had been so extravagant. So easy. Baba always carrying my suitcase and Ahsen taking my carry-on when I complained. Mama packing snacks and all of them ushering me forward, carrying me along their tide.

While comfort was, in fact, comfortable, I had been so spoiled that it was unnecessarily uncomfortable now to shift from a life of ease toward a life of small difficulties, from a life of dependence to independence.

My life had been so full, so why had I felt so empty in it, even Before? There were family and friends, a pretty face, and good grades. We were well-off; we always had enough to eat and good things to buy.

Inside me there was a valley between what I felt and the happiness that was expected of me, and I wasn't sure when it got there, what glacier carved it into my soul.

All I knew was that it was ever-growing. It had been, ever since March, when I had told Ammi I decided to get married. She'd been happy—it was a step forward. But I was a wilted flower, and with each day that passed, I lost another petal, until I was a rotting stem from which nothing could grow.

I boarded the plane and found my seat in silence. *When was the last time I spoke?* My breath tasted old, but I didn't have a toothbrush. I was in the same clothes as yesterday.

I set my bag down, melting into invisibility. Fright crept through me. Every time somebody entered the compartment, I expected it to be somebody looking for me. I was as jumpy as a felon, which felt accurate, for it was a crime for brown girls to disobey their families. It was a felony for them to run away.

Somebody sat next to me, and I turned to see a young guy a few years older than me. He was good-looking. Despite his appeal, I squirmed. All I wanted was to sit next to an old woman or a girl my age, anybody kind and placid and nonthreatening.

He settled into his seat. I must have looked frenzied because he gave me a strange look.

I forced a smile that manifested more like a grimace and turned my attention away. However, in my peripheral vision, I kept my sights on him, and he kept looking. Was it because he thought I was cute or because I looked like a Terrorist? *The woes of being a hijabi.*

Realistically, it was probably the latter because I looked as shitty as I felt. Despite how much sleep I'd gotten, my clothes were rumpled, my skin was dry, and my hair—although covered—was greasy. Beyond that, I had lost almost fifteen pounds in the last six months, which maybe didn't sound like a lot, but I was short. It meant I had gotten really skinny, to the point of looking sickly.

Ironically, I had considered this to be a plus side to the

misery of the past months. At least I was finally thin. All my life, I had been plump, and Ammi had been at me to lose weight. She was at least glad I was losing weight "for the wedding," as she thought.

To me, getting thin was ultimately underwhelming. I thought when I finally got skinny that my life would change for the better, but it didn't. It was just strange. I would wrap my arms around my body and feel how little there was left, feel straight to the bone where before there had been *more* to me.

It was like I was disappearing, even physically.

"Where are you headed?" the boy next to me asked, pulling me from my thoughts. He flashed me a charming smile. My eyes must have relayed a stream of question marks because he half-laughed. "I mean, in New York."

"Oh. Um . . . to visit a friend?"

"Cool! My family lives on Long Island."

"Um . . . okay."

I reached into my bag and pulled my headphones out but realized too late that I didn't have a phone. Resisting the urge to physically facepalm myself, I pulled my bag into my lap and then stuck the earbuds into my ears, pretending that I had a phone in my bag.

"Enjoy your flight," I said, smiling because I was a Muslim and had an image to uphold. As a Muslim, if you treated one person badly, they might blame your entire religion. *No pressure, though.*

"Thanks," the guy half muttered to himself, deflating. I felt guilty. Why did I feel guilty? I didn't owe him my company, and I didn't want to talk.

I pulled a blanket up around my shoulders, curling my body into a tight ball and turning my back to him. I nestled into the wall and gazed out the window, until the plane began moving and my ears popped. I saw the world as I knew it shrink until I was above the clouds.

I took a deep breath. *Peace at last.* This was a suspension of time. For the next six hours I would be on this plane, and there was nothing to worry about yet because I was on my way to the future, taking an infinitesimal step closer than I had ever been before.

Cotton candy clouds filled the sky. It was so beautiful to see them from above, the rounded peaks, the shadows over land far below. I could have stared, mesmerized, for hours at the clouds we passed by, just as I could watch snow fall or fire crackle. Nature was brimming with majesty, and it was so raw and pure that I believed all man-made beauty was surely molded after the blueprints of Allah's architecture.

I was lost in the world so much bigger than I was, lost like a star in the galaxies. I was so small, and the world swallowed me whole.

Sometime later, I tried adjusting my legs and collided with another's. I looked down to find that the boy beside me had spread his legs, obliviously infiltrating my personal space. Even after my foot accidentally kicked his ankle, he did not move, impervious. He didn't care.

It was a trivial detail, but irritation flashed through me.

Sighing, I squeezed into myself, pressing against the wall so there was no physical contact between us, but he didn't seem to notice. I was uncomfortable. The cool air from the window pinched my cheek and nose, but I didn't make a remark or push back.

Sticky tears bubbled in my eyes. I wasn't crying—it was just emotion, seeping out in a tangible form. I wiped the tears away with the back of my hand and focused back on the clouds, the perpetual movement of them, the flow of white in an impossibly blue sky. Relaxed, I melted into torpor and eased softly into sleep.

I was insatiably tired. I woke hours later, mouth rancid with the aftertaste of slumber.

In my sleep, my limbs had unwound, and one leg had fallen off the seat. My leg rested against his, our limbs overlapping.

Bile flooded my throat, and I tentatively turned my head to look at him. He was asleep, facing me, his head resting on the edge of my seat. I eased my leg back up into my stomach, slowly so not to wake him, and bit my lip to hold back my revulsion.

He sleepily opened his eyes, and, seeing me, smiled politely. I pulled my blanket up around my face again and held back a cry. In another life, it may have been exhilarating to sit next to a cute boy on a plane, to have him pay attention to me.

But at that moment, it wasn't—not at all.

Abruptly, I stood, jaw set, eyes blank, to get out. I was hyperaware and paranoid, a hunted, starved animal. He looked up at me and pulled his legs in, but hardly. As I passed through, contact was inevitable. His knees knocked against my thighs, and I nearly toppled into his lap. Bile rose in my throat again.

I held it together until I entered the bathroom. The door shut, and something within me burst open. Tears filled my eyes then overflowed. I quickly brushed them away, wetting my hands and my gray hijab, but it was no use. I began to cry.

I was tired of crying, of always being on the verge of tears, a lump perpetually clogging my throat. But I couldn't stop it, the hot tears burning my cheeks, the mucus pouring out of my nose, the feeling that my heart was being held and squeezed and squeezed. Everything within me rattled and I felt so brittle, on the verge of collapsing.

I held my face in my palms, and tears gushed onto my knuckles, into my mouth, salty and sharp. Finally, I looked in the mirror. I didn't recognize who I saw.

In my memories, in the photographs and videos, there was a girl with a crooked-toothed grin and chubby cheeks. She always smiled; she always laughed. In her dark-brown eyes, there was light.

Who is she? I couldn't reconcile her with who I was now. That girl was me, but I didn't feel like her—not anymore. I wondered what happened to her. I missed her. I was envious of her. I wondered when I became someone else.

When I looked in the mirror now all I saw were sullen cheeks, a clenched jaw, apathetic eyes, and snarling lips. There was death smoldering beneath my skin, turning it gray, like I was a corpse rotting within myself.

The instant I left the bathroom, I collided with a flight attendant. Her eyes filled with alarm.

"Oh!" she cried, hand flying to her heart. "Is everything all right?"

I shook my head, eyes filling with tears again. I didn't trust myself to speak without melting into sobs.

"What's the matter?" she asked, pulling me aside. A comforting hand fell to my shoulder. I felt eight rather than eighteen. I rubbed my eye with a fist and sniffed.

"Are there— Can you . . . change my seat? If you can't, it's okay!" I stuttered.

"Of course, darling," she responded. "Why? Is somebody bothering you? We can file a report together." Her countenance shifted into a no-nonsense disposition as her eyes hardened and her lip straightened.

"No, ohmygod, no it's—I just . . . I want to be alone for a bit," I stammered. The flight attendant's eyes softened.

"I understand, honey. Luckily, the flight's half-empty. Follow me."

"Let me grab my bag," I said.

Setting my jaw, I walked back to my aisle. When he saw me approach, he lifted his legs back slightly to let me through.

"Could you hand me my bag, please?" He pulled out his earbud and I repeated myself. Nodding, he reached over and offered it to me. To avoid any finger-brushing, I awkwardly held it from the bottom.

I met the flight attendant, and she led me to an empty row

in the back cabin. Because it was a Tuesday morning, it wasn't difficult to switch my seat.

"Thank you so much," I whispered to her, eyes tearing again at her kindness.

She shook her head and smiled a dazzling smile. "Don't worry about it! If you need anything let me or one of the other girls know," she told me.

I offered her a turn of my lips, trying my best to smile. Then I was alone. I didn't need to put up any facade. Loneliness was like an old pair of socks I should have gotten rid of ages ago—though worn and slightly scratchy, they were somehow comfortable despite the discomfort.

Hours later, my ears were popping again, and my stomach was flopping as we landed. People filed into the aisles, grabbing their bags and their children. There was a funnel surrounding my sight, blocking off anything that didn't have to do with myself. I clutched my bag and ran off the instant I could.

Technicalities ensued, boring and seemingly endless. Still, I felt the prickly fear of being alone, the disheartening discomfort of having to do everything myself, but finally—*finally*—I exited the terminal.

There were families and escorts and people with signs but nobody for me. So I walked, watching my swollen brown feet move in my sandals across the white tile, until I reached the door. A little voice whispered in my ear, *brown girls don't just run away. Go back, go back.*

I thrust open the door and there it was: New York.

A world away from the home that was no longer my home.

Chapter 5

What struck me first was the air: pollution mixed with rain and smoke. It tasted different, and it was definitely chillier. What struck me next was the hour: darkness had already descended, swirls of spilled navy ink. The East Coast was three hours ahead, I recalled.

New York seemed like an entirely different country. For a moment, I felt the bliss that came from visiting an unseen land. Standing in JFK almost felt like home—I heard aunties speaking in Urdu, I saw hijabis, and men with long beards, and people dressed in shalwar kameez. There were children leaping into the arms of family members, their laughter filling the air like ringing bells.

It almost made me smile.

Until I thought about my parents. I couldn't even remember how long it had been since we were happy with one another. Goodness toward parents was obligatory in Islam. There was a hadith, a Prophetic saying, that heaven lies beneath the feet of one's mother.

Tearing my eyes away from the happy families, I looked around, trying to figure out where to go from there. I saw a sign leading to the AirTrain, which dropped passengers off at Jamaica train station. From there, it connected west to Manhattan or east to the Long Island Rail Road.

The idea of New York City frightened me; it was dangerous there. And I'd always been a suburban girl. Plus, I missed the ocean already.

So I headed to the AirTrain, bought a MetroCard, and boarded with everyone and their luggage. At Jamaica, I got off and bought a ticket at the kiosk for the LIRR going toward Port Jefferson, the last stop. According to the map, it was right by the water. I guessed I could get off there. It seemed as good a place as any.

When the train came, I boarded in a daze. Clutching my bag to my chest, I stared out the window, looking for stars.

There were so many, floating in the rich, cloudless sky. I felt like I could drink it all up, like I could reach out and catch the stars like fireflies. I wondered what it would be like to have wings, to have a perpetual light inside me. Wondered what it would be like to fly.

I watched and wondered for a while as we passed through various towns and suburbs. Since it was dark, I couldn't make out much, but it didn't look too different than the suburbs I was used to. Sleep stole over me once more, despite how much I had already slept. I let it drown me in its darkness until the train reached the end of the line at Port Jefferson.

I piled off the train with everyone else, but unlike them, I had no car waiting for me. Thankfully, there was a taxi idling. I was surprised to see it wasn't the iconic yellow taxicab I associated with New York. *Maybe things aren't as glamorous as they show on television.*

"Where to?" the taxi driver asked.

"Um ... is there a hotel nearby?"

"In Port Jefferson? Nope."

How are there no hotels?

"Um ..."

"There's a couple of bed-and-breakfasts close by, if that helps?"

"Oh, yes. Can you take me to the nearest one? Please?"

The B&B was expensive, but it was too late for me to back out, and I was too awkward to argue. I couldn't go back outside, anyway, not into the dark and silence.

I unlocked the room and was met with the comfort of a clean, crisp room. Pulling off my hijab, I set down my bag and sighed. The air tasted fresh, and everything felt foreign and new, but soft too.

I could finally breathe.

I tousled my hair—it was matted down and gross from travel. Kicking off my shoes, I collapsed onto the bed, sinking into the pillows.

Before I could get too comfortable, my stomach growled in protest. I hadn't eaten since lunch yesterday, and it was already almost 10 p.m. with the time difference. I had refused any food on the plane except for coffee and peanuts, lost as I was in a haze of sleep.

I had no appetite then, but now I could eat. I opened my laptop, connected to the Wi-Fi, and ordered some food, feeling a little bit relaxed.

I was in the middle of nowhere, across the country. Yesterday felt like it was thousands of miles away—like the past was back in Sunnyvale, California.

Until my email started pinging with notifications. There were some from the bank, alerting me urgently of my previous purchases.

I used the hotel's phone to call them back, telling them not to worry and to unlink my phone and home address in their records. I wondered if they had called first ... would Ammi know now where I was?

What if they find me?

My stomach knotted, and the air tasted sour. I thought back to the past few months—how every time I was late coming home, Ammi would scream and scream, shaking me, asking where I'd been.

Legally speaking, I was an adult, and I wasn't missing—I had run away. *Can they still give information about my whereabouts to my parents?*

I wanted it all to stop: these thoughts, these emotions, the constant pulls on my heart and the constant pain in my chest and stomach. *Why does everything hurt so damn much?*

And then I saw it: an email from Ahsen.

z where the hell are you??? mama's freaking out and
i've been out looking for you for hours. not cool. at
least respond or something.

My heart rate accelerated, and I thought of the people I
had left behind. The real repercussions of my actions. How
worried they must be. I quickly drafted an email in response.

don't worry. I'm safe. I'm not coming back. don't look
for me. I love you guys.

I didn't even realize that I was crying until tears plopped
onto my keyboard, wetting my fingers. My heart splintered—I
wanted to go home. *Maybe I still can.*
I hit Send.
I got a response almost immediately.

the FUCK do you mean you're not coming back???
WHERE ARE YOU???

And I knew I couldn't go back. Not if Ahsen was mad too.
I blocked his email, wanting to collapse. I felt disgusting, my
insides bitter and vile. All I had consumed was coffee, and I
could nearly feel the burns in my stomach's lining. My breath
tasted awful. I smelled and felt worn and wasted.
Then I heard knocking on the door.
My heart leaped into my throat, and I ducked behind the
bed, hiding.

Maybe I am imagining things.

Until I heard the knock again.

The worst thought ran through my mind—*they've found me, they're going to drag me home.* My entire body shook.

"Um, hello?" It was a girl's voice. "I have your order?"

Relief washed over me. I clutched my heart, trying to cease its fervent beating.

"C-Coming!" I called, trying to compose myself. I slipped my scarf on loosely and answered the door. The delivery girl gave me a weird look.

"Here's your food."

She placed the pizza box in my hands. I attempted an apologetic smile.

"Thanks so much!"

I closed the door and opened the box. But once the smell of cheese hit me, I found that I no longer had an appetite.

So I turned on the shower, losing everything to the sensation of hot water scalding my skin. It awoke every nerve within me, reminding me that this body was still alive. My thoughts drowned in the furious pitter-patter of water, a rush of liquid pouring over me, enveloping me in a warm embrace. I let it consume me, erase everything I was, until I was just a body, just skin being burned.

After, I felt better. Clean. I wrapped my hair in a towel and shrugged into a robe. I threw my clothes into the sink and let them soak in warm water before washing them with soap and setting them out to dry. There wasn't much else to do.

Ordinarily, my post-shower routine lasted half an hour:

moisturizing, cleaning cuticles, rubbing away dead skin, brushing and oiling my hair, breathing. But I had none of my things, not even a brush. No clothes, no toothpaste, no deodorant, no underwear.

I tied my shower robe tight and crawled into bed, lying down in the center and surrounding myself with pillows, by cotton and feathers and white and warmth. I ate some pizza and watched television until I felt sleepy again.

It was strange to sleep almost naked. I felt so small in this vast bed, almost like a baby.

Like I had been reborn.

Chapter 6

*T*he next day, the sun was out and I was clean, so the black clouds looming above me faded to gray for a bit. I exited the B&B in yesterday's clothes, still rumpled and damp from last night's washing. The sun was warm on my face.

It wasn't sticky and humid. Rather, the weather was warm with an undercurrent of cool. A soft breeze kissed my cheeks. *It's nice*, I told myself, over and over again, until I began to believe it.

This is okay. You are okay.

I was in New York! Maybe not the *New York* New York of movies and books, but even so, I was on the opposite end of the continent, away from anything I had ever known. A fleeting feeling of euphoria filled me. I was on my own, ready to explore, ready for adventure.

I walked to find some food. The town was right on the water, with meandering streets up and down, canopied by lush green trees. Sunlight peeked through the cracks in the leaves, glistening and shimmering. The town had a nautical vibe, with white seaside restaurants and the smell of seafood heavy in the air, fish and shrimp.

I wasn't hungry before, but now I could eat. There was a cute café nearby, and walking in, even the air made me feel a little better—the strong smell of coffee, the sweet scent of baked goods.

"Can I have a small coffee and a croissant, please?" I ordered.

"Sure thing, one small coffee and a croissant," the barista repeated. I almost laughed at the way she said coffee—it was so different! Like on television. *Kaw-fee.* I always thought they were exaggerating about Long Island accents, but apparently not!

As I waited for my order, I noticed a man in a suit adding half-and-half to his coffee. I used to make Baba's coffee like that.

What day was it now? Wednesday? Baba was probably at work, Ahsen at his internship, Mama at home, cooking and cleaning.

They wouldn't miss me.

What would *I* do now?

I could do anything. What did I want? *I just want to be happy.*

I said *just* like it was a small thing that I wished, but happiness was such a great desire, contentment so elusive. I wanted to be at peace, not at war. I was too tired to fight anymore.

I walked from the coffee shop toward the pier with my

breakfast. I was on the northeastern side of Long Island, which was much quieter and sparser than the suburbs I had passed closer to the city. Here, it seemed like everyone was a local: men pushing strollers, kids eating ice cream, and middle school couples holding hands. The docks were visible from the apex of the slanted road, the water a sparkling blue. A ferry was docked, and the white sails of smaller boats bobbed in the water.

I walked along the boardwalk, staring into the water. It was so different here: the water more gray than cerulean, the air not as sharp with salt. In California, you could taste the salt with every breath; here, it was subtler. There were barely any seagulls squawking, and the water was very still. Another strange thing was the flat land. There were no mountains lining the horizon. I could see far, far away, into what must have been Connecticut.

It was different but still nice. I sat by the docks a while, letting my skin bake in the sunlight. Ammi always said I was too dark and needed to stay out of the sun, but she wasn't here to stop me.

After a while, being surrounded by everyone with no one of my own made me lonely. I needed people.

So I went back to the B&B and looked up the nearest masjid on my laptop. I walked and took a bus and walked some more. Public transportation was a little complicated, and it would have been much easier to have a car, but I didn't mind walking—I had all the time in the world.

I walked until I saw a peaked minaret and a brown-skinned

woman in a hijab, walking with brown-skinned children. A bunch of boys played basketball in the parking lot, while younger kids chased one another, laughing and squealing with glee.

My heart soared, and I remembered it was nearly time for Zuhr, the midday prayer. The masjid would be full of people.

My people, my people.

I entered, and there were people and people and people. So much noise after days of quiet. I heard Urdu and Bengali and Arabic, and I nearly sobbed in relief, my ears happy.

This was home. Headscarves and skirts and laughter and prayer and little kids running around. I didn't know anyone, but still this was home. This was the beauty of masjids, of the ummah, the Muslim community. These were my people.

I sat down in the front row and grabbed a tasbeeh. All around me was beautiful calligraphy, spelling out the ninety-nine names of Allah and other adhkar. I absentmindedly repeated "Allah hu Akbar" while watching the environment around me churn. There was nearly peace.

Until somebody tapped me from behind.

Chapter 7

Holy shit, it's Ammi.

I yelped and scrambled forward, falling to my knees as I turned around, only to find that the face behind the hand was not Ammi but an alarmed girl.

"Oh, I'm sorry! I didn't mean to scare you!"

Her voice was soft and kind. She was wearing a long-sleeved maxi dress with a crinkle hijab wrapped around her head. Behind pink-rimmed glasses, her brown eyes were warm.

"It's—it's okay."

"Are you new in the area?" she asked, smiling. "I thought I'd say salaam since I haven't seen you before."

Another smile, this time toothy and sugar sweet.

"Yeah, I'm . . . new around here," I responded.

"Salaam," she said, waving. "I'm Haya Chaudry."

"Zahra."

"So, what are you doing here? Visiting family or . . . ?"

It was a good question. An excuse was ready, but I didn't want to lie. "I don't—no—um . . ."

"Okay, cool," Haya said, nodding as if I had given her a legitimate answer.

She looked around my age, though a good few inches taller than me, with brown skin and a heart-shaped face. My ghastly demeanor must not have frightened her, for the next thing I knew, she sat beside me, our knees touching. While we waited for the iqamah, she stayed beside me. Despite all the aunties who came and said salaam to her, despite all the children whose foreheads she kissed.

And she looked at me with such unassuming openness that I wanted to speak. I was so desperate to talk to anybody who would listen, and here she was, eyes attentive.

Sometimes you just need a stranger. Somebody who doesn't know you, who doesn't have any preexisting notions of how you should be. No expectations or reputations to live up to—a clean canvas for you to paint your words onto.

So after Zuhr, when she was still sitting beside me, I found myself speaking.

"Do you live around here?" I asked. "Like, is this your masjid?"

"Yep," Haya replied, smiling fondly. "I've been coming here for ages. Since I was in the womb, probably."

"Oh, cool, cool," I said. "I just got to New York yesterday and sort of stumbled here by accident."

"Ohmygod, nice!" she said, grinning. "Well, I'm glad you decided to pop in here and we met! Where are you from?"

"Sunnyvale, California," I told her. "It's by San Francisco? It's a suburb."

"A West Coast gal," she said, wiggling her eyebrows. "I've never been, but please tell me you know how to surf."

"Ah, not exactly," I told her, nearly laughing. She was so bubbly—I felt light. "But I have been waterskiing, and it is *amazing*."

"Stop, I want to go waterskiing so badly!" she squealed. "Unfortunately, I don't know how to swim, so my mom is totally against the idea, which is literally so lame."

"You don't have to know how to swim!" I told her. "You get a life vest and stuff. My dad is so particular we keep it on even though we know how to swim."

A little knife poked my heart at the mention of Baba, at the memory. Baba was always scolding us not to take our life vests off for selfies or pictures, telling us to stop trying to be so cool because we would never be as cool as him anyway. Ahsen and I would roll our eyes, but we couldn't help but laugh too.

Those memories seemed so far away now.

"Do you and your siblings go often?" Haya asked.

"Uh, it's just me and my older brother, and we don't go that often," I said, voice cloudy. I cleared my throat. "Only a few times."

"I have one sibling too!" she said, shifting the attention to herself. "My older sister, Sadaf. She's twenty-one. She might be coming here, actually! You got lucky showing up today—in the summer, we have a Youth Group meeting after Zuhr on Wednesdays. You should join!"

I noticed other girls around my age had started gathering in the back of the prayer hall.

"Oh. Um . . ." I started to think out loud. I didn't want to intrude.

"It's open for everyone! Mostly girls aged fourteen and up," Haya told me. "We discuss life and give advice and are one another's sisters in Islam. You'll love it. It's a really lovely community. Most girls stop coming after high school, since they get busy with college and stuff. Even though I just graduated in June, I'm still trying to come because it's so nice!"

Before I could protest, Haya grabbed my hand and pulled me toward a group of girls who were standing around, chatting. She introduced me to two girls who were talking loudly over each other, laughing and high-fiving through their conversation.

"Madiha, Imaan, salaam! This is my new friend Zahra, and she's joining us today!" Haya told them. They grinned at me.

"Hey! Welcome to our masjid. I'm Madiha," one of the girls said to me. She was really tall, taller than Haya, and had a strong, athletic build. She was also a hijabi, with black eyes and medium-brown skin. "Everyone here is super chill," Madiha told me, "so don't worry at all about being new."

"And you're lucky, Haya introduced you to the coolest girls here," the other girl, Imaan, said, doing a hijab flip. She was petite and around my height and was wearing a lilac abaya with a matching scarf. I laughed.

"Cool? *Please*," Haya said, laughing too. "You guys are still little babies. Whereas *we* are mature adults."

Haya turned to whisper to me, "You're eighteen, right?"

I nodded.

"See!" she said. "Us? Adults. You guys?" She pointed to them. "Babies."

"Quit playin'. I'm like half a foot taller than you. And our sweet sixteens have passed," Madiha said.

"Yeah, you tell 'em, Diya," Imaan added. "Which means . . ." She paused for emphasis, voice solemn. "*We* have reached *womanhood.*"

"Yeah, I'll be sure to mention that to your training bra," Haya said, cracking up.

"*Ooh!*" Madiha called, bursting into laughter while Imaan pouted, covering her chest with her hands.

"Ohmygod, stop!" she said, but she was laughing too. "Why'd you have to violate me like that?"

"I mean, she's not wrong, in your case," Madiha joked.

Imaan smacked her friend.

"Salaam, everyone!" a voice called, interrupting our laughter. We turned to see a girl in a floral hijab standing up in the front of the prayer rows. She looked like she was a year or two older than me. "Can everyone please sit down so we can start? Try to get as close together as possible!"

"Let's sit," Haya said, and we followed the others as they sat down, cross-legged, in a circle. There were about fifteen girls total, some younger than me, some older. But everyone looked . . . kind: warm eyes and sunlit smiles.

The prayer area had cleared out, so it was only our group in the women's section of the masjid. The sweet scent of bakhoor burning over charcoal filled the air-conditioned air. Beneath our feet, the masjid carpet was soft and worn.

"Bismillah . . ."

In the name of God, the Most Merciful, the Most Beneficent.

We started off by praying to Allah to bless us and give us strength.

"I see some new faces, so to everyone whose first week it is with our Youth Group, welcome!" the leader, Uroosa, said. "Let's all go around and say our names, ages, and our favorite cake flavor!"

I was glad Uroosa wasn't asking me for a more personal detail, like what I wanted to be or what I was doing with my life. Cake flavor I could handle.

As everyone began introducing themselves in the circle, I pictured a Black Forest cake with pineapple filling instead of cherries and chocolate syrup drizzled on top—exactly like how Mama always made it for my birthday when I was younger.

I hadn't had that cake in years.

"My name is Zahra, I'm eighteen years old, and my favorite cake is . . . vanilla." Shaking my head, I blinked away the memories and focused on the other girls.

"Now that we're all acquainted, let's begin today's discussion. Today's topic is dua," Uroosa said. "What is dua?"

"A supplication," one of the younger girls, Umaymah, answered.

"Yes, true," Uroosa replied. "But more than that—something deeper."

"Dua is a conversation with Allah subhana wa ta'ala," a girl wearing a blue hijab, Hamnah, said.

"Yes, good!" Uroosa replied. "That's important—we have to think of praying and making dua like a conversation with Allah, like a conversation with a loved one. Remember, there is no being that loves us more than He does. Allah created us. He is always with us. So, when we make dua, we have to remember that Allah is listening to us, that He understands us, and He just wants what is best for us . . . because He loves us."

That was what everyone always said—that God loved us, that He was always with us, near to us. But lately it felt like He was so far away.

It made me wonder. About how I used to be so strong in my faith, so reliant on it as fuel to get me through this life. Until things got too stressful, and I didn't have any time to think about God anymore. Maybe leaving my prayers and letting my relationship with God dwindle contributed to why things got so shitty, so fast.

Even now, I didn't talk to Allah because I was ashamed. Why would He listen to me after what I had done? After everything? How I had treated my mother? I had disappointed Him, turned my back on Him.

He wouldn't listen even if I spoke.

Who would listen to me?

"I know it's way easier said than done to have that trust and faith in Allah," Uroosa continued. "How about we go around, and everyone mentions something they think is difficult about making dua? And no pressure if you can't think of anything."

"Oh, I'll start!" Haya volunteered. Uroosa smiled warmly at her.

"Perfect."

"Okay, so something I find difficult about dua is the crying part," Haya said. "Like, when you really start making dua and talking to Allah and letting all your emotions and frustrations out—I always end up crying. And no one likes crying."

I felt that way too—I was sick of crying.

"Definitely!" Madiha added, and my focus shifted to her. "Opening your heart like that—it *hurts*."

It was unbearably painful, which was exactly why I avoided it. It just made me feel worse.

"But I guess that's the point, right?" Imaan said, joining in. "Like, being vulnerable with Allah to sort of prove that you love and trust Him too?"

I did love Allah—but I knew He could not love me.

"It's like that hadith, where if you go to Allah walking, He will come to you running," Umaymah added on. I had heard that hadith too, but surely it wouldn't apply to *me*. The thought almost made me laugh because it was so ridiculous.

"Yes, it's narrated in Sahih Bukhari that Allah said, 'If my servant draws near to Me a hand's length, I draw near to him an arm's length. And if he comes to Me walking, I go to him at speed,'" Uroosa said, pulling up the reference. "We just have to take that first step."

Those words raised a lump in my throat. It was hard to believe. After everything I had done, the sins I had committed—would Allah truly come running to *me*? If only I took a step toward Him?

No, it couldn't be. It wouldn't.

"But it's so hard!" Madiha said. "That first step."

"It definitely is," Haya agreed.

I tried to focus on her, on what she was saying, rather than being lost in my own guilt. The other girls started adding in, as well, and the conversation picked up. They talked about how hard it was to be vulnerable, to feel, to hurt, and while I didn't add in any of my own commentary, all their words rang true within me.

For the first time in a long while, I felt a little less alone.

I didn't deserve relief, but I felt it anyway, and I was—for that moment—happy.

Perhaps that was why I dreamed that night when I slept— to remember.

We were at a party, but the moment I entered, I knew something was wrong.

The room was quiet, and the first person I saw was Baba, but he wouldn't meet my eyes. He looked ten years older, shoulders crumpled, eyes downcast and ashamed. Then Ahsen, shaking his head, eyes filled with venom and fists curled. I felt my heart drop into my toes.

They hated me—all of them. I knew it. My family and my friends and my cousins, all gathered in that room, watching me. They had known me since birth, since forever, but all that love was gone. I could see them whispering, see their stolen glances and snickering smiles and countenances of horror. All directed at me.

I had been their princess, the perfect daughter—always obedient, always sweet and kind and pretty and complacent. How could I fall so far? How could one thing change everything? Change my whole life? One stupid mistake that didn't seem like a mistake until it was already made.

Mama wouldn't even look at me, wouldn't even spare me a glance. I went to her, stood before her, directly before her eyes, but it was as if I didn't exist.

"Mama," I cried, but it was a squeak, barely audible. My voice was trapped in my throat, lodged behind a growing sob. I didn't know what to do. How could I make them stop viewing me with such disgust? How could I convince them it had been a mistake? That I was sorry, that I was so, so sorry.

Then he came, the catalyst, who split my life into Before and After. He stood out from the onset: white skin and blue eyes and blond hair. And the way he looked at me, in front of everyone—it made my heart stop with fear.

It was the way I had always wanted to be looked at, but not here. Not in front of everyone.

I wanted to hide.

Mama would see; everyone would see. You could tell from his eyes what had happened between us, could tell immediately, but he didn't stop—he came forward, in front of everybody, and he grabbed my waist. Dread curdled my blood, and I wanted to push him away but I couldn't.

I couldn't.

He leaned in, and I closed my eyes. Before the kiss came, he was thrown away, replaced by Ammi.

"Slut," she hissed, and my sight went black.

When I woke up, my cheek stung, and I felt dirty and stained. The pillow beneath my cheeks absorbed my tears like a sponge.

How to expunge this humiliation from my veins? How to retract this guilt from my bones?

Uroosa had said yesterday that Allah was always with us, but I couldn't feel His presence. I was alone in my empty bed-and-breakfast room, swallowed by darkness.

I craved comfort. I wanted my bed, my books, to eat a snickerdoodle and wear my favorite pajamas, to hear the San Francisco rain outside my window. But I was thousands of miles away, and it made me so sad I could just about scream.

I wanted to scream at the top of my lungs that this pain was not poetic. Nothing about what I felt now could be described in pretty metaphors and flowery imagery, painting the sad girl as complex and beautifully broken—there was nothing beautiful about this.

It was fucking ugly.

I smothered my face in my pillow and opened my mouth wide, but the scream never came. I could feel it inside me, sharp, shredding me apart from within, decimating all there was, until it echoed in the vast emptiness left in its wake.

It felt like death, but I didn't die.

I just filled with longing for a home that no longer existed.

Chapter 8

$\mathcal{W}$ith no clothes, no toiletries, and no food, I walked and then took the bus to Walmart. The least I could do was to stock up on supplies. I got a cart and started shopping, grabbing the necessities and some comforts too. As I walked through the aisle, I saw all sorts of people—old couples, young mothers, children and their siblings.

I had never really been to Walmart by myself like this, never really been so alone. Mama was always in charge, or Ahsen, and I usually only came along to help, never for the heavy lifting.

I could see the same characteristic in the moms who were here, and I wished I could ask one of them to hold my hand and guide me too. I saw a little brown girl waddling through the aisle, holding her older brother's hand. They couldn't have been more than two and five, and for a moment, I thought the little girl looked familiar.

Maybe I saw myself in her, holding onto Ahsen's hand when we were little.

But no, it was something more.

I didn't realize until her mother turned to call her.

"Fatima!"

I ducked behind a row of clothing, heart beating fast.

It was Fareeha, Zayn's sister.

Zayn, my fiancé.

Zayn, who I was supposed to be marrying next week.

I swore to myself. *This* cannot *be happening.* Maybe I was imagining things. Gathering my courage, I slowly peeked my head out from the aisle, trying to catch another glance.

Our eyes met.

Shit, shit, shit.

Ducking my head, I made a run for it, praying she didn't recognize me. It was definitely her. *What the hell is she doing here?*

Then I remembered—she lived in New York. I had completely forgotten. What a cruel twist of fate.

Grabbing my purse, I speed-walked away from there, not even bothering to get my cart, maneuvering my way through the racks. It sounded like there were footsteps following me, but I didn't want to look over my shoulder in case it was her. I couldn't let her see my face.

Heart beating faster and faster, I rushed to the dressing rooms and entered the first one I saw. I locked the door, breathing hard.

What if Fareeha saw me? What if she tells? Maybe I should go talk to her, I considered. *Maybe I could explain.* But explain what?

"As-salaamu Alaikum!" Baba said, shaking hands with Zayn. It was March, a week after my eighteenth birthday, and he was to be my future husband, if all went well. He was a family friend who lived nearby. His sister, Fareeha, was married and lived in New York, so it was only him and his parents over for dinner.

We actually didn't know his family that well, but Ammi knew his mom from the masjid. He was twenty-one and was graduating college in May. He was supposed to start medical school in the fall.

As the dinner went on, I snuck glances at Zayn, but we didn't talk. He was nice, tall—handsome even. Later, Ammi said he was raised right, had good family values.

"Haan kardun?" I heard her ask Baba, asking if she should say yes.

This was how it was done in the olden days, and Zayn's family was straight from Pakistan, moved here a few years ago, so he didn't think it was strange or anything.

"Jo aapko sahi lage," Baba replied, telling Ammi to do what she thought was best.

"Abhi nikkah, then later, shaadi," Ammi decided.

After, when she came to talk to me, her face was surprisingly kind for once.

"Acha hai na? He is a good boy," Mama said, voice gentle. "What do you think?"

Maybe getting married would give me freedom; at the least, it might make Mama happy.

"Yes, he's nice," I said, my voice barely a whisper. "Whatever you think is best."

It was decided. Sweets were fed and gold was given.

We were going to have our nikkah—the Islamic wedding ceremony—performed, but I wasn't going to move in with him until after I finished undergraduate school and he was done with medical school. Our nikkah was supposed to be like an engagement, except we would be Islamically married.

Then I had run away.

I heard someone knocking on the changing room door. Gripping the wall for support, I swore under my breath, hoping it wasn't her.

"Ma'am, is everything all right in there?" a voice asked. Just an employee.

"Everything's great, thanks!"

But everything was terrible.

Mama must have dealt with an absolute shit show with Zayn's family when I ran. I had managed to bring shame to the family, after all. I felt nauseated, thinking of Mama calling his mother, coming up with excuses, and trying to make sense of something she did not understand.

How would she explain it to them and save her own skin? How would she deal with it all alone? Baba would be no help—he never was in matters like these. And Ahsen was never home, so expecting anything from him was futile.

It was terrible of me to abandon Zayn like that, just days

before the ceremony. No one deserved that. And what about all the preparations? All the payments and cousins flying in and clothes made and sweets delivered? What about all that? It was impossible to have any Pakistani wedding function without it being a big deal.

But I couldn't have gotten married. No matter how nice Zayn was, I barely knew him. And I couldn't take care of myself, let alone a whole husband—even if it would have only been like an engagement.

Sighing, I finally left the changing room, only to realize I had ducked into the men's side instead of the women's. A few people gave me strange looks, but I didn't care.

I speed-walked to the corner of the store, hiding out for an hour until I could gather the courage to restart my shopping. I had abandoned my cart when I ran, and when I went back to look for it, it was obviously gone.

I started over, hoping I wouldn't run into her again.

Chapter 9

Where do I go from here?

I had no clue.

What do I want?

There were too many things.

What I really wanted was not to think. I wanted the world to swallow me whole, for the sky to paint me blue, for the sun to scorch me red until I was nothing but a piece of this earth, existing inevitably, motions innate and thoughtless. I wanted to sleep for eternity and awake if everything was fixed and fine.

So I rented a car. I bought snacks, a phone for good music, and a journal. And I drove. Toward the horizon, with no destination in mind, through canopied local roads, along the ocean, until I stumbled upon an expanse of nature that could engulf me and make me forget. Fleeting moments of beauty and happiness, of perfect weather and the sun on my skin.

I drove and was scared out of my mind, but I drove until even that feeling left me. I drove until I could breathe again. I drove until my mind was blank. I drove and I forgot, and I drove and I was nothing but a speck of dirt on the earth, nothing but a puff of cloud in the sky, nothing but nothing.

I was alone with the world and God, but I didn't think He was really there. Was I a bad Muslim? Is that what this was? Was I being punished for my sins?

Sometimes, He would try and talk to me, sometimes whispering in my ears, in my heart, but I pushed Him away, too embarrassed and guilty to speak. Sometimes, He would try, but then He left too.

Sometimes, he visited my dreams, and I awoke crying, feeling filthy and stained. Sometimes, I stopped breathing. Sometimes, I watched the blood bubble from my skin in a gorgeous, grotesque shade of maroon.

Sometimes, I felt so free I wanted to kill my parents for restraining me. Sometimes, I felt so lonely I wished for my mother's arms and embrace. Sometimes, sadness suffocated me. Sometimes, beauty elevated me. Sometimes, I thought about Ahsen. Sometimes, I thought about Zahra.

Sometimes, I nearly died.

Sometimes, I nearly lived.

On the sixth morning, I woke up in a quiet bed-and-breakfast and checked my bank account to see that I had drained nearly half my resources. *You need to be smart now*, logic told me. No more nothingness. I had to think about who I was and who I wanted to become.

Why can't I just be apathetic?

One day if I ran out of money, I'd be forced to go home, and I couldn't have that. I wouldn't go back, I swore it. So I needed a plan. But I didn't know a thing about myself.

For the last six months, I hadn't been living. But it was worse after March, after making the decision to get married. It was like, after that, everything inside me went numb. I had stopped feeling because when I did, it hurt too much.

What was the life I wanted for myself?

When was I the happiest?

I could remember summers in Pakistan with my extended family, how everything was peaceful. There was the vibrant culture and my grandparents' love and my family and my roots and my home and—

I could never go back.

I would never see my grandparents again. The thought made me want to tear my hair out. Tears pricked my eyes as I thought about my daadi's face. The love with which she always smothered me. How happy she always was when I was in her arms.

Would I never see her again? Never make chai for her or feel her brush my hair? Never?

Similar to how I felt the cord connecting me to my parents sever, I felt the cord connecting me to my grandparents shatter. No longer a daughter. No longer a granddaughter.

Who was I, then? Who was I?

I pulled out my journal to write and expunge everything awful from my mind, but the words refused to come. All I could hear in my mind was Ammi's voice, broken and raw, yelling—*how could you? how could you?*—over and over, and it made me want to rip my heart out of my chest, knowing that I caused her that pain, knowing those tears were because of me, knowing that anger in her eyes was directed at me.

I had run away from my life, but I couldn't run away from myself.

Was it selfish of me to leave? Was I the problem? Ammi always said I was too sensitive. Baba didn't understand how I felt. Ahsen mocked me for being too dramatic. Maybe I was.

But how could self-love be selfish? Ammi thought it was. A girl's duty was to her parents, her brothers, and then eventually to her husband and his family. That was all I was meant to be. Nothing more. There was no sense of *self*. Ammi had been drilling these morals since birth—they were tattooed onto my skull.

Why did I keep fighting it?

I didn't hate Mama or Baba or Ahsen. I loved them, actually, but I just didn't like them anymore. Living with them, always suppressed, always suffocating, always holding my breath—I couldn't do it. Always on the edge, always one step from crumbling, like the switch from light to darkness.

It was then I noticed a little red "1" floating over my email icon. I clicked open the message and found it was from Uroosa—the Youth Group coordinator. It was a reminder that there was a meeting today, Wednesday, after Zuhr salah. I had spent a full week aimlessly driving around.

I had only signed up for the emails because I hadn't wanted to awkwardly refuse when the little signup sheet was being passed around—Haya had been watching.

Everyone had been so sweet and kind last week. *Should I go back?* Could I make myself a home there?

What if Fareeha was there? Or someone else who could recognize me? I couldn't ever truly escape.

Then I saw another email from Haya.

> hey zahra! I totally forgot to ask for your phone number, but it was so nice meeting you last week! I hope I'll see you again at the yg meeting!! :)

I was running out of money. I needed to figure out my next move.

So I went, hoping for a sign.

Chapter 10

"Zahra! Salaam!"

Haya's voice called out to me the moment I entered the masjid. Relief washed over me. The entire bus ride and walk over I had been worried. I had returned the car—it was too expensive to keep, even though it did make traveling much more convenient.

Haya motioned me over to where she was standing with a couple of other girls, and I recognized the pair of best friends from last week, Imaan and Madiha. They were always together, attached at the hip, and the sight pinched my heart, making me all too aware of how lonely I was.

"Ah, I'm so glad you came!" Haya said, interrupting my thoughts. She threw her arms around me in a hug, taking me aback. I couldn't remember the last time I had been hugged. My body instantly relaxed.

"Salaam, Zahra," Madiha said, giving me a kind smile.

Imaan and Uroosa welcomed me as well. My spirits lifted. They remembered me! Perhaps I wasn't a ghost after all.

"Zahra, please chip in with your opinion," Imaan said, voice serious. Today she was wearing really cute wide-leg pants and a ruffled blouse. Like last time, she was dressed so nicely. "We're discussing television shows. Diya and I are pushing for *Gossip Girl* as the best."

"Please!" Haya cried. "*Gossip Girl* is so trashy."

"Um, hel*lo*, that's what makes it good!" Madiha replied, holding both her hands up. "The tension, the anxiety, the *drama*! Meanwhile, *The Office* is so boring. And sad! They're so mean to the main character, what's-his-name—the guy played by Steve Carell."

"Boring? I'm offended," Haya said, shaking her head. "*The Office* is amazing. Zahra, back me up."

I looked from Haya to the girls, laughing. "I'm with Haya on this one. *Gossip Girl* is way too dramatic."

Imaan and Madiha both gasped dramatically.

"That's it!" Imaan cried. "I've had enough of you people!"

"You're fired! You're all fired from being our friends!" Madiha added.

I could see why they liked *Gossip Girl* so much.

We laughed and continued talking. Imaan told us about a BuzzFeed article she had read, and how she wanted to see her words there one day.

"I'm really into journalism," Imaan said. "I've been reaching out to places for freelance work but haven't gotten anything yet, so I'm trying to work my way there."

"She's so smart," Madiha told us proudly, showing off her best friend. Imaan shoved her playfully.

"As if you're not?" Imaan said. She turned to me. "Madiha's a total rock star in science. I made her do all my chemistry lab reports for me last year because I simply could not deal."

"Ohmygod, chemistry lab," I said. "I hated that."

Madiha waved a hand. "Pshh."

"She's a total jock too," Imaan added. "But we love her anyway, even though jocks are insufferable."

"Hey, girl jocks are fine," Madiha protested. "It's guy jocks who are *jerks*."

We continued chatting and were interrupted only when the iqamah for Zuhr rang out. We stood in line and prayed together in jamaat, and after, when the rest of the crowd had left, Uroosa called the meeting to start. Like last week, we sat cross-legged in a circle on the carpet. A tray of fresh cookies someone had baked was passed around. I gladly took one, biting into the sweet chocolate.

"Salaam, girls!" Uroosa called out warmly. "I don't see any new faces, so we can skip the introductions. Today we're going to do something a little different. There's no topic; I'll leave the discussion open for anybody who feels they have something to say. Imaan, would you like to start?"

I shifted my attention to her, ears perked to hear what she had to say. I didn't feel quite brave enough to say anything myself, but I wanted to really pay attention to these girls, to listen.

"Yes, sure! Salaam, everyone. So, I was thinking about

marriage because my aunt is looking for my cousin to get married soon," Imaan said. "And my cousin was telling me how scared she is. Isn't that outrageous? She's scared. It made me wonder. Isn't something wrong with the world and society if women are afraid of getting married?"

She paused, and we all considered it for a moment.

"Have you ever heard a man say he doesn't want to get married, or he is afraid what will happen when he does?" Imaan continued. "You never hear that. Probably because things never really go bad for men. They always benefit. Isn't that wrong? How afraid we are of something that is meant to be so amazing?"

"Not to mention the abominable desi wife standards," Madiha said. Most of the girls in the Youth Group were desi, so we all immediately knew what she was talking about. "Like how we have to be fair-skinned and thin? You must know how to cook. You must be submissive to be a good wife. Don't be too loud or too opinionated and give him whatever he wants, whenever he wants—even yourself. Stay quiet. Compromise. Women must give in. Pamper him and never give him an opportunity to be upset with you. But what about the wives? What about us? I mean, there's definitely a lot of awareness and good change going on, but it's so slow! And why is the culture so messed up to begin with?"

"Even if the culture is messed up, you can't help but miss your home country, right?" Hamnah said with a sigh, jumping in. "It's like, I always feel this pulse within me, pulling me back there, across oceans and continents. I miss hearing my mother tongue. I miss the halal food everywhere and the sound of the adhan throughout the day wherever you are."

"Tell me about it," Haya added. "Don't you guys miss your family? How somehow you are related to everybody and even those that are not connected to you by blood are somehow connected by marriage or proximity? Do you ever miss the culture, the richness and the vividness of it? The clothes, the music, the sounds and smells and flavors and sensations—I miss it all. I wonder if I will miss my roots forever."

"It's hard being the child of an immigrant," one of the younger girls, Umaymah, said. "You don't really feel like you have a home. Are we American because we were born and grew up here? Or are we Pakistani—or Indian, or Bangladeshi, or Arab—because that is our ancestral homeland, where our grandparents and great-grandparents died and are buried?"

"Exactly!" I said, before I could think twice and stop myself. Everyone's attention shifted to me. My heart rate quickened, and I swallowed, nervous. I turned to Haya, who gave me a reassuring smile, and then I continued speaking. "Like, um, I was thinking—where is home for us? When we go to wherever is 'back home,' our families laugh at our accents and our adjustment to the mechanisms there, and when we are here, they tell us to go back to where we came from. I wonder if we'll ever find the perfect balance between the two—if we'll ever find *home*."

Someone else spoke up, and the girls' attention shifted once more. My heart was still beating quickly. That was nerve-racking. But I was glad to have spoken, glad to have participated beyond only listening. It felt good to talk.

And it made me wonder, and it made me think, about the great vastness of life. These were wide topics we all related to; everyone had anecdotes. It was nice to talk—to feel the solidarity among us all and the understanding. I saw girls hold hands and squeeze strength into one another. There weren't many solutions, really, but we all talked and gave advice and tried to deal with the sometimes harsh realities.

There seemed to be a singular cord connecting us all, threading through each of our hearts, as we cracked jokes and talked about serious things and laughed and nearly cried all by turns.

It was a mess of a meeting, really—there was no specific aim or goal to be reached.

We just talked. And I became a part of this community, another vein the heart pumped blood to. I felt connected to them through my own struggles and experiences.

At the end of the hour, Uroosa did a closing dua, and the meeting was adjourned.

"How did you like it?" Haya asked afterward, when people began leaving the masjid.

"I loved it."

"Great!" she said, squealing. "You have to come every week, okay? I love when YG gets new members!"

"I'll try," I responded. I didn't know yet if I was staying.

I wanted to—but I didn't know. What if I saw Fareeha again? What if this was her masjid?

"Hey, do you want to go grab some food?" Haya asked, interrupting my thoughts. "I'm starving and there's a Panera nearby. I need mac and cheese in an IV, stat."

She wants to hang out with me? Maybe this was my sign.

"That sounds great."

We walked out of the masjid and into the sun. It was hot, the sky a beautiful, pure blue, and the trees a vibrant green. We headed over to her car in the parking lot. As I sat in the passenger seat, I was overwhelmed by the sudden feeling of normalcy. How long had it been since I went out with a friend? Sat in the passenger seat as they drove? Too long. Not since last fall, maybe, before the pressure and frenzy of college applications set in.

"What brings you to New York?" Haya asked, starting her car. Cool air immediately flowed out of the vents, and she directed one to my face, another to her own. "You ran out so quickly last week, I feel like I didn't get the chance to properly talk to you!"

"I just graduated high school, and I'm going to NYU in the fall," I lied. It was a plausible reason. I had been accepted—I could still go. But I had missed the deadline, and I didn't know the first thing about student loans or if they would even let me still attend.

Well, maybe not this semester, but maybe next? It would be good to have it as an option. My whole life stretched ahead of me, a blank canvas, and I needed to fill it with something—map a path to somewhere.

"That's great!" Haya replied, eyes on the road. She was

sitting ramrod straight with both hands firmly on the wheel, a very responsible driver. "And we're the same age—I just graduated too, and I'm starting the pharmacy program at St. John's in the fall."

"Cool! You must be so smart."

"Ah, not really," she answered, shaking her head. "So are you staying with . . . family or something? You said you're from California, right?"

"Um, well," I began, but I didn't know where to go. "Actually . . . my parents passed away recently, so I came here early—I needed a change of scenery."

"Inna lillahi wa inna ilayhi ra'jioon," she replied, reciting the Arabic prayer Muslims say upon hearing of loss or tragedy.

I had become mendacious; the lie came easily.

It sounded about right. Sounded okay. They were dead, so I left California because I couldn't deal with it anymore. Sounded true. Tasted okay.

Was it a lie if you believed it? Maybe my parents were dead. Maybe they had died while I was gone. *Maybe, maybe, maybe.*

"I'm so sorry, Zahra," Haya said, face melting with grief as she turned to me. Since we were at a red light, she reached out to squeeze my hand, and I felt my eyes well with tears.

Even if they weren't dead, I was probably dead to them.

"Thank you," I replied, voice muffled.

"And what about your brother? You mentioned you had an older brother, right?"

What about my brother?

"Ahsen, yeah. He goes to school up in Boston," I told her.

"That's good!" she replied, brightening. The light switched to green, so we continued driving. "He's close by. My cousin from Pakistan, Hamza, just finished his first year up in Boston! I wonder if they've crossed paths. What's your brother studying?"

"Finance."

"Hamza's civil engineering. He's a nerd like that. What are you interested in studying?"

"I'm not really sure yet," I told her. "I'll probably go in as undecided and see what fits."

"Don't worry about it," Haya replied. "You've got time."

For the first time, I realized I did. An entire life full.

We arrived at Panera and parked, then headed inside, where it was moderately busy. We ordered some food, though I didn't really have an appetite. Truthfully, I missed Mama's food. I missed my own food, even. I used to help Mama with cooking a lot back home, and we always made something fresh every day.

Something I wouldn't experience again.

"That's our order," Haya said, pulling me from my thoughts. We grabbed our trays and sat down, and Zuhr somehow turned to Asr as I found myself talking to a stranger. I hadn't spoken in days, and it was such a relief to feel the vibrations of my own voice, my tongue fumbling to keep up with the words that poured from me.

I didn't tell her everything—not about running away or why. I didn't want her judging me for what I'd done. Those memories were better suppressed.

Nonetheless, it was nice. I realized some things about myself then, just speaking to her, and it was interesting because she didn't know me at all, so I could very well exaggerate. I could make myself whoever I wanted to be, no longer a Paracha or Ahsen's younger sister or Momina's daughter.

Was this a fresh start? Yes. And no.

But it was nice to laugh, once we got past the sticky details of reality. We just talked. I wasn't sure exactly what about, but we just talked—about life and the vast spectrum it encompassed, the beauty and the horror. Haya was so sweet, her face filled with laughter and light. *What would it feel like to be that content?*

"Won't your parents be worrying?" I asked, when some time had passed and our cappuccinos were cold. Haya shook her head.

"No, they're pretty lax about that sort of thing," she told me. Haya hadn't gotten a single call in the past few hours. I couldn't relate in the slightest.

"Hey!" Her eyes brightened behind her glasses. "Come home with me for dinner! You can meet my sister too. She's crazypants but hilarious—don't tell her I said that. The hilarious part. Her head is already too big. Feel free to tell her she is unhinged."

I laughed, then paused. "I'm not sure . . ." I didn't want to impose.

"Wait, where have you been staying?" Haya asked suddenly. "With family?"

"Uh . . . ," I began. "I've been driving around the past few days, staying at random places, but I just got back in the area today, so I was thinking of getting a bed-and-breakfast nearby to stay in tonight. I don't have any family here."

"Wait, are you serious?"

I nodded.

"Bed-and-breakfasts are so expensive!" she cried. "Please come stay at my place for a day or two."

"No, no, it's okay," I said quickly, completely mortified at the thought of being such a burden.

"Oh, please come! Please, please! We can look for a place for you to stay for the summer before the semester starts," Haya said. "My mom is great at finding things like that—she can help you out! And we get to have a little sleepover too! I haven't had a sleepover in literally forever! We can do face masks! I just got a new set, and they smell so good you'll want to eat them."

"Um . . . ," I started again. Before I could concoct a plausible excuse, Haya held up a hand.

"It's done!" she said. "This is going to be so fun!"

Maybe she could see I was struggling, maybe she was taking pity on me, or maybe she really was thrilled and I wouldn't be imposing. Somehow, I didn't care—I felt excited too.

I smiled at her. "Thank you. That's so kind of you. And it does sound really fun."

"Ohmygod, don't even mention it. Are you renting a car or something? I can drop you by your car at the masjid, then you can follow me to my place?"

"No, I've been taking the bus and walking places."

"Okay, so I'll be your chauffeur," she said. "Please give me five stars on Uber."

"You are an excellent driver," I told her, laughing. We threw out our garbage and headed out to her car. I only had a big tote bag of things that I'd been carrying around, so it was easy to transport.

Haya's house was about fifteen minutes away, and we took local roads until we drove into a gated community with houses close together. All the streets were named cute things like Blueberry Lane or Tulip Place.

I was surprised to see how narrow the streets were, and the overwhelming greenery everywhere. In our suburb, the streets were wide, with thick trees neatly spread out, and things felt drier. Here, everything was overflowing, bushes and thickets of trees and the rustling of leaves. In the evening, the weather wasn't even hot—it was pleasant.

"Have you asked your parents if it's all right?" I asked, as she pulled me to the door. Haya waved a nonchalant hand.

"It's fine. They adore company," she said. Panic ran through me. Before I could stop her, she was pushing open the door.

We were home.

Chapter 11

$\mathcal{I}$t was home but not mine—Haya's.

As we entered, I was overwhelmed by the scent of fresh lemon filling the air. In the distance, I could hear the sound of Geo News from the living room and smell roti cooking in the kitchen.

"As-salaamu Alaikum!" Haya called out, warranting a chorus of wa alaikum salaams.

We walked through the corridor straight into the kitchen, where her parents were. Her father was a tall man with thick, curly hair, and her mother was a short, round woman, with a long braid down her back.

They both wore shalwar kameez, and Auntie had a dupatta across her neck. Haya's mother was cooking while her father was chopping the salad. The air was filled with the smell of ginger and meat and onions, like food and comfort and home.

"Agayee meri, beti?" Her mother turned and, upon seeing me, smiled. "As-salaamu Alaikum, beta," she said, voice older but as sweet as her daughter's. "Haya, ye kaun?"

"This is my new friend Zahra from Youth Group!" Haya said, leaving my side to join her mother's. "She's from California! I invited her over for dinner. She said she'd be staying at a bed-and-breakfast, but they are overpriced anyway so I asked her to stay with us until she can find someplace better. So, Mama, this is Zahra, and Zahra, this is my mom, Nabila."

I cringed at Haya's words—how could she so easily launch plans onto her mother? Spontaneity was unappreciated in my house and near forbidden. But Haya's mother was unfazed.

"Of course," she said with a laugh. "So nice to meet you, beti."

"Are you sure, Nabila Auntie?" I asked, voice small.

"Of course!" she said again, shaking her head. "You are most welcome here."

"I don't want to impose."

"No, no, please." Nabila Auntie waved an aata-covered hand, sprinkling flour in the air. "Anyway, the Prophet would always house travelers, you know, so really you're giving us an opportunity to do good, and we should be thanking *you*."

I smiled, and relief pushed me forward into her open arms. She hugged me hello. She smelled like clean cotton and powder, that certain auntie smell.

"Salaam, beti," Umar Uncle said to me, giving me a warm smile from under his curled mustache.

"HAYA?" A voice screamed from atop the stairs. I assumed that was Sadaf, Haya's older sister. "Haya, you will not *believe* what happened to me today. Matlab, it's unbelievable, truly."

A tall girl entered the kitchen, hands waving in the air dramatically. She had curly black hair pulled up messily into a bun with a few loose tendrils falling down. She wore a T-shirt and shalwar. A gold nose ring pierced one nostril, giving her a very striking, pind-desi look.

As Haya took her scarf off, I noticed her hair was similar to her sister's—black and curly, though longer and curlier. They both had light, wheat-brown skin and took after their father in the looks department.

They mirrored each other in looks, but even more so in mannerisms. Their facial expressions and confident manner of talking resembled each other's, for one thing.

Everyone always said Ahsen and I looked similar, but our personalities couldn't have been more different.

"Ooh, friend!" Sadaf squealed, running to me. Before I could react, she wrapped her arms around me, but because I was so short, she was basically hugging my head. Sadaf and Haya were both tall, though Sadaf was taller than Haya. I inhaled the scent of her piney perfume, which was slightly masculine.

"Hi, salaam," I said, and I couldn't help but laugh.

"Sadaf, you're *such* a weirdo," Haya said, pulling her sister off me. At the same time, Nabila Auntie said, "Uff, Sadaf, you couldn't wear a kurta with that shalwar? T-shirt zaroori thi?"

"Mama, please, this is so much more comfortable," Sadaf

replied breezily, gesturing to the T-shirt her mother didn't approve of.

"Sorry, Zahra," Haya said. "Like I said, my sister is crazypants."

"Um, who are you calling crazypants? And *Zahra*! Oh, I adore that name! Did you know it means beauty? Totally true in your case," she said, draping an arm across my shoulder, leaning in as if to tell me a secret. "Did you know Mama was going to name me that? It's said when I was born, I simply *radiated* beauty—still do—but Mama's grandma's name was Sadaf, so I was named for her."

"Oh, please!" Haya exclaimed. "More like Mama *wished* her daughter would radiate beauty, but you didn't—so she had to have me for that dream to be fulfilled."

Haya stared off into the distance smiling while Sadaf rolled her eyes. "As if. You were such a fat little baby, nobody could distinguish any facial features. Like you legitimately didn't have a chin. I swear, I couldn't hold her after she was a month old because she was simply too heavy."

"That's because you were a weak little three-year-old!"

"Excuse me!"

"Oh, stop it, the both of you," their father, Umar Uncle, interjected. "You're both beautiful, regardless of your name, and you very well know it too. I mean, whose daughters are you?"

"Mine, of course," his wife interjected coolly, stirring the food.

They all laughed. *Are families actually like this?* Full of light-hearted jokes and laughter and love? Weren't there meant to be hard lines of respect and bowed heads and quiet voices?

I went to the bathroom to clean up, catching my breath, before coming out for dinner.

Nabila Auntie made gosht karahi and fresh phulke, and when I took the first bite, I almost started crying. It was so good, the chunks of mutton cooked perfectly in tomatoes, coriander, and ghee, and the roti perfectly thin and airy. A little different from how Mama made it, but still, it was a home-cooked meal, made fresh and with love. In that moment, I ached for home, but I tried not to think of it, focusing instead on the merriment of the sisters' conversation.

All throughout dinner, Sadaf and Haya spoke loudly over each other, most of the time being physical about it, pushing one another and gesturing enthusiastically, and their parents didn't say a word to scold them. They were not reprimanded for their impropriety—not told that *good* girls never spoke too loudly. Rather, their father laughed, and their mother listened.

Umar Uncle finished dinner first, and after he ate, he got up and quietly went to the back door. I wondered why.

"Baba!" Haya cried, noticing. "I have told you one hundred thousand times to quit!"

"I have quit, jaan, I'm just going out for some . . . fresh air."

Nabila Auntie shook her head in disapproval. "Don't get any ideas about coming near me if you're going out for a smoke."

"Ah, but how could I possibly stay away?" he asked, tossing her a wink before slipping outside.

Haya met my eyes and shook her head. "He's so bad about smoking," she told me.

"It is terrible for his health, I agree, but God, do cigarettes smell good," Sadaf said, taking in a deep breath. Umar Uncle hadn't closed the door all the way, so we could smell the cigarette smoke a little. "I'm, like, definitely secondhand addicted."

"You're deranged, is what you are," Haya told her sister, then turned to me. "Once Sadaf liked this guy purely because he smelled like cigarettes and gasoline."

"Ohmygod, I completely forgot about him." Sadaf's eyes went all dreamy as she recalled, then she shook her head. "He was such a tool, but he smelled sooo good." Haya made a disgusted face. Sadaf turned to me. "He had a motorcycle too," she said. "I've always wanted to ride a motorcycle with a man."

Nabila Auntie cleared her throat. "Seriously?" their mother said, shaking her head.

"Yes, Mama Dearest." Sadaf and Haya laughed, unperturbed.

I was shocked by how frank they were being in front of their mother, doubly so by how calm she was in response. I would have never said anything even relating to a boy in front of Ammi, let alone openly talk about crushes and smells and cigarettes and *motorcycles*.

"You girls are grown up, so I trust you not to do anything foolish," Nabila Auntie said, taking a bite of her food. "But, Sadaf, please no motorcycles."

"Motorcycles?" Umar Uncle said, coming back inside. "Who's getting on a motorcycle?"

"Me!" Sadaf said, cheeky and unashamed. My mouth almost dropped open at the candid way she spoke.

Umar Uncle made a face. "You can't get a motorcycle until you're thirty-five," he said, waving a finger.

"Baba, come on, we're not kids anymore. You can't keep using that logic," Sadaf said.

"Baba always says we can't do things until we're thirty-five," Haya explained to me. "It's so random! And makes no sense!"

"Like when we were little kids, he would say, 'No watching scary movies until you're thirty-five,'" Sadaf added. "And we'd be like, 'But *Mama* isn't thirty-five and she watches scary movies!' and he'd amend it to, 'Until you're thirty-five or have two kids, whichever comes first.' As if that has literally any logic!"

"I still stand by it," Umar Uncle said.

We all laughed. I was glad they were including me in their little stories and jokes, letting me in on their flow of anecdotes and commentary and love.

Haya must have told them something about me when I went to the bathroom, for they didn't ask a single prying question, nor did they force me to speak.

After dinner, everybody picked up their own plates and pushed in their own chairs and there was no big production of cleaning the kitchen. Haya, Sadaf, and I cleared the table and handed the dishes to Nabila Auntie and Umar Uncle, who washed and dried and put them away.

It was all done in no time at all, and I thought about how back in California, every night I would stand for nearly an hour washing everybody's dishes. How pointless when everybody could do their own share.

"Okay, bachay," Nabila Auntie said, when everything was clean. "You girls have fun. Baba and I are going to bed. Haya, take care of Zahra, okay? Zahra, jaani, if you need anything, do let us know."

"Of course, Mama," Haya responded.

"Thank you, Auntie," I said. Then ensued a chorus of goodnights and kisses, and I received a hug as well. But it was not one of those disingenuous hugs aunties give you when you greet them at parties—the slight squeeze of the shoulder, the lightest brushing of cheeks, so as not to ruin anyone's makeup. Nabila Auntie squeezed me to her, and I felt enveloped by the security that exists only in a mother's arms. For the first time in the longest time, I felt full.

We went upstairs, and Haya led me to her room while Sadaf went to hers. Haya's room had sunrise-pink walls and was decorated in a very beach house aesthetic. It smelled like sea salt and hibiscus, courtesy of a plug-in air freshener. I recognized the scent. It's how Haya smelled too.

"The bathroom is just through there." Haya showed me, pointing. "There's face wash and toothpaste and everything in there, but if you need anything, let me know! And get in there before Sadaf does—she takes forever doing her skincare routine. Do you want to shower? I'll get you a fresh towel."

"Oh, um, yes, a shower would be good," I said. Haya

got me a towel and I went to the bathroom with my tote bag. I only had one other outfit that I'd been wearing, which I'd picked up on that Walmart run, and one pair of pajamas. While I'd washed my clothes once in the hotel bathroom, they weren't properly laundered.

I also had the toothpaste I bought, but when I went to the girls' shared bathroom, I immediately wanted to use their things. There was an array of lotions and face washes and different skincare products, and in the shower, I used their shampoo and conditioner, my hair and scalp instantly feeling better and cleaner than it had in the past week of using hotel shampoo.

I took my time cleaning myself and after, brushed my teeth and moisturized. It was the closest thing to my Californian routine I had had since I'd run away.

It felt good. Really good. My stomach was full of home-cooked food, I was clean, and I was someplace safe.

When I exited the bathroom, I went back to Haya's room, holding my clothes. "Can I throw in a load of laundry?" I asked, and she showed me downstairs to the laundry room. I tossed all the articles of clothing I had in the machine. They barely made half a load, but the detergent smelled lovely, and I was already excited for clean, fresh clothes.

Then we went back upstairs and prayed Isha. It was a thoughtless set of actions on my part, done in five minutes. But Haya spent some time on her prayer, so I pretended to make dua until finally she was done.

I wondered what she had spoken to Allah about for so long, but I didn't ask. I wouldn't know how to relate, anyway.

"It's still sort of early, so let's watch a movie," Haya suggested. "Sadaf!" she called from her room. "Let's watch a movie!"

"Let me finish praying!" Sadaf hollered back.

"Let's go get snacks," Haya said to me. We went back downstairs to the kitchen and loaded up, then set up on Haya's bed. While we waited for Sadaf, we slapped some sheet masks on.

"Ooh, these do smell really good," I told Haya.

"See, I told you." She looked funny talking with the mask plastered over her face. I giggled. "Stop, don't laugh," she said, trying not to move her face and mess up the mask, "or I'll start laughing too."

"Sheet masks! Where's mine?" Sadaf asked, coming into Haya's room from the opened door.

"You're too late so you don't get one," Haya said. Sadaf ignored her and grabbed one from Haya's drawer, smoothing it on.

"Did you get the cookies and the—?" Sadaf asked.

"Doritos? Yes!" Haya held them up. "Now *hurry up* and close the door so Zahra can take her scarf off."

Sadaf did as she was told. When the door was shut, I took my scarf off and we all climbed into bed. Haya was in the middle with her laptop on her lap. Sadaf and I surrounded her with the snacks.

"What movie?" Haya asked me. I paused. I hadn't watched a movie in so long, I couldn't remember any of my favorites.

"You guys pick," I told them. "No horror though, please. I'm absurdly unbrave. Romantic comedy if possible."

"I agree," Sadaf chimed in. "Get something heavy on the rom and heavy on the com, sis."

"I've got just the thing."

The movie began and it was so easy to slip back into the cracks of what life used to be like. There was nothing unfamiliar about being in a bed with too many people, huddling together in front of a screen and sharing snacks. I used to do this with my cousins, with my school friends, sometimes even with Mama when there was a Pakistani film we both wanted to watch.

There was nothing unfamiliar about making remarks and swooning and adding commentary. Haya drew hearts onto the screen when Sam Claflin appeared, and we had all seen the movie so many times we knew most of the words.

"Ugh, they keep missing each other!" Sadaf cried, frustrated even though she knew they would end up together in the end. "Personally, I cannot handle this. Just shoot me if this ever happens to me."

"I will shoot you right now if you don't shut up!" Haya threatened suddenly as Lily Collins came on screen.

We all paused in silence at Haya's aggressive comment, then all burst out laughing at the same time.

"Omygod, okay, I'll shut up," Sadaf said, jokingly abashed as she threw her hands up in innocence.

"Sorry, these movies get me so emotional!" Haya covered

her face with her hands. "I can't believe that jerk hid the letter! I'm going to cry!"

We continued laughing, and my stomach hurt, but in a good way. I felt breathless, my chest tight. Then, Haya grabbed my hand and squeezed.

And it was as if she were squeezing me through time.

I remembered nights with my cousins, watching movies, squealing and laughing. I remembered days with friends, falling into one another, heads on shoulders and eyes shut tight and arms grasping and smiles wide. Those memories were vague and out of focus but still there.

And when Haya squeezed my hand, it felt so normal—so painfully ordinary—that I started crying.

Silently at first, just tears scorching my cheeks with their trails. There was finally a moment of peace, a semblance of contentment in my heart. I was so overjoyed, I couldn't handle the sudden surge of positive emotion.

Tears turned to sniffling and shuddering breaths, but I told myself to be quiet, to stop. Otherwise it would seem like I was seeking attention. I told myself to bury my sadness and smile.

But I couldn't hide it anymore—it was too late in the night, and I was too tired. So I bit my lip and suffered in silence until Sadaf handed me a tissue.

"I always cry at this part too, don't worry," she said gently, eyes still on the screen. I was infinitely thankful she didn't cause a scene—stop the movie, switch on the lights, turn to me, ask me what was wrong.

"Same," Haya said, eyes unwavering from the screen as she handed me a donut.

It made me want to cry even more, their kindness. What had I done to deserve this? What great stroke of luck was I experiencing to have stumbled upon the kindest girl in the world and her family?

Is it You? I silently wondered. *Is this a setup for a punishment I'm going to face? Or is this relief?*

I didn't believe I deserved relief, but I made the choice to accept it anyway, and I was—for that moment—happy.

Chapter 12

When I woke up the next morning in Haya's bed, Haya was gone. I stretched, taking in the sunrise-pink walls and the slants of sunshine coming in through the gaps in her blinds.

I got my (freshly laundered) second outfit and toothbrush, and went to the bathroom. Halfway there, I paused.

I could just make out voices discussing something seriously downstairs, and I had a feeling I knew what. I edged down the staircase until the words became clear. I listened.

"Haya, you have to take care of Zahra, acha?" Nabila Auntie said. "I don't think she's well."

"Of course, Mama." I heard Haya kissing Nabila Auntie's cheek before lowering her voice a bit. "I'm glad she ate a proper dinner last night. When we went for lunch yesterday, she barely ate. And the things she said to me yesterday—I think she has depression and perhaps anxiety as well. And there were fresh wounds across her arms, Mama, and they didn't seem accidental."

"Oh, bechari," Auntie said, voice worried. "We must help her as best we can and pray that she will be all right. Whatever it is that's caused this is deeper than any of us can penetrate, but we can help her move toward self-healing. And remember, be kind."

I walked back to Haya's room, head spinning. They were talking about me. I was Zahra, the girl with depression and perhaps anxiety as well. When did that happen?

I'm depressed? I'm hurting myself?

No, I'm fine. Perfectly fine, just a little sad, that's all, but everyone gets sad sometimes, right? I was still convinced I was being dramatic, overreacting.

But it was true: I was depressed. I was hurting myself.

The realization made me disgusted with myself. I didn't want to be broken. I didn't want them to worry about me. I didn't want to be a burden to them.

Ammi said depression wasn't real anyway. She said it was simply an excuse to be ungrateful. That it was all in my head—this sadness—and if I wanted, I could get rid of it. I just had to want to be happy and I would be.

You have control of your emotions, she would say. S*top being so sad. Stop being ungrateful. Allah hates those who are not happy for what they have. Look at all you have, and still, you are unhappy? Look at those children in Palestine and Syria, living in war. Look at the girls with acid thrown on their faces in Pakistan or the women starving in Yemen.*

Still, you are sad? Still, you complain? Even after your Baba and I gave you everything? This house, this privilege, this pretty face?

What is there to be sad about? Tell me.

I never had anything to say. All I knew was how awful I felt. I had no explanation for it. I pushed up my sleeve and looked at the fingernail-shaped scabs indented in my skin, like seeds sown into the earth.

But nothing would grow from this, not even when I picked one and a gorgeous, grotesque maroon bloomed from the wound. It didn't even hurt anymore. Nothing more than a pinch. Nothing more than a little reminder that I was still alive.

Footsteps moved toward me. I rubbed the blood into my skin and pulled my sleeve down as Haya entered.

"Morning, love," she said, jumping onto the bed beside me. Her laugh was infectious, so I smiled. "How'd you sleep?" she asked.

"Well," was the automatic response. Polite and well-mannered.

"Great!" She beamed. "Now get dressed! Let's have some breakfast and head out."

"Okay. Where are we going?" I asked.

Haya wiggled her eyebrows. "For some awaragardi—time to explore."

"Okay."

I got dressed, and when I was ready, we went downstairs. As we descended the steps toward the kitchen, I could smell melted butter and hear sizzling as Nabila Auntie cooked parathas and fried eggs.

Mama used to make parathas every Sunday morning

without fail. My childhood memories were full of family breakfasts of crispy, pizza-pie-shaped bread with salty milk. Ahsen would tickle me, and I would squeal with delight, my giggles bubbling through the house. Baba would tease Mama and she would laugh, and ten years would drop from her eyes.

Would they still sit together at the dining table, even with the missing chair? One half of Mama's children gone.

"Come eat," Nabila Auntie said, so I sat down in another family's life and ate. It was a balance of teasing and chatter and love, but I fit nowhere in the equation. I was factored out, sitting alongside a parenthesis looking in.

After we ate, Haya and Sadaf put on their scarves, pinning them in place. Sadaf grabbed the keys, and it was time to head out. Cheeks were kissed and goodbyes were said, but I was an awkward stranger out of place.

"Let's bounce," said Haya, throwing an arm across my shoulder. We stepped outside into the heat, heading straight for Sadaf's car. Haya sat in the passenger seat, and I sat in the back. "Brace yourself," Haya warned me.

Once Sadaf started the car, loud Punjabi music blared from the sound system. I wondered what Haya meant until Sadaf started driving, whipping out of the Chaudrys' driveway with alarming speed. I clutched the door, eyes wide. Sadaf adjusted her mirror, winking at me.

"Let's rock and roll," Sadaf said.

"Sadaf, please!" Haya cried as we sped down the street.

"Oh, don't be a baby!" Sadaf called back over the sound of

music. "Now who wants coffee? I need an iced latte like I need air. It is. So. Hot."

We stopped at Dunkin' to get iced caramel lattes, then drove over to the nearest mall, which was about half an hour away. Despite her chaotic manner, Sadaf wasn't an entirely reckless driver—she only ran one (maybe two) red lights. It would have been alarming if she wasn't so confident, but it was that confidence that made me blindly trust her. I knew we would be okay.

It was a nice feeling. Sadaf was the cool and caring older sibling I had always wanted—striking the perfect balance between responsibility and fun—whereas Ahsen could barely take care of himself, let alone anyone else.

Sadaf was the same age as Ahsen, both about to be seniors in college. Sadaf was three years older, but she and Haya were best friends. More than best friends. They were like two branches sprouting from the same tree.

I hated Ahsen sometimes for not knowing me. For being an idiot and fighting with Baba over things that could have been ignored. For every time Mama sighed when he came home late or came down from a high. Every time he was arrogant and entitled and a man who believed the world was his to take.

The hate hardly lasted because I always felt bad for him. And I knew things were rough for him. With Baba especially. As many times as Ahsen picked a fight with Baba, Baba picked a fight with him. So I let Ahsen be imperfect even though it meant I had to make up the difference.

There was only ever room for one screwup in the family.

"Oooh, turn this song up!" Sadaf said, pulling me from my thoughts. It was a throwback song, from years and years ago, and the sudden tune struck a chord within me, triggering memories of the time in my life I had heard it last. The world was suddenly full of tart lemonade and sizzling chicken and splashing water and summer sunshine.

Then Haya began to sing, and the world was then and now, past and present, and I straddled them both to sing along to the words I had known for years but forgotten until this exact moment.

So we sang, the three of us, at the top of our lungs, but it wasn't loud enough to drown the melodic sound of the singer's voice and the bass and the drums. We sang and our voices were one, and for an ephemeral moment, I didn't feel so alone anymore.

For the rest of the car ride, we sang. We sang old Disney movie songs and dramatized the different characters.

And I wondered how I remembered all the words when I could hardly remember the last six months. But some things, I guess you never forget, and being a kid is one of them.

And you never forget the Bollywood songs they play at weddings, either. We sang Hindi and Punjabi songs even though we hardly knew the words, except the parts where they broke out in English.

Haya serenaded Sadaf.

We sang and we laughed and we exchanged stories and sat in silence and smiled, and I wasn't sure, but I thought this was living—being in good company and talking about nothing and everything.

It was familiar as life used to be Before, when I had friends and we went out for crepes or to the mall or for coffee or for walks or just lay nestled in bed together.

In the car with Sadaf and Haya, I felt buoyant.

Maybe the reason I had spiraled so much farther down in the last six months was because I had shut everyone out: my school friends, my family friends, anyone who tried to get near me, even people who I wasn't exceptionally close to but still liked being around. I had isolated myself, pushing them all away, until eventually they stopped trying too.

When we got to the mall, we headed inside and started browsing. I watched Haya and Sadaf, observing their choices. Haya gravitated toward pastels and pretty pieces, while Sadaf liked darker colors and more striking styles. Both of them had good taste, and I trailed behind them, carrying a pile of sweatpants and loose shirts. They had no shape and were nothing but cloth to bury myself in.

"Okay, I'm basically done," Haya said, arms full of blouses and skirts.

"Same," Sadaf said, holding jeans and two tops. They both turned to me.

"Yeah, I'm done too," I said.

"Let me see what you've got," Haya said. I showed her my armful of clothes. She and Sadaf exchanged a glance.

"Darling Zahra," Sadaf said. "You must appreciate the little things in life." She plucked a T-shirt from my hands, holding it up gingerly. "And one of those little things is dressing cute as hell."

"Look good, feel good, babe," said Haya, pulling the sweatpants from my pile. "There's nothing wrong with wearing sweatpants and sweatshirts, but they don't make you feel gorgeous, do they?"

I shook my head. She handed me an orange skirt. My eyes widened.

"This won't look good on me," I said upon seeing the color. A little voice popped in my head. It told me my skin was too dark to wear coral, that my skin got washed out when I wore yellow. I couldn't pull off this color or that; they didn't complement my skin tone—I was too brown.

"What gives you that idea?" Haya asked, confused. I shrugged.

"Do not listen to societal bullshit that tells you you can't wear certain colors," said Sadaf. "You are gorgeous and can pull off any damn color you want. You like it, you buy it."

"I don't know . . ."

"Listen. When you look amazing, you feel confident, right?" Haya asked.

It was true. I nodded, then paused. "But I'm always worried about being modest too," I said. "Sweatpants feel like the easiest way to accomplish that."

"You can dress cute and still be modest," Sadaf said, and she and Haya were proof of that. They always looked nice but still dressed modestly. "I mean, of course everyone has a different meaning of the word, and we all try in our own way, but don't feel like Allah wants you to not dress nice in the name of modesty."

"I agree," Haya said. "Plus, when you feel great, you appreciate something that you often forget to, aka yourself. Like, Allah made you beautiful, and while clothes cover us, they also adorn us, reflecting the beauty of Allah's creation."

"And if you appreciate your beauty and yourself," Sadaf added, "I feel like it helps you appreciate life and God to a greater extent too. So, you can look nice, be modest, and be appreciative, which is a win-win-win."

"Huh," I replied. It did make sense. Maybe I was using the modesty thing as an excuse not to try. "I've never thought of it that way."

"At least, that's how I think about it," Haya said, giving me a comforting smile. "Do what makes you happy and comfortable! And if these clothes"—she gestured to the sweatpants and shirts—"are that for you, then that's great! But it's okay to try new things too."

I wanted to listen to her, but my main issue was the voice in my head, locked in my memories, sewn into my soul. I tried to ignore it, but it was so loud—drilled in for so many years. It was Ammi's.

No, don't wear that. Nahi, you can't wear this color. Uff, this doesn't look good. Go change. Return this. Hai Allah, why would you buy this? No, no, no.

But Ammi wasn't here. I could buy whatever I wanted, and she would never see it. I could wear whatever I pleased.

I didn't have to worry if it was too loud or obnoxious or unappealing.

Ammi wasn't here, but as I put down my pile of clothes and started fresh, I was still afraid.

I could imagine her reactions to every article of clothing I stumbled upon—the pursed line of her lips, the arch of an eyebrow, the slight nod of approval or the sharp *no* of disapproval.

I could hear her voice in my mind as I picked up a dark-red lipstick. I could see her look of disgust when I picked up a black dress. *Don't*, she said in my mind, but I did.

After the first act of disobedience, my fear waned, and I picked up silky dresses and bright tops and everything else Ammi would have disapproved of for being too loud.

I will buy these things, I told her in my head, buzzing with defiance. *You can't stop me anymore.*

It was such a small thing, my appearance, but finally having full control over the way I looked made me happier. Such small things made such a huge difference.

"Come on, let's go try this stuff on," Haya said, when I had a new pile of clothes. We all went to the dressing rooms. I stripped and before trying something new on, stared at my body in the surrounding mirrors.

I really had lost a lot of weight. When I took a deep breath, my ribs poked out. Before, I used to think if I ever got skinny, I would be so pretty, and everything would look good on me, but now, I sort of missed the way I used to look. It felt more like *me*, whoever that was.

Exhaling, I tried on the clothes. There were a few pairs of boyfriend jeans that I tested to see which fit best. I settled on one medium-wash and one light-wash. Then I tried some tops, and I liked the layering combinations best—thin cardigans with shirts underneath, or long-sleeved shirts with a slip blouse on top, or a button-down shirt open with a graphic tee underneath.

Most of the clothes were practical, for everyday wear, but I tried on some fun blouses and dresses too, which I could save for special days. I didn't know if I would have any special days coming up, so I put most of that stuff in the not-buying pile, but there was this one gorgeous shirt I absolutely had to get: it had dramatic sleeves and was covered with fuchsia and bright-blue flowers. It was eye-catching, and the fabric was incredibly soft.

"Okay, I think I'm done," I said, leaving the dressing room. Sadaf and Haya were waiting for me outside, laughing at a video on Sadaf's phone.

"Ooh, yay, let me see!" Sadaf said, putting her phone away. I showed them the clothes I had settled on, and they both nodded in approval.

"Very cute," Haya said. "I love it."

"Much better than before," Sadaf agreed. "I love a good shopping spree!"

"Thanks, guys." I smiled at them. "This was really fun. Not the amount of money I'll be spending, but the rest of it."

Sadaf waved a hand. "It's an investment! At least that's what I'm telling myself . . ."

We laughed and went to check out, and while I was paying a pretty penny for all these clothes, it was worth it. It would be an investment. Besides, I couldn't keep wearing the same two outfits forever.

I replaced Ammi's voice with Haya's: *Look good, feel good, babe.*

After we checked out, I went back to the dressing rooms and changed into a new outfit—the light-wash jeans, a white shirt, and a sage-green cardigan on top, which tied in the front with three tiers of strings.

I put my gray scarf back on, since it was the only one I had, but it didn't clash with the outfit. It actually all looked really good together.

You are beautiful, I told the girl in the mirror, just as Haya and Sadaf had told me. For the first time, the girl in the mirror smiled back at me, and she looked like somebody I used to know.

I smiled. It was a brittle smile, near shattering, but it was not a lie.

"Ooh, so cute!" Haya said when I came out.

"Very nice. I love it," Sadaf agreed. I beamed at them both.

"Where can I buy more scarves?" I asked. "I only have this one."

"I'll send you a link for where we get ours," Haya said. "You can get ten for like thirty bucks. It's such a steal."

"And they have basically every color," Sadaf added.

"Not that you wear anything other than black," Haya told her sister.

"Hey, a black hijab is essential and classic," Sadaf replied. "It's like the Muslim version of a little black dress."

"So true."

We shopped some more, spending an exorbitant amount of time at Sephora trying samples, until it was time for Zuhr, the afternoon prayer.

"Let's go to the dressing rooms," Haya said, reminding us. She led the way to one of the handicapped dressing rooms to pray, pulling out a pocket janamaz for us to spread on the floor.

I was surprised at her and Sadaf's dedication to prayer. A long time ago, I had been that dedicated, and it had been nice to have structure to my day. There were five prayers around which my hours revolved. Then I had gotten so caught up in everything, I had forgotten about Allah.

Will He forgive me after all this time? Something told me He would. I promised myself that the next time I prayed, I would make it good.

We got lunch at the mall's food court, then browsed some more, and afterward, drove to a park to take in the beautiful weather. The heat of the day had passed by then, and there was a lovely breeze in the air.

At the park, my gaze caught on the swing sets, where children soared up toward the sky no matter how many times gravity pulled them down. There was mesmerizing beauty in that oscillation, the perpetual fluctuation of up and down, high and low. Children's laughter filled the air like birds chirping. They were all chubby cheeks and sticky hands and curly hair—messy, messy little beings, but adorable and pure. The sight made me smile.

When it was time for Asr, we were in the park, so we prayed there. I took a deep breath and began. It was hard. It was difficult to focus on the Arabic I could not translate, on the motions so trained they were automatic, but I tried. Each moment my mind wandered, I pulled it back.

It required a lot of effort, but it was a step forward. I felt a semblance of peace and clung to it.

Chapter 13

The peace lasted until we got home—and I remembered this wasn't *my* home.

I was in Haya's room, putting my shopping bags away, when I realized the sun was setting and another day had passed. Sadaf and Haya had been with me all day, but under what pretense? I was not a childhood friend coming to visit after years. I was nobody to them.

Elation faded to despair, a chemical switch being turned off in my mind. I wanted to vomit.

That night, after another wholesome and heartwarming dinner, I made sure my things were packed for departure in the morning.

"Where are you going?" Haya asked, watching me zip the new duffel bag I had bought.

"I can't stay here forever," I replied, avoiding her eyes. "I'm going to find a place to rent for a bit and sort things out."

"In one day? Just stay here awhile. We've been having fun!"

"No." I shook my head. "Thank you, but I have to go."

Here I was, thrust into Haya's life like an old family friend, staying at her house, eating her mother's meals, letting her pay for my lunch. I didn't even know her—I didn't know anybody.

Who am I to them, anyway? Nobody.

Who am I to anybody? No one.

"Where will you go?" Haya asked. "What's your plan?"

Learn how to live.

"Find a place to stay. Get a job."

Survive.

"Not much of a plan, girl," Haya said, offering me a small smile. It was a smile you gave to a child when she was being foolish, and I knew I was, but I couldn't stay. "At least stay until you've found a place for rent, okay?"

"*No*, Haya," I said, voice sharp. She was taken aback by the bite in my tone. *Don't you know?* I wanted to scream. *Don't you know I'm nothing but acid? Nothing but poison and shame?* "I said I'm leaving, so I'm leaving."

"Zahra." Haya's voice was calm as cool water. "We—*I* can help."

"I don't need help!" I snapped. "I'm not broken, so don't try fixing me! I'm fine. Everything is fine. I've always been on my own. I can handle this."

I couldn't deal with her sympathy or her kindness. What an entitled, spoiled brat I was.

"Oh, honey," Haya said, and I wondered how she understood. "It's okay to be vulnerable. It's okay to be human and scared. You don't have to be perfect."

Her words made me flinch. "Yes, I do," I whispered, looking at my hands.

"You don't," she said.

I didn't believe her. But I knew being mean to her wasn't right—not after all she'd done for me. I took a deep breath, calming myself. "Okay," I said. I turned my lips up. "I'm sorry for snapping at you."

"It's cool, babe." She squeezed my hand. "Now let's make your plan."

We sat down cross-legged on her bed, and she clasped her hands together, prepared to organize and plan.

"How much money do you have?" asked Haya.

"A couple thousand, probably. Which always seemed like a lot, but now, it doesn't feel like that much."

"Basically, you need a place to stay and, more importantly, a job, right?" Haya said. I nodded. It felt good to take control again, at least over something. "What are you good at?"

"I don't know . . . I'm not good at much." I shrugged.

"Do you have your résumé on you anywhere?"

I opened the document on my laptop, and she read through it, nodding to herself. She finished, whereupon she promptly smacked my arm.

"*I'm not, like, good at much*," she mimicked in a terrible California Valley accent. "Pagal, this is so impressive!"

I laughed at the accent. "That is *not* how I sound! I'm not Sally from the Valley. And what's impressive?" There wasn't anything impressive about me, honestly. It was all mediocre.

"Your grades are straight As? Your standardized test scores

are way above average?? You have loads of extracurriculars???" she said, mouth open. "What part of this isn't impressive? Moreover, how did you deal with all this? It must have been overwhelming! I'm stressed just looking at it."

I shrugged. It had been, but I had never given voice to those thoughts, though I had felt it deep in my belly, where my anxiety always simmered. I leaned back against the pillows on her bed, sighing.

"It doesn't matter, anyway," I said, shaking my head. "I ended up committing to a college I would have gotten into with half these credentials so I could be close to home."

But Ammi wanted to brag, and Baba wanted to be proud, so I tried to reach their expectations. Tried.

"What do you mean?" Haya asked, eyes confused behind her glasses. "I thought you were going to NYU?"

Shit. I'd slipped.

"Yeah," I said, fumbling for words. "But I only decided that recently ... I was originally supposed to go somewhere close to home."

"Oh, okay. Damn, anyway," she said. She adopted a faux auntie voice. "Masha'Allah, beta. Khush rao, jeeti rao." She pinched my cheek and grinned.

"Yeah, yeah." I shook her off, but I smiled.

"It's July right now, and classes start the first week of September, right? Or the last week of August? Either way, you really only need to find a place to stay until then, at which point I'm guessing you're going to the dorm?"

"Uh, yeah," I replied, looking at her bedroom walls to

avoid her gaze. I didn't want to lie, but I didn't know what else to do. I couldn't tell Haya that I had lied to her from the beginning, not when we were getting close.

"I think we can definitely find you a temporary place to stay. There are loads of students who stay close to the university near here during the summer for summer classes," Haya said, pulling out her phone. "I'll ask Sadaf and my parents what they can find out, and that shouldn't be too expensive, since it's meant for students."

"Oh, that would be . . . perfect. Thanks."

Haya waved her free hand, the other occupied with typing something on her phone. "Okay, done. I texted them. That leaves us with how to pay for it. You've clearly demonstrated great work ethic and dedication, so probably anybody will hire you. But what do you want to do? What do you like to do?"

"What do I *like* to do?"

I hardly knew anymore. All I did at home was chores and homework, really, or lying on my bed in nothingness. I used to adore cooking, trying new, fun recipes—but there was no time for that anymore. Not with my full-time job being a student.

"Chores and homework, really," I said. "Once Ammi left for Pakistan for two weeks when I was thirteen and I held everything down in her absence—cooking, cleaning, etc."

"That's promising! Maids get paid decently."

My initial thought was: *A maid? I did all this shit in high school to become a maid?* Then I realized there was actually nothing wrong with being a maid. It was a job, not a definition. So I tucked away my supercilious thoughts and nodded.

"I can babysit, cook, and tutor as well, probably," I added. I realized how archaic my skill set was then—so perfectly groomed for being a housewife and mother.

But again, there was nothing wrong with being a housewife. They were no less than working women or men. It was just a job. I shoved my pretentious thoughts away once more.

"Let's make you a fancy flyer," Haya said, pulling out her laptop. "I'm a Canva *pro*."

Together, we made flyers to hang up at the masjid, and Haya made a little online graphic for Nabila Auntie to send in her WhatsApp groups.

"I swear these WhatsApp groups cover, like, half the aunties on Long Island," Haya told me. "I'm sure one of them will be looking for a tutor for her kid or extra help around the house."

It was so strange. I had my entire future in front of me uncharted, a blank canvas primed for strokes to be made, and I had all the colors and possibilities in the world at my disposal—to do whatever I wanted.

"Let's check Facebook too," Haya said.

"I don't have one," I said. "I'm not really on social media."

"No worries; we can use mine." Haya pulled up a new tab on her laptop. "I literally only use Facebook to chat with my cousin Mina in Pakistan."

We searched through Facebook pages for Muslims in the area, seeing if they had any job postings, and when we found some, we sent my résumé out. Haya suggested I also apply at the mall, and even though I was worried about running into Fareeha again—*what if she shops at this mall?*—I couldn't come up with a plausible excuse for Haya as to why not. And deep down, I didn't want to live in fear anymore.

"Now back to apartment hunting, though I vote for you staying here." She gave me a pointed look. "We can check the local Muslims' Facebook group or look around online. Even though I adore having you here, truly."

I raised an eyebrow. "You're being too nice, Haya. I'm sure you want your room and personal space back."

"I do *not*! I like you being here! My parents don't yell at me when guests are over! And it's like having another sister, but nicer—since you're not annoying and don't STEAL ALL MY CLOTHES LIKE *SADAF*."

Upon hearing her name, Sadaf came bounding in from the next room.

"Ex*cuse* me? What did you say about me?"

"I said I like Zahra better than you because she doesn't smell bad."

"Say that to my face, Haya," Sadaf dared, getting in Haya's personal space. "Say it to my FACE."

Haya threw a pillow at her sister.

"You little—" An assault ensued, though it was unilateral because Sadaf simply jumped on top of Haya. Haya shrieked.

"Say you love me!" Sadaf shouted.

"No!"

"Say it!"

"Fine! I love you! I love you!" Haya conceded. I was dying

of laughter watching them, and I wanted to squeeze them both for the life that spilled out of them, onto me.

After we composed ourselves, Sadaf's gaze fell upon my packed duffel bag. Her lips puffed into a pout.

"Aw, you're leaving?" She frowned. "Excuse you, I know my name is Sadaf but that doesn't mean you have to make me sad af."

"Don't worry," I said, getting comfortable on Haya's bed. "I'm not going anywhere just yet."

Chapter 14

The next morning, I looked into more places to rent, just out of formality, but really, by then, I didn't want to leave either. So I stayed, and I was glad for it. It might not have been my home, but it was the closest thing to it I could get.

After Nabila Auntie made us breakfast and kissed our faces—even mine—we went to the masjid. Every Monday, Wednesday, and Friday, Sadaf and Haya volunteered there at the summer camp, where they taught manners and basic Islamic principles from the Sunnah and Qur'an.

"Okay, Z, listen up," Sadaf told me when we got to the masjid. Students were beginning to arrive, aged five to twelve, and they congregated into small groups on the carpet. They sat on the floor with little tables in front of them, all of them with identical drawstring bags from the masjid. "You're going to help babysit the little kiddies who are too young for class— the toddlers and babies and in-betweens," Sadaf said. "They're in that room in the back." She pointed.

"Watch out for three-nagers," Haya warned me, adjusting her glasses.

"Ah, three-nagers," said a voice behind us. "More dramatic than actual teenagers, if you ask me."

I turned to see a pretty black girl who looked around my age. She was wearing a purple scarf and a gorgeous matching abaya.

"Mawa!" Haya exclaimed, and they wrapped each other in a hug. "You weren't here on Wednesday! I haven't seen you in *forever*."

"Yeah, I had a family thing! Four days is four days too long," agreed Mawa, before turning to me. "As-salaamu Alaikum, I'm Mawa. You must be Zahra, right? Haya texted me about you! I can't wait for us to work together."

I didn't doubt her sincerity. I smiled at her.

"I'm excited too," I told her. "I adore babies."

"Fantastic!" Mawa took my hand. "Let's go meet them, then."

She led me to a room full of toys and children playing and running, and the chaos of it struck me suddenly as beautiful because of the raw life in all these children's faces. There was another volunteer in the room, and it was our job to watch these children for the next few hours—to play with them and to feed them and to love them.

We did.

An hour in, I learned what three-nagers were like when little Batool started to cry because a strand of hair fell from her head and she thought she had gone bald.

"It's okay, Batool," Mawa told the little girl. "Look, you still have such beautiful hair!" Mawa brought Batool to the mirror. Batool petted her own head, feeling the hair, then sighed with relief.

"Thanks, Mawa!" Batool shouted, engulfing Mawa in a hug before running off.

"The kids get wild," Mawa told me, shaking her head. "But they're so cute, it's worth it." I agreed, and a few minutes later, a curly-haired girl approached me asking for a cookie.

"Here you go," I said, giving her one. I crouched down so that we were at eye level. She looked at my lips and her eyes widened in wonder. I was wearing a new lipstick.

"Me want!" she said.

"Okay, honey," I said, pulling out my ChapStick. I lightly applied it to her lips, and she grinned.

"Yay!" she cheered, erupting into giggles then running away.

"Please tell me you're throwing that ChapStick away," Mawa said, noticing the exchange. "Kids are so germy! I mean, it's sweet, but *yuck*."

I laughed. My heart nearly burst, being surrounded by these kids. They were sticky and loud, and it was annoying sometimes but amusing more, and relaxing most. For once, I didn't feel the heavy eyes of judgment on me, just the sparkles and rainbows of innocence.

I found myself pleased. There was something so enjoyable about playing with children—the exaggerated voices, the dramatic acting, their laughter. It was nice to escape the confinements of adult life and slip into the innocence of childhood. There were no limitations, and imagination was the only requirement for success.

We got lost in our own worlds, pilots and pirates and princesses. Chases ensued, as well as tackles and tickle fights. We floated in the clouds of our minds, leaving the real world behind.

When two-year-old Ammar held my face in his hands and said, in his slurred toddler-speak, "Zahrapi, you're so glittery," I almost cried at the cuteness overload, even though his spit had landed on my forehead. He had yet to learn how to properly pronounce "pretty," so glittery was his best replacement.

When a five-year-old explained to me what high-fives were—"Like hi," she waved her hand, "and five because five fingers!"—we giggled and she hugged my head with her little arms.

And at the end of the day, I was a sticky and slightly wet mess, but it was okay because my cheeks and lungs and stomach hurt from laughing. My heart felt full of sunshine.

Since it was Friday, the day camp ended early for Jummah prayer. We all listened to the khutbah and prayed together, and afterward, I was vaguely distressed watching the kids leave. I already loved them.

"Don't worry," Haya told me with a knowing laugh. "You can volunteer again on Monday."

I nodded, grinning.

"Good," I responded. "They're so cute I want to squish them all forever."

"It's a good thing you love kids," Sadaf said. "Now I know who I'll be leaving my kids with when I get tired—with dear old Zahra Khala."

The thought warmed me to my core, that I would know these girls until we were married and had kids, and after that, that I would be a beloved aunt. Would I know these girls for the rest of my life? Suddenly I could see an entire life stretched before me, and it didn't seem too awful.

After Jummah, I figured we would head home, but Haya had a different idea.

"I want to take you to the park!" she said. "The weather is nice, so it shouldn't be too humid."

There was a park across the street, so we walked over, the sun warm on our backs but not insufferable. The park had a playground where children were running around. We walked along the pathway until we reached an area covered with trees. Sadaf broke off then, saying she'd be right back.

"Let's sit," Haya suggested. We went over and sat in the grass, which was cool against my palms as I leaned back on my hands. In the shade, it was even lovelier as I watched the glitters of sunlight shifting between the leaves. The air was sweet with the smell of flowers.

From here, I could see the masjid, and even the structure of it—the distinctive architecture with the minaret—gave me comfort.

"So, do you like our masjid?" Haya asked me, following my gaze. "It's chaotic, but everyone's really nice, right?"

"I love it," I told her honestly. "Everyone's so kind and

welcoming." I smiled, but she must have detected the sadness in my eyes.

"What?" she asked, confused. "What's wrong?"

For as long as I could remember, *my* masjid had been a second home to me. I could picture myself running through the halls with my brother, imagine myself sitting in class, see myself with my parents and other adults breaking our fast. The masjid was the center of the Muslim community, and since forever, it had provided me with the support and care that anyone could ever wish for.

And while there were strengths and weaknesses to the mechanisms of the masjid community, I loved it and everyone in it—they were family to me.

Every year since I was six years old, I had attended Islamic school on Saturdays, just as I attended an ordinary school during the week. Every Ramadan, we would pray taraweh together in the masjid. My family and I frequented the masjid so often that I knew nearly everyone who came there—all the mothers and daughters and friends and families.

I missed them.

"It's nothing," I said, shrugging. Haya bumped her shoulder with mine.

"Don't do that, jaan," she told me, face patient. "Don't cut your thoughts off. Talk to me."

"It's just—" I started, finding my voice. "I miss my own community, you know? All the girls there, all my friends. I haven't seen or spoken to them in months, but I miss them—or the idea of them, I guess. Even though I was angry at them for a while. What good are friends who couldn't be there for me when I needed them?"

It isn't as though we were *best* friends, but they were girls I had known since forever and saw pretty often. I liked being around them.

"Well, you've got to understand," Haya said, "everyone has busy lives, and sometimes it's hard for them to make time. Even if they want to. Maybe that's what it was."

"But for so long there was nobody there. Not at all . . ." As I said the words, I caught the whine in my voice. "No—I'm sorry." I shook my head. "They were." And I remembered. "They were there, but I pushed them away. I wanted more."

I always wanted more. I wanted people to fix my life for me. I wanted them to be everything for me when I couldn't even be anything for myself.

It's my own fault, really, for needing so much. When any of my friends or cousins asked if I was all right, I told them everything was fine. Why *wouldn't* they believe me? It was unreasonable of me to assume they would catch on to the lie when I had perfected my act.

It wasn't fair of me to expect others to understand the machinations of my mind when I myself did not. *I* shut down—*I* shut everyone out. How could I expect them to help me when I wouldn't let them? It was me who kept pushing and pushing, no matter how determined they were, and it was no wonder they stopped trying eventually.

"Don't apologize," Haya told me. "And don't blame your-self either. Sometimes we get caught up in the all-or-nothing state of mind, and we don't want to settle for anything in between. It's easier that way, to be stuck in one static emotion. But life doesn't work that way, not always. We are complex and contradictory beings, so don't try defining and thus confining yourself."

"Yeah, I guess," I agreed, unsure of what to say. We sat in silence a while, simply looking around. A few minutes later, we saw Sadaf walking toward us, one hand carrying a big brown bag.

"I brought food," Sadaf declared, sitting down next to us in the grass. Our bodies made a little circle. "Z, it's a chicken burger—that's cool, right? And a Coke?"

"Yes, thank you, that's perfect," I said.

"You got mine with—" started Haya.

"No pickles, extra onions, and ketchup? Also known as the most obnoxious thing to order ever? Yeah, yeah, I know what you eat, kid," Sadaf interjected, waving her hand. She reached into the bag and handed Haya her sandwich, then handed me mine. Haya handed out napkins, then the drinks, giving me a Coke.

As I bit into my burger, I watched as Haya wordlessly split her Sprite in half and mixed it with Sadaf's cranberry juice, giving her sister half and keeping the rest for herself. Routine and history and transcendence of words—I ached for that.

It made me think of my own sibling.

Even though Ahsen and I weren't close now, when we were kids, we used to do everything together. But then he grew up and couldn't be bothered with his stupid little sister. He started fighting with Baba over stupid shit. He started going out all the time and partying and doing things he knew he shouldn't, like drinking and drugs.

"What are you thinking about?" Haya asked me.

"My brother," I said. For the first time, it dawned on me that I had left him too. They must have been wondering why I wasn't with him if my parents were dead as I had told them.

"Are you guys close?" Sadaf asked, eating her fries. I shook my head.

"Not anymore," I said. "He went to Boston for college and never really bothered with visiting except in the summer and sometimes over winter break."

"Ah, so you didn't see him much these past few years?" Haya asked.

"Nope, and I was sort of glad for it." I paused, feeling guilty for saying that. "He's not a bad person—I think he's really good at heart, deep down. He's just so . . . I don't know. Angry and lost. So it's not always pleasant when he's home."

I sighed, not liking the narrative I was creating about my brother. I didn't want Haya and Sadaf to have a bad impression of him. I didn't want them to judge him—that protective sibling instinct kicking in. I could think as badly of him as I pleased, but no one else had that prerogative.

"I think being a firstborn son was really hard for him," I said. "Which is ludicrous to say, because obviously being a brown girl is worse, and guys are so privileged, but it was still tough for him. My dad expected everything from him, and

I think it made him bitter, which is why he can be such a jerk sometimes."

"Being a firstborn is hard," Sadaf agreed. "I went through this phase when I was sixteen and I was a total nightmare at home."

"Ohmygod, I remember," Haya said, shaking her head. "She was the worst. Like, always super upset and getting mad at everyone."

Sadaf pinched Haya's arm, earning a squeal in response. "Growing up sucks, okay! And not everyone is as good as you. Sometimes you just feel like shit, and there's nothing you can do to make it better."

Don't I know it.

"Yeah, I think Ahsen would agree with you," I told Sadaf. "And I know it was just as bad for him to go to an all-white school as it was for me. Like, he was teased for the way he grew facial hair much quicker than his blond classmates and for his braces. And he was notorious for his good grades and told that he must have been smart because he was 'Indian,' which completely discredited his own hard work."

"That would piss me off so much, my God," Sadaf said.

"Yeah. It got a little better when he went to college, I think, because he sort of grew into himself, and he got loads of attention from girls. But then he got cocky and arrogant and partied all the time. I mean, I love him—of course I love him, he's my brother—but my God, he is so annoying."

Sadaf and Haya listened, and when I was done speaking, neither of them knew what to say. We sat in silence for a few moments, until Sadaf spoke. "He sounds like a tortured tool," Sadaf said. "So, basically, my type."

"Ohmygod, Sadaf, you're ridiculous," Haya said, shaking her head, but Sadaf's comment had gotten a laugh out of all of us. "I genuinely cannot deal with you."

"Truthfully, though, dealing with younger siblings is tough. I used to *hate* it when Haya told me what and what not to do," Sadaf enlightened us.

"I do not tell you what to do!" Haya objected, sitting up. Shocked by Sadaf's statement, Haya's mouth fell open in a wide O. Sadaf gave her an unimpressed look.

"Yeah, but you look at me with your judgy little eyes and I know what you're thinking."

Haya thought about this for a moment, closing her mouth, then eased back down. "Okay, that's fair."

"Like when I was getting this." Sadaf pointed to her nose ring. "Haya was totally against it, but now look how fantastic I look!"

"You do look fantastic," Haya and I agreed.

"As I was saying—it's embarrassing when your younger sibling is a judgy little know-it-all. *We* are supposed to be older and smarter, guiding *you* little losers, but when you reverse the roles, it's proof that we don't actually know what the hell we're doing, either."

I paused, thinking that over. "So, what did you do?" I asked Haya. "When Sadaf was in her little phase?"

"It was difficult but . . . I left her alone for a while, subtly voicing disapprovals and critiques until she figured it out herself. Really, you just have to be patient and not give up on them, no matter how idiotic they get."

"Aw," Sadaf threw her arms around Haya. "That was so cute, little sis."

"That's because I *am* cute."

"But yes," Sadaf agreed. "It takes us some time to figure things out, but eventually we do. I guess . . . don't give up on him? Maybe play friend, and not moral police? Even if he is doing stupid shit?"

It would have worked, in theory, I thought, but boys didn't notice subtleties. I had tried it with Ahsen, never clearly voicing my censure, and instead hinting at it, but he never caught on. "But boys are dumb," I said, frowning.

"So true," Sadaf agreed. "I guess then you could be outright with him, call him out on his bullshit, you know? Like, *why are you having a big temper tantrum? Why are you being mean? Quit being such a dick*, you know? And be matter-of-fact about it. Once he realizes it doesn't make him cool, he'll probably stop. Praying also helps. In the end, it's all up to Allah."

If I ever went home and saw him again, maybe I would try that. It always annoyed me how soft Mama was around Ahsen—babying him the way Pakistani women often babied their sons. But I never realized that I was just as soft, just as forgiving—feeding into his entitlement. It made me think about internalized misogyny.

But thinking about Ahsen filled my heart with an ache so volatile I felt on the verge of bursting into flames.

He was annoying, but I did love him.

Chapter 15

That Sunday, there was a dawat at the Chaudrys' place. One thing about Pakistanis was they loved throwing dinner parties.

"Zahra, beti!" Nabila Auntie's arms were around me the instant I entered their home after a day of job searching.

From the kitchen, I could hear the chatter and clatter of words and dishes and the soft music in the background. It was all so familiar: the smells, the sounds, the colors. Saalan and naan and chicken tikka and pulao. Brown skin and gold jewelry and red lips. White beards and clean white shalwar kameez. The quick, smooth Urdu flowing like the wind, soft and sweet in my ears. The Bollywood tunes, the drum, the rubab.

It was a little foreign too. Tastes slightly different. Faces not the same. Jewelry and accents and music all not quite what I was used to back in California.

It felt like a new pair of shoes—slightly tight and uncomfortable—even if they looked like all my old pairs. They weren't scuffed, didn't have the same stains or worn smell. Even though they were similar, the differences were glaringly, painfully obvious.

"Salaam, Nabila Auntie!" I hugged her back, swallowing the foreign familiarity. Before I knew it, I was passed to Haya's arms, then Sadaf's, and then across the row of aunties waiting in the formal living room and kitchen. Curt smiles, slight pats on my shoulder, brisk salaams.

And then I saw her.

Fareeha.

We both froze. This time, there was no mistaking it—she recognized me. She knew *exactly* who I was—the girl who was supposed to marry her brother. Her mouth fell open, eyes full of emotion, but she said nothing. She simply sat there, regarding me with shock.

"Nabila, ye kaun?" someone asked, after I had smiled and said salaam.

"Haya's friend," Nabila Auntie said. My heartbeat accelerated, pounding. I resisted the urge to run, to get out as quickly as I could.

Bechari, they tsked, when she told them my parents were dead. Nabila Auntie slid me into her side and rubbed my arm, but all I could see was Fareeha: the disbelief on her face. The anger.

Oh God.

She won't make a scene here, will she? I couldn't let Haya and Sadaf and Nabila Auntie and Umar Uncle find out the truth. They had shown me so much kindness. And for what?

A girl who ran away from home and left her fiancé? They would hate me.

I smiled nervously, trying not to look at Fareeha, but she was staring at me, not saying a word. *Run, run, run.* My lower lip trembled, smile faltering. But I didn't want to leave. Not when I was finally making a place for myself. Not when I finally had friends again.

Finally, Fareeha spoke. Her attention was hyper-fixated on me, and I flinched beneath her gaze.

"Where are you from?" she asked, voice clear. I couldn't lie.

"California," I replied, trying to smile innocently.

"Oh, what a coincidence!" Fareeha replied. "My brother's ex-fiancé was from there."

My smile faltered.

"It is a big state!" Sadaf said easily, coming to my side. She gave Fareeha a strange look, wondering why she had brought up such a thing.

An awkward beat later, the conversation shifted to Sadaf.

"Sadaf ka rishta dhunda?" somebody asked Nabila Auntie.

I caught Sadaf exchanging a knowing glance with Haya before she smiled a sugary smile.

"*Auntieee*," she protested, drawing the end out in a near-whine. "I'm not ready to get married yet! I can barely manage myself, let alone a whole relationship with somebody else."

"Well, that's why you marry and learn, darling," another auntie said.

"Uffo, Auntie," Haya drawled, scrunching her nose. "Ye kya logic?"

"Aaj kal ke bache," one of the aunties tsked. "You kids are too modern now."

"Acha, bas," Nabila Auntie said, changing the subject. She turned her attention to one auntie. "How's Ahmed's job going?"

The conversation shifted from weddings to sons and the life of mothers, so we girls went to the kitchen to get appetizers. I could feel Fareeha's eyes on me, but I guessed she wouldn't say anything, at least not tonight. But who knew how long she would keep quiet? Would she try to talk to me? I was dizzy with anxiety, my breaths short and quick.

"Are you okay?" Haya asked me, holding a hand to my shoulder to steady me. "You're pale."

"Yeah," I said, waving her off with a laugh. "I think I'm just hungry."

"Here, take some more," she told me, piling another samosa onto my plate. I smiled, then followed her and Sadaf up the stairs to where the other girls were. But not before looking over my shoulder.

Fareeha was watching me go.

I swallowed.

I followed Haya to Sadaf's room, where the girls were hanging out. Sadaf's room was a deep blue, with black furniture and gray accents. The color scheme wasn't the only thing that made it different from Haya's—where Haya's room was clean and orderly, every surface in Sadaf's room was covered with artwork, trinkets, jewelry, books, and/or movie/concert tickets.

Haya and I entered and sat on the floor, where Madiha and Imaan from Youth Group were perched on floor cushions. They said salaam and I hugged them, happy to see them again. Madiha was wearing a simple shalwar kameez suit, while Imaan was wearing something fashionable and a bit dramatic. There were also two other girls sitting on Sadaf's bed with her. I didn't recognize them, but they were dressed beautifully and wore delicate gold jewelry.

"This is Zahra." Sadaf introduced me to the two girls. "Z, this is Naadia Mirza, and her younger sister Humaira." I had heard Sadaf talking about them before. Naadia was Sadaf's best friend from college—they were both psychology majors and were going to be seniors in the fall. They were also both very loud, and together, the pair was definitely obnoxious, but they didn't care.

Humaira was a year older than me and Haya and looked nothing like her sister. They were about the same height, a little taller than me, but Naadia had a deeper complexion and runway-model looks. She had thick brows, massive eyes, a small face, and an artsy touch to her style. Her hands were covered in rings, and several layered necklaces hung from her neck.

Humaira was curvier, with a round face and more delicate features. She had a small nose, pouty lips, and arched brows on a face that looked like it never lost its childhood chubbiness. She had an elegant style and wore a few key, delicate pieces of jewelry and dark-red lipstick. She had a very classic look—a bit like Mahira Khan, whose dramas Mama and I used to watch. (I wondered if Humaira would meet her Fawad Khan.)

Even though Humaira was only nineteen, she seemed to have it all together. She looked like a perfect doll—the way she sat, dressed, ate, talked. She was wearing a chiffon scarf that paired perfectly with her shalwar kameez, and somehow it wasn't slipping off every five seconds.

According to Sadaf, the Mirza girls were obscenely rich, and while Naadia didn't look like it that much, it was evident on Humaira. She had the air of a princess.

"Salaam, it's nice to meet you guys," I said, smiling up at them. They smiled back in response, until Sadaf released a loud sigh.

"God, the never-ending interrogation that begins once you reach your twenties," Sadaf said, shoveling a spoonful of chaat into her mouth. Naadia reached over to give her hand a squeeze. They both slouched together against the pillows.

"Damn, that means I'm almost there," Haya lamented beside me.

"Oh, please, you're a baby," Naadia told her, waving a hand. "You have plenty of time."

"You shouldn't fret—you've got Sadaf to shift the attention for now," Humaira said from her position on the bed. She spoke very properly, like a character in a Jane Austen novel. "I'm counting on Naadia for that entirely. It's one of her only uses."

"You're such a brat," Naadia said with a laugh, kicking her sister gently.

"What?" Humaira said easily. "I have no interest in being interrogated by our five phuppos—you can bear that burden."

"No thank you! I am focused on applying to medical school," Naadia said.

"Well, when you are of a mind to be married, *do* let me know," Humaira said, a mischievous gleam in her eye. "I'll be sure to set you up. I have someone in mind already . . ."

"Not the matchmaking again!" Sadaf said, breaking out into laughter. "Humaira, you must be stopped."

"I see no reason to relent!" Humaira quipped, smiling. "Not with such a success rate." Humaira turned to us girls sitting on the floor cushions. "If you ladies are ever in need of a setup, do let me know. Matching people is one of my favorite pastimes."

"I'm good for now, thanks," Haya said with a laugh. "And anyway, per your earlier logic, I've got Sadaf to occupy my parents' attention in the matter of marriage, and no one's going to want to marry her, so I've got loads of time before I have to think about it."

"The disrespect I am shown in my own home!" Sadaf said, exchanging a disgusted look with Naadia.

"Truly despicable," her best friend agreed. They both sank deeper into their pillows.

"Oh God, who are we going to depend on?" Imaan asked, fluffing her organza dupatta. "We don't have any older sisters!"

"Yeah, I only have stupid brothers!" Madiha cried. "And they don't get pressured the same way!"

"I hear you," I told them with a sigh. "I only have a brother too." Madiha and Imaan's faces slipped into pouts at the exact same time. The sight made me smile. They had been best friends since they were kids, and I was glad they had each other. They could exchange a glance and burst out laughing at something only they understood. I wished I had someone like that.

And just as I thought it, my eyes met Haya's, and she gave me a smile.

"Honestly, I want to get married sometimes because I'm lonely," Sadaf said, and our attention shifted back to her on the bed.

"Same, but loneliness isn't a good enough reason to get married," Naadia said. "That's not what marriage should be about."

"Then what is?" I asked, curious. "What's a good enough reason to get married other than your age? I mean, aren't we *supposed* to get married in our early twenties?"

"Darling, no," Humaira said, shaking her head.

"Yeah, that's cultural bullshit," Haya said.

Mama got married when she was seventeen and moved across the globe with a man she barely knew. She said that's just how it was.

"Tell her what Mama always tells us," Haya prompted her sister. Sadaf snapped her fingers and nodded.

"Oh, I do love this story!" Humaira said, eyes dreamy.

"Same," Naadia added. "Nabila Auntie is amazing."

"Okay, so we would always ask Mama how she got married—" started Sadaf. She shook her head and smiled. "Wait, I can't tell this story! Haya, you tell it."

"I can't tell it, either! We'll ask Mama later tonight," Haya said.

The conversation shifted as Sadaf asked Naadia how her medical school applications were going.

"They open on August first, so I'm trying to finish everything before then," Naadia replied. "It's been a nightmare. I can't wait for it to be done."

"I can't wait for them to be through, either!" Humaira added. "She's been entirely neglecting me."

We laughed. "What are you studying, Humaira?" I asked.

"Civil engineering," she replied. "I'm starting my second year in the fall. What about you girls?"

I paused, unsure of how to respond, and Haya cut in before I had to, saving me from the awkward silence.

"I'm starting a pharmacy program in the fall!" Haya said. "Madiha, Imaan, do you guys have any idea what you want to do yet?"

"Journalism," Imaan replied, and Madiha said, "Biomedical engineering."

"A whole bunch of smarties," Sadaf said. "Look at us."

It made me think about what I wanted to do with my life, but I couldn't think of anything I was passionate about. It was good I wasn't going to college come fall. I needed more time to figure things out.

We all continued talking: Madiha told us about playing basketball on her school's team. Humaira described a couple she had set up. Naadia talked about their father and his ridiculous antics. It was nice chatting with these girls.

Maybe I wouldn't be close with all of them, but it was nice being together, like how it used to be at dawats at my house. I wasn't super close with the girls back home, either—they were family friends I had always known but it was still fun hanging out and catching up. Comfortable.

Later, when we went down for dinner, I noticed as all the aunties fawned over Humaira, which soured Naadia's mood a little. It was obvious they adored Humaira—she was easily likable. She always knew exactly what to say and how to say it—the perfect girl.

It reminded me of how hard I used to try to please Ammi and her friends, to please society and all these people who hardly knew me. I always tried so hard to please everyone else that I forgot about myself.

From the outside, maybe other girls had thought I was perfect, just like I thought Humaira was, but I knew all the cracks in the porcelain.

How easily porcelain could shatter.

When we were cleaning up later that night, we finally asked Nabila Auntie how she got married.

"Mama Dearest, tell the story to Zahra!" Sadaf said, hanging off her mother's arm. "Tell her, tell her!"

"You want to know about my wedding?" Nabila Auntie asked me.

"Yes, but more than that . . . I guess, *how* did you know

when to get married? I mean, were you just at that age? Or . . . ?"

Setting the broom aside, Nabila Auntie smiled and walked to me. I put down the cloth I had been using to wipe the counters, and we all sat around the kitchen island.

"Well, it didn't have to do with age but with feeling," she began, holding a hand over her heart. Her face was calm. *What does it feel like? To be so at peace?*

"You never know, really, when the time is right. But sometimes you get this feeling. It only comes after you've gone through all your mental and emotional sorting, and one day you think, I am ready. I am full of so much love, and I am ready to give that love to another. My heart is open and ready to link with another's, to form that intimate relationship.

"You think, I want to love and be loved, and finally, I can, because I love myself and I love life and all that's left, really, is somebody to share these moments with—somebody to crawl inside my mind, somebody to sleep inside my heart.

"And then one day he walked into my life, and I felt a little nudge. My breath caught. It was like Allah was saying, *Look at this one. Look at him right in front of you.* This is going to be your husband. You will love him, and he will love you. And I knew. Somehow. It was like Allah was speaking right to me."

And I understood then—that marriage was not an escape. It was not meant to be what you went to in the lowest moment of your life, as I had. It was not meant to be an end, but a beginning.

After a little while, I made an excuse and shut the lights

off to go to sleep. It was like the snap of a finger, how quickly I fell back into my depression, how easily comforted I was by the deep sadness, like it was an old friend, one who would never leave me.

In some fucked-up way, I belonged here, in this vast emptiness. It was okay to cry and to cave. I didn't have to try to smile or seem okay.

I missed home.

I missed my bed and my worn flannel sheets with the lemons. I missed my moccasins and my fuzzy socks and Ahsen's sweatshirt that he gave to me when he started college. I missed my town and knowing exactly where everything and everyone was.

I missed my favorite comfort foods and I missed knowing exactly where to go to see the sunset or get a coffee or to be alone. I missed the wide streets and the salted air and the mountains. I missed my books and my journal and my things, my everything. I felt so much more lost without them, all those little pieces of me.

All the big pieces. I missed Mama and how she smelled like powder and cotton. I missed Baba and the way his veins wrinkled and moved in his hands while he typed. I missed Ahsen and the way his eyes closed when he laughed too hard.

I missed them.

I missed me.

Chapter 16

$\mathcal{I}$ spent the whole next day on edge, waiting to see if Fareeha would call.

Of course, she wouldn't have made a scene in front of everybody last night, but there was no reason she wouldn't call Nabila Auntie the next day and tell her everything: that I was the girl who left her brother, who left her family—the girl who ran away.

And I knew Nabila Auntie and Haya and Sadaf would all want to hear my side of the story before jumping to any conclusions, but what would I explain to them? The truth? That nobody had forced me to say yes to marriage. That it had been my decision. And I had still run.

Since it was Monday, we spent most of the day at day camp, volunteering. I spent time with the children, and after, took the bus to the mall to apply for some jobs there. I didn't come back to the Chaudrys' until around dinnertime, and by then, I felt the tension ease a little bit. If Fareeha wanted to blow my cover, she would have already, right?

If I could just make it through the day, maybe I would be in the clear.

I almost made it.

"Oh, Zahra, before I forget," Nabila Auntie told me after dinner, when we were sipping chai in the living room. "Fareeha called. She was one of the young women here last night? She was asking about you."

"Oh?" I replied, trying to remain calm, but my hands began shaking, almost spilling my chai onto my lap.

"Why was she asking about Zahra?" Sadaf asked, confused. She was sitting beside me on the couch, and Haya sat on my other side.

"I think she may be interested in her for Zayn," Nabila Auntie said.

"Oh, poor Zayn." Haya sighed. "He's Fareeha's brother. He was supposed to get married, but the wedding fell through, like, a few days before."

"He's such a sweet guy too!" Sadaf added with a pout. "We met him when he came to visit Fareeha once. It's so sad his wedding fell through, and no one really knows why."

"Oh?" was all I could say. My throat was clogged.

I felt tears prick my eyes and clenched my jaw to hold them back. I couldn't cry, not here, not now. There would be too many questions. And I couldn't tell them the truth, that I was the girl he was supposed to marry, the girl who had left him for no good reason. I was the villain in this story.

"Beta, I know you're so young, and your parents aren't here, so I told Fareeha I would speak with you before saying anything to her," Nabila Auntie told me, her face gentle. "There's no pressure at all. I can tell her you're not comfortable with the situation, but I thought I would run it by you before doing so."

Nabila Auntie was asking so carefully for my opinion that it made me want to cry even more. There wasn't any pressure at all. *Where did Nabila Auntie come from? Why couldn't my own mother have been like this?*

Nabila Auntie was the true manifestation of what it meant to be a good Muslim—to be caring and careful and kind. To never make another human being feel uncomfortable or upset. To treat others with respect.

I hadn't even learned to respect myself yet.

But I was trying.

"Um, it's okay, Auntie," I said. "I guess I can talk to her myself and see what she wants to say? Would you be able to give me her phone number?"

"Yes, of course," Nabila Auntie said. "You let me know if you need anything, jaan. I can talk to her with you if you would like."

"Thank you."

Nabila Auntie texted me Fareeha's number, and I saved it.

"I'll let her know that you'll call her when you get the chance," Nabila Auntie told me.

Now all I needed was the courage.

Chapter 17

*L*ife was awful, but then life was great.

I avoided calling Fareeha, and hoped she wouldn't tell Nabila Auntie the truth if she hadn't already. I was under the illusion that I had time.

Time to breathe, time to heal.

The next day we went to a park by the Chaudrys' house, the same one we had gone to after the mall the other day. It was a regular park, with open fields, trees, bushes, flowers, and a playground. Every color shone with beauty—the greens and pinks and yellows.

The park was brimming with kids and teens and adults and oldies. The weather was gorgeous—so sublime I wanted to bottle the soft air and warm sunshine and keep them in my pocket. I wanted to save them for the dead of night when everything was dark and bleak.

"We used to come to this park as kids," Haya told me,

smiling to herself. "And some summers we would have soccer camp here, as well."

"I remember that!" Sadaf interjected. "You would come home a sweaty mess and fifteen shades darker, and Mama would just laugh, saying it looked like the sun had smothered you with kisses even though you smelled truly disgusting."

"I didn't peg you for a sporty girl," I said to Haya.

"Trust me, I was not," Haya said with a laugh. "Of everyone we know, Madiha's the sporty girl. I only did that soccer camp once because I thought the uniform was cute."

"She also tried lacrosse and ice-skating for the outfits," Sadaf added, as we walked down a winding pathway. Around us, kids zoomed past on bicycles, their laughter ringing in the air.

"The outfits!" Haya emphasized, clapping. "Sports get such cute outfits. In soccer camp, we got these little purple and green jerseys with matching shorts and socks!"

"Mama used to braid her hair and stick little green bows in it too," Sadaf said. "And then during the game, Haya would literally stand on the side, not getting any dirt on her."

I could see it clearly—Haya standing on the sidelines, looking adorable. We were walking by the soccer field now, and it was filled with teen girls playing soccer. We kept walking, and when we got to the swing set area, it was full of laughing kids falling all over themselves but getting up no matter how scraped their knees got. I wished I had that kind of energy again.

We walked around, watching the kids, their parents, the sun, the slides, the grass, the monkey bars.

"I haven't been on swings in forever," Sadaf said, leading us to a string of empty ones. I plopped down and immediately felt so overgrown, too old for swings, but Sadaf was already a pendulum in the air.

"What are you waiting for?" Haya asked, laughing. She looked like a carefree kid, and I wanted to follow suit. I was hesitant at first, not sure if I would remember how to get so high, but my body remembered.

Everything inside me remembered how to be a kid, and suddenly I was up, up, up too—soaring. It made me catch my breath, the wind cool on my face and the cold metal in my hands turning warm.

"Throw your head back and look at the clouds!" Haya urged me, and her words threw me back a decade. In my mind, I saw Ahsen telling me the same thing when I was a kid. In memory and in the present, I threw my head back, and suddenly I was flying. It was incredible. I was entirely weightless. I was floating in the air, invincible.

I could stay like this forever.

"I haven't done that since I was a kid," I said when we finally got off the swings to let some waiting children have a turn.

"You are still a kid." Haya laughed.

We linked arms and walked to the ice-cream truck at the edge of the park, then ambled through the pathways, sun warm on our skin, ice cream cool in our hands.

The air was thick with the aroma of flowers. Bright pink and yellow flowers dotted bushes and trees, singing to us. The sky was a perfect blue, and the ice cream was so sweet it made my teeth ache. But it was perfectly cold and tasted like years ago, so I ate it happily. We continued walking, talking about this and that, until Sadaf suddenly gasped.

"Oh. My. *God*," she said, hitting Haya on the arm. "Is that Carlos?"

"*What?*" Haya shrieked, instantly alert. She turned her head, searching. "Where?"

"Stay cool, but like right in front of us. Walking this way with a little kid," Sadaf responded. I could see plenty of people walking our way but couldn't discern the specific Carlos they were talking about. I was suddenly on the defensive at the prospect of a boy entering our calm circle of friendship.

"This is wild. We were literally just talking about soccer camp." Haya turned to me. "He was *at* that soccer camp with me. Once when I kicked the ball, he deflected it so wrong it fractured his wrist," Haya said. She bit her lip, embarrassed. "He sort of cursed me out in Spanish, I think. But that was years ago. I wonder if he remembers me."

It was evident that he did. When we got close enough on the pathway, he smiled wide, dimples cutting into his cheeks, and waved at us. He did not at all look like a boy who was upset Haya had fractured his wrist. Instead, he looked incredibly pleased.

"Oh no," Haya said. She waved and smiled back, but her voice was tragic. "He got so cute." He was a little taller than Haya and well-built, with a head full of pretty curls. "Not the curls," she muttered.

Sadaf and I laughed, but I felt a little pit form in my stomach thinking about cute boys. Thinking about the last cute boy in my life. I couldn't dwell because he was calling Haya's name.

"Haya! How are you?" Carlos said. In my head, I gave him one point for saying her name correctly. We were close enough now that we stopped walking and faced each other. *He really does have great hair.* He held the hand of a little boy with similar golden curls and even deeper dimples.

"Carlos, hi!" Haya squeaked. Sadaf elbowed her, and Haya cleared her throat. "I'm well, how are you? This is my sister, Sadaf, and our friend Zahra."

We exchanged hellos, and even I was a little winded by his charming smile. I could understand why Haya, chewing on her lip, wasn't doing so well.

"Ivan, say hello," Carlos told the little boy. "This is my cousin," he told us.

Ivan smiled at us, and while Sadaf and I were awed by how cute the kid was, Haya was more awed by how cute his cousin was.

"Hello!" Ivan said.

"Hi, cutie-pie," I said, bending down to reach his eye level. He smiled shyly, half-hiding behind Carlos's leg.

"I won't bite, I promise," I said, holding out my hand. Ivan hesitated, but eventually offered his hand to shake. I rattled his arm, and he giggled. *How absurdly adorable.*

"Do you mind if we join you?" Carlos asked Haya. Her eyes widened but being sweet was her default.

"Of course not!" she said, voice high. He fell into line beside her on the pathway.

"Great," he replied, giving her a half smile as he ran a hand through his hair. Haya's eyes tracked the movement of his arm muscles. Sadaf and I exchanged eyebrow raises, trying not to laugh. We quickened our pace a bit so we were walking in front of Carlos, Ivan, and Haya. But we were close enough to hear how nervous Haya sounded.

"Why is Haya freaking out?" I whispered to Sadaf. "He's cute, but like . . ."

"Haya had this massive crush on him during soccer camp," Sadaf explained, laughing. We walked down the winding path, passing women with strollers and middle schoolers on bikes. "When she fractured his wrist, she was mortified and skipped the last week of practice to avoid him."

"Ooh, saucy," I replied, shielding my eyes from the sun as the path turned to the sun's direction. "Kismat?"

"Definitely," Sadaf affirmed.

"This is actually wild. What are the chances of running into him a decade later?"

"To be fair, we run into people all the time on Long Island, and this park is the nicest one in the area, so it's not weird he's here. But still, the serendipity is something to be appreciated."

"If Haya would calm down." I turned around and glanced at her. "She's twirling her hijab."

Sadaf snorted. "She's such a loser."

Our conversation was interrupted when Haya called my name. Sadaf and I stopped walking and turned to face them.

I registered the SOS she was sending me with her eyes, but I shook my head at her and smiled.

Ivan tugged on Carlos's shirt, diverting his attention as they caught up with us. He whispered something in Spanish, and Carlos smiled.

"Claro, chiquito," he said, then turned to me. "Ivan wants to know if he can hold your hand."

I felt like the Chosen One. My heart nearly imploded.

"Of course," I said, holding my hand out for him. Ivan bounced toward me and grabbed it. Sadaf and I swooned.

"You're pretty," Ivan informed me. "I like you."

My heart definitely imploded. I loved little kids.

Ivan held my hand, and Sadaf pouted, sighing dramatically.

"How I wish *I* had someone's hand to hold," she told Ivan.

"Ooh mine! Mine!" he said, giving her his other hand.

"Wow, he really likes you guys," Carlos said, grinning. But then he turned to Haya. "Smart kid."

But the way he said it . . . Haya's face paled, and Sadaf raised an eyebrow at me. I swallowed back a laugh. The pathways in the park looped around, so we were back by the soccer field. The game was over now, and different small groups of people were using the field to kick around a ball or race on the turf. That gave me an idea.

"Hey, Ivan, let's have a race! Me, you, and Sadaf," I said, looking down at him. He nodded enthusiastically.

"That's a great idea!" Carlos said. "Ivan, show your new friends how fast you are!"

From behind Carlos, I saw Haya frantically shaking her head.

"Come on, let's race from here to the midfield point," Sadaf said, leading us to the goalpost. We stayed on the edge of the field, so not to bother the people kicking their soccer ball around. Sadaf, Ivan, and I got in line.

"I'm gonna beat you," I told Ivan, wiggling my eyebrows.

"No, I'm gonna beat you!" he replied, laughing.

"And—*go!*" Carlos called. We ran across the field, Sadaf and I obviously slower than Ivan to let him win. When we crossed the finish line, he jumped up, cheering.

"I won, I won!" he said.

"Good job!" I beamed at him. "Let's sit down and rest now."

I took his hand and sat down cross-legged on the turf, and Sadaf joined us. Across the field, Carlos and Haya were too busy chatting to come over and join us. Haya looked less stressed, laughing at something he was saying. The way he looked at her, it made my heart ache. It was so pure.

"I reckon we're babysitting now," Sadaf said. We began playing tag with Ivan, who was surprisingly fast for a five-year-old. It took Haya and Carlos a considerable amount of time to reach us in the center of the soccer field, but when they did, Haya looked buoyant. Carlos did seem a little nervous, though, his fingers playing with a rubber band, but his eyes were all on her.

Until the rubber band suddenly snapped and hit Haya on the forehead. Her skin flashed red. We all froze. Carlos was stunned, face horrified. Haya was equally mortified.

"Damn, Carlos," Sadaf said, quick to react. "If you wanted to hit on Haya, you didn't have to literally *hit her*."

Carlos's face turned red, and Haya laughed.

"I guess we're even for the whole fractured wrist debacle," she offered.

"Definitely not," he said, mouth turning up in a smile. "But don't worry! I'll think of some other way you can make up for it."

Sadaf and I exchanged wide-eyed looks, but before we could remark, Ivan bounced over to Carlos and said in a loud whisper, "I have to go to the bathroom."

Carlos looked at us. "I guess it's time for us to go."

"Bye! It was nice meeting you," Sadaf said, and we all waved. With a final lingering look at Haya, Carlos left, following the path away from us. When he was out of hearing distance, Sadaf pinched her sister's side.

"Ow!" Haya squealed, smacking Sadaf back.

"HAYA," Sadaf cried. "What just happened?"

"Who *is* he?" I asked. Haya smiled shyly, sitting down on the edge of the soccer field. We sat down, both of us across from her.

"What do you mean?" she asked, acting nonchalant. But we saw right through it.

"*HAYA!*" This time it was me who shouted her name. An elderly couple walking past us shot us a look, and we all burst out laughing. I lifted a hand in apology.

"Okay, fine!" Haya conceded. "He's even sweeter than I remember. And he *converted*."

"*What?*" Sadaf cried.

"What?!" I yelled. "No. Way."

Haya nodded, holding her hands to her chest and sighing. "Is that fate or what?"

"Don't be dramatic, princess." Sadaf snorted.

"Is that what you talked about? I need details," I urged her. "I thought running into him was crazy, but the fact that he *converted* is even more insane."

"I know! Basically, he told me how he converted last month, and he was really curious about learning more and being a proper Muslim, which is why he was so, like, excited to run into me, because he remembered I was Muslim, and he hadn't really known any other Muslims or didn't know who to talk to, especially since he's so new," she rambled. "He gave me his number because I said I could help him out if he needed it."

"*Wow*," Sadaf drawled.

"*Smooth*," I chimed in.

"Oh, hush!" Haya said, standing up. "He's cute but this is, like, strictly professional. I'm helping a fellow Muslim, okay? This is, like, dawah. Now let's go home. It's getting hot."

"Someone's hot and bothered for sure . . . ," Sadaf teased. She got up, and Haya shoved her.

"Shut up."

We all walked back to Sadaf's car. The humidity was setting in, and the weather was getting warmer. In the car, we played music, but Haya couldn't keep the goofy smile off her face.

"He has such nice dimples," Haya remarked. "Unreal. And the hair? Amazing."

"How about you lower your gaze next time, Sister?" Sadaf said.

"Hey," Haya said innocently. "I'm appreciating Allah's creation. Is that such a crime?"

We all laughed. It was exciting, the prospect of this cute boy who seemed interested in my cute friend.

But I couldn't get rid of the discomfort in my chest, stinging like acid. It was the discomfort that came from being scorched, and not wanting my friend to make the same mistake. Even though it wasn't me getting involved in a relationship, I was immensely protective of Haya and this boy who seemed decent but could be anything but.

I hoped she wouldn't get scorched.

I hoped she wouldn't even get close to being burned.

Chapter 18

A few nights later we went out for dinner to this cute little restaurant in Hicksville, which is home to all the halal food on Long Island. It was a bit of a drive, since it was in Nassau County, not Suffolk County, where the Chaudrys lived and where the masjid was. As we drove over, I was shocked by the highway, which was just straight.

I still hadn't adjusted to how *flat* Long Island was, no mountains, no hills. It was a far cry from the towering skyscrapers I associated with New York. The highest point around here was a place called Bald Hill, which was basically a pillar painted with the American flag, and let's just say, I wasn't impressed.

In Hicksville, we went to this long street filled with various halal food places—from Afghan to Persian to Pakistani. There were a few desi supermarkets and shalwar kameez stores too, including a Junaid Jamshed, which I thought was a nice touch.

We went to Chai Shai, which was a typical desi restaurant: there was a fluorescent sign outside that said "Halal" and a big kalima decal in Arabic on the window. Inside, the decor was sparse, but multicolored and gold, plus the dishes were stainless steel and simple.

Chai Shai was owned by Lubna Auntie—a short, older woman, who had known Haya's parents for two decades.

"Meri bachian!" She beamed at us, coming out from behind the counter to give us all hugs. "And this must be a new friend! You girls are always bringing me such good business!"

"Auntie, no one makes chicken makhni like you do!" Sadaf said.

Haya introduced me, and we sat down at one of the tables. The place wasn't busy, and I could hear a Rahat Fateh Ali Khan track playing in the background. The air smelled like coriander and garlic and sautéed onions and meat—homey smells.

"What should we eat?" Haya asked, eyeing the menu. "Like, obviously papri chaat, but what else?"

Everything on the menu was familiar. There were Pakistani dishes and some Western items like burgers and fried chicken as well. I shrugged at Haya. When I turned to Sadaf, she was staring into the distance.

She was quieter than usual. Haya and I exchanged a glance before Haya snapped her fingers in front of her sister's face.

"*Hellooo*," she said. "Focus, Sadaf."

"Okay, okay, sorry," Sadaf said, clearing her head. We decided what to eat, and it was only when we had placed our order that Sadaf gave us any clue.

"I'm so stressed," she groaned.

"Is it graduation?" Haya asked, voice knowing.

"The usual." Sadaf nodded, and her sister frowned. I guessed this was something they'd discussed before.

"But you still have loads of time until then, right?" I asked, confused as to why graduation was stressing her out already.

"It's just—so much," she explained. "I'm off to the Adult World next May, and I've no clue what I'm going to do. I need to start applying to jobs this fall, which is only a few months away. Naadia's already applying to med school, and it's like everyone else I know got offers from their internships or knows exactly what they're doing, and I'm still figuring it out."

"Do you want to work or go to grad school?" I asked her.

"Ideally, I want to work for a bit, then maybe go back to school when I've saved up a decent amount," Sadaf replied. "But it's so difficult to get a good job, you know?"

"You're a psych major, right?"

"Mm-hmm. I want to go into speech therapy later on. Ideally with kids who have gone through trauma at a young age," she told me.

"Maybe you could get a job as an assistant or something at a practice doing the kind of work you're thinking about, to get good experience?" I offered. She nodded, resting her head on her arm.

"That's probably what I'll end up doing," she said. "It's just stressful. I have no idea what my life will be like after college."

"Don't worry too much," Haya told her. "One, you'll get

wrinkles. Two, you're smart and have done well for yourself, so I'm sure you'll get a great job."

"Mmhh," Sadaf mumbled. I could see her deflating, and I understood exactly where she was coming from. I had been in a similar spot last fall, though I was graduating high school and making plans for university.

It was the same fear, the same crippling anxiety that came from an unknown future. I had made so many plans, detailed what my life would look like in each scenario. I guess it didn't even matter in the end because now I was here, in New York with no plans and maybe no future.

Anxiety crept through me, but I pushed it back.

I would take this day by day, week by week. I would make this work. *It will be okay.*

But I couldn't calm the discomfort simmering in my tummy. I wanted to know what the future would hold too.

"Let's talk about something else," Sadaf said, bouncing back. "Like your cute boy, Haya."

Haya hid her face behind her hands.

"No," she said. "Let's talk about something *else* something else."

"Haya," I drawled, pulling her hands away. "Give us the tea. We *are* at Chai Shai."

"Don't think we haven't been noticing the sudden intense interest you've had with your phone the past few days," Sadaf said, waving a finger.

"Look! Food!" Haya called. One of Lubna Auntie's sons set the food down at our table family-style. Our attention was diverted by the intoxicating aroma wafting from the dishes. There were fresh, buttery naans, deep red chicken makhni topped with green coriander, and plates of papri chaat and masala fries.

"Ooh," Haya cooed. She immediately reached for the fries, squealing when she burned her fingers.

"Why are you freaking out? He's literally just a guy," Sadaf said, waving a spoon threateningly in Haya's face. "And remember, all men are trash."

"I'm not freaking out!" she protested, enunciating each word with a red-chili-powdered fry in Sadaf's direction. Haya popped the fry in her mouth then sighed. "I just don't know how to deal with it. He's always texting me! And it is mostly questions, but not all the time. He wants to get coffee some-time, to talk more, but like—I'm stressed! I don't know how to handle boys!"

Sadaf laughed. She poured a spoonful of chaat onto her plate, then crushed papri over it. She handed the chaat to me next, and I made myself a serving as she had, though I poured green chutney over for extra spice. Haya dove straight into the chicken makhni, the sauce thick and creamy.

"Oh my God, relax," Sadaf said, taking a half naan from Haya as she cut them. "One, you'll get wrinkles at the ripe age of eighteen. Two, he's just a person. And of course he wants to get coffee—you're so cute and nice and charming. I mean, whose sister are you?"

"Ha, ha." Unamused, Haya scooped chicken makhni onto a piece of naan and stuffed it into her mouth.

"But be careful, because crushes are dangerous territory," Sadaf warned.

Haya frowned, shoveling more makhni into her mouth.

"Again, I reiterate, men are trash."

"I don't have a crush," Haya protested, the words muffled due to all the food in her mouth.

Sadaf and I paused our eating to give her a pointed look.

"Haya, be serious," I said, pouring water into our cups.

"Okay, fine, *maybe* I have, like, a baby-baby-*baby* crush on him," she conceded, not meeting our gazes. "Baby times three crush. So tiny, it's hardly there."

We were unconvinced.

"What kinds of stuff is he asking you?" I asked, grabbing some fries from her.

"Stuff like how to pray properly and about dua and how he can get more involved in the community," she replied, moving the fries closer to me. "I think I'm the only Muslim he knows so far because his parents are Chilean and super-super Catholic, but I told him to come to the masjid for Jummah and stuff."

"Do his parents know he converted?" Sadaf asked.

Haya winced. "Not yet, and he's majorly stressed because he wants to respect them but knows they'll probably hate him once they find out," she said, frowning. "I told him to just give it more time. That's what people usually need—more time."

After we had eaten and drunk our chai, Haya went to Lubna Auntie to pay. When she came back, she had an immense smile on her face.

"Who's the best friend you will ever have?" she asked, sitting down beside me. "Spoiler alert—it's me! I got you a job here!"

It took me a moment to react. When I did, my mouth tasted sour. I didn't want Haya pulling strings and doing all this for me. *Doesn't she know she's already doing too much?* I wanted to curl into myself, to take up less space.

"I worked here for a bit, before I got my gig at the health center, and it's a great job!" she said. "Auntie is the sweetest and her sons are majorly nice too. The pay is good, and the job is not too difficult! I gave her your number. You can start tomorrow."

"Haya—" I started, but I didn't know what to say. I released a breath. I didn't know if I should have been angry or ecstatic or sad.

In the end, all I could muster was, "Thank you. So much. Really."

I started the next day. The restaurant opened at twelve, so in the morning, I took the train and then a bus to get there. It was a bit far out, but I didn't mind. I had all the time in the world.

When I arrived, I took a deep breath and pushed through the doors.

"Salaam, Zahra, beti," Lubna Auntie said when I entered. Putting her arm across my shoulder, she led me to the kitchen, where a handful of older men and women were busy chopping vegetables and cooking at the stove. Lubna Auntie steered me to the back of the kitchen, where her two sons were washing and drying dishes.

"Muzzamil! Yaseen!" she called. They both looked up and smiled as she introduced us. One was a tall, wide, dark-brown man with a thick Sunnah beard and short hair. That was probably Muzzamil, the older one. Haya mentioned to me that he was married and had two little girls.

His brother, Yaseen, was also tall and well-built, but with a short beard and long, wavy hair. He was in college, I think a year older than Haya and me. While they seemed nice enough, I felt wary.

"We'll have you helping around wherever you can, acha beti?" Lubna Auntie said to me. "Serving, cleaning—can you cook?"

I nodded. "Just about anything on your menu, and anything else you want me to," I told her with a bright smile. "I'm a quick learner."

Lubna Auntie smiled warmly, her face wrinkling softly.

"Great! Do you know how to make spring rolls?" she asked. I nodded.

"You can do that today then. The recipe for the mix is by the stove so you only have to make that up and then wrap it in the sheets," she said, leading me to the kitchen. She set a pot on the stove and showed me where things were, telling me that if I needed anything, I could simply shout for her or her sons.

"Have fun, beti," she said, then she was gone.

I got to work, following the recipe, and calling upon what I remembered from making them at home with Mama. It wasn't a difficult task, and it was actually nice to be cooking. I forgot how much I enjoyed it. It was calming, just stirring the mixture, feeling the warm kitchen air on my cheeks. Here, dicing onions and slicing carrots, I couldn't mess up.

It was only when I began to wrap the rolls that I faced a problem. They kept breaking. After a few failed attempts, I considered calling out to Auntie, but when I popped my head out of the kitchen, I saw that she was busy serving food. I chewed on my lip and reentered the kitchen.

One of her sons, Yaseen, was at the sink, washing dishes, but I didn't want to bother him. While we had been in the same space the entire time, I hadn't spoken a word to him or made eye contact.

But he must have sensed me struggling because a few minutes later he came over to where I had helplessly destroyed another spring roll.

"I see Mama has you making rolls," Yaseen said, running a hand through his long hair. I had a pile of broken roll sheets beside me at that point.

"Yeah," I said, biting my lip. He smiled at me. The way he spoke and looked at me made me feel normal, not defensive or worried. He stood with his hands behind his back, not invading my personal space at all. "More like trying," I admitted sheepishly. "They're all falling apart. I think these are different from the ones I'm used to." I held up a broken sheet. Yaseen laughed.

"I can show you if you want," he said. I nodded. He pulled a headband out of his pocket and pushed his long hair back. The sight of the headband made me snicker, but I bit my lip.

"Hey, don't make fun," he said, pointing a finger. "Everyone thought it was cool when Zayn Malik did it, and I'd been doing it for years before that poseur caught on."

That really made me laugh. I started to relax.

"Oh, yeah, sure," I said. "And where's the rest of your boy band?"

"Hey, you want my help or not?" he said good-naturedly. He washed his hands, then stood beside me in front of the counter, leaving a healthy amount of space between us, and showed me the technique—folding the sides in first, then rolling. He held up a perfect roll.

"Ooh," I said, realizing my error in folding. I had rolled first, then done the sides. "That makes sense!"

"Is my brother bragging about his perfect rolls?" Muzzamil asked, coming to stand next to Yaseen. "Don't believe him. I'm the real expert in the family."

"Yeah, sure you are, Muzz Bhai," Yaseen said, rolling his eyes. To me, he whispered, "My three-year-old niece can make better rolls than this guy."

"Let's have a go, then," Muzzamil challenged. "Me, you, and the newbie. Let's see who can make the most."

I laughed.

"It'll for sure be me," I said sarcastically.

"Oh yeah?" Yaseen said. "Let's go then, for sure!"

We all stood together and began making rolls, seeing who

was the fastest. Both boys were rooting for me, I could tell, because whenever Muzzamil wasn't looking, Yaseen took some rolls from his brother's pile and added them to mine. And when Muzzamil "accidentally" knocked over Yaseen's spoon, forcing him to go get another one, he winked at me.

In the end, I did win, and the boys had cut my work to less than a third of what it should have been.

"See, I knew I would win," I joked. "You guys just aren't on my level."

"It's only because I taught you everything you know," Yaseen said. Their mother came in then, and seeing the pile of rolls, smiled at me fondly.

"Well done, Zahra! Excellent," she said. I nearly interjected to tell her the truth, but her son cut me off.

"See, Mama, I told you hiring more help was a good idea," Yaseen said.

"Yes, and I'm sure you boys have done none of your work, nikamme," Lubna Auntie said, tsking at her sons. She shook her head, going to whack Yaseen with a wooden spoon. He dodged it easily and instead planted a kiss on her cheek.

"Too slow, Mama," he said.

"Batameez," she said, laughing. "Chalo, kaam karo."

She sent them off to work, and even after they were gone, I felt warm inside. They were innocuous and sweet. It made me miss Ahsen a little, how we used to joke around sometimes, during the rare occasions he was home and in a good mood.

But I didn't miss him nearly as much as I missed my mama. In the kitchen, I continued working, making samosas and chicken patties, and all I could think about was standing in the kitchen beside my mother, learning from her. Every year, we would spend days before Ramadan making dozens and dozens of samosas and patties to be frozen. Then, throughout the month, we would cook the little treats for iftaar.

It was always the most peaceful time of the year. It felt like forever and ever ago.

I missed her. Despite everything, I missed my mama.

Chapter 19

*J*uly slipped away as I started building a life for myself, and it was funny how some things didn't change. I was still here, still wanting, still craving, still breathing, living, dying. People made me sad, and people made me happy, and I loved them all and resented them too, but nothing had changed. People kept changing around me, growing, learning, evolving.

And here I was, just wanting. I had run away from my life, but I couldn't run away from myself.

All these feelings, so many, and then—none at all. And the people, so many, and then—none at all. And this life, so busy, so full, and then—empty.

How did I talk to Allah? That was supposed to make it better. I was craving love and security right now.

On the plus side, I made enough money to get a little studio apartment to rent. It was small and cheap, and in a not-too-nice area, but it was alright. And close to a bus station. The apartment was attached to somebody's house, which is why I got such a good deal without needing roommates. It was near a university, so there were loads of places like it, meant to be affordable for students.

I didn't want to stay with Haya and Sadaf anymore. In part, I didn't want to be an unwelcome guest, and in part, I wanted to be secluded from them. It was hard always smiling and talking and pretending to be okay.

At least at night, I could be alone on my single mattress, surrounded by the vast emptiness, and in some strange way, feel like I belonged. It was such a contradiction because, during the day, when I was with people, I felt like I belonged too.

I had a routine and girls who were my friends. Volunteering at the masjid summer camp, attending Youth Group, going to the Chaudrys'. Working at the restaurant, getting a job at the mall, getting some part-time tutoring jobs as well.

Madiha and Imaan and the other Youth Group girls were fun. Lubna Auntie at the restaurant was nice, and Muzzamil and Yaseen were sweet and funny. The Chaudrys were amazing, and when I got to know Naadia and Humaira, I realized they were wonderful too.

I was part of the community . . . but not really.

One foot in, one foot out, I always felt the transience within me. How quickly I could pull the rug out from beneath my own feet and land safely to disappear. I was not a thread woven into the cloth of their community, but rather, a scrap sewn haphazardly onto the side. I could easily be ripped off.

Be careful, don't get too comfortable, don't start caring, because they might leave—or you will.

So I kept myself at arm's length from everyone, every-thing, because once I cared, I cared too much.

And that was too scary for me to bear.

Chapter 20

$\mathcal{I}$ wanted to run as August went on. It made me feel not rooted in my life.

It felt like things were ten times harder, took ten times the effort, as the summer became a downhill slide toward fall and school and regular routine. I wasn't going to college this year—I still needed time to figure things out—but Haya and Sadaf and all the other girls would be busy with school come September.

Every time I took a step forward, it felt like I tripped and fell to the floor. Each time, it was harder to get up again. Like things were okay but could easily crumble any second— like I was holding on to a fraying rope that could break any moment, leaving me to fall off a cliff's edge.

Everyone I knew was great—the ones I was close to and the ones I wasn't—but they weren't there with me in the darkest shadow of night. They couldn't pick me up when I fell, but I wished they could. It was hard being your own cheerleader all the time.

I tried not to dwell on the past, but the bones of my sins came back to haunt me, and I could do nothing to stop them.

After volunteering one day, I was leaving the masjid, laughing with Haya as we headed toward her car, when I saw a ghost.

Zayn.

I stopped dead in my tracks, the laughter dying on my lips. My heart beat violently against my chest. For a moment, I thought I was hallucinating—*he can't be here.* Everything froze, until Haya's voice rang into the air.

"Zayn! Salaam, how are you?"

Everything shattered all at once.

He was here, looking straight at me.

"Wassalaam," he said to Haya, tearing his eyes from me. He gave her a warm smile, but his gaze kept flicking to me. I couldn't believe he was here, but here he stood, wearing a blue T-shirt and jeans, the wind tousling his dark hair.

"Visiting Fareeha Baji?" Haya asked him. He turned to me, about to open his mouth to speak. My throat was dry. *This cannot be happening.*

By then, Sadaf had caught up with us as well. We all stood in the masjid parking lot by Haya's car. The sun felt blistering against the skin of my hands as I fidgeted with my fingers. I felt faint.

"Hey, Zayn, what's up?" Sadaf said, smiling warmly at him. "Are you here to see Fareeha Baji and the kids?"

"Actually, I'm here to see Zahra," he said. He turned

directly toward me, gaze intense. Haya and Sadaf exchanged a confused glance.

"Zahra?" Haya repeated with a nervous laugh. "What do you mean? You two know each other?"

I felt a wave, rising, rising . . .

I swallowed the lump in my throat. "Um . . . ," I managed to say, as Zayn nodded.

"We were supposed to get married," he said, voice flat.

The wave crashed.

I saw the realization dawn on Sadaf's and Haya's faces, the pieces falling into place and the stories aligning. Confusion and betrayal and anger. Tears burned my eyes. I hastily blinked them away.

"Zahra, is that . . . true?" Haya asked, facing me. Her eyes were wide behind her pink glasses, her voice small. "You're the one who left him right before the nikkah?"

She waited for me to reply, but I couldn't speak. I avoided her glance, looking behind her at the blue sky, much too bright and blinding.

"Um . . . ," I tried again.

"Z, what the hell?" Sadaf said, upset. My gaze went to her, and there was strong emotion written on her countenance. It wasn't good. I shrank away from her. "Why didn't you tell us? When we were talking about it a few weeks ago?"

I didn't know what to say. My voice had disappeared.

"Uh, well . . . ," I tried yet again, but he interrupted.

"Can we talk please?" Zayn asked, scratching the back of his neck. "I'm sure your parents are worried about you too."

"Your parents?" Haya repeated. "You said they died in a car accident."

"Is that what she said?" Zayn asked, puzzled. He turned to me. "Why would you lie?"

"Yes, Zahra, why *would* you lie?" Sadaf asked, voice hard. She was confused, but there was clear anger on her face as well.

"I'm sorry—I'm sorry, I didn't—" I stuttered, but I couldn't manage any words.

"Zahra, what's going on?" Haya asked, face full of hurt. She took a step away from me. "Who are you?"

"I ran away from home," I said, finally telling the truth. My voice broke. "I didn't know how to tell you."

"You've been lying to us this whole time?" Sadaf asked, shaking her head. "Zahra, we vouched for you. You stayed at our house! I thought we were friends."

"We are!" I insisted, sight blurring with tears. "We *are*."

"Friends don't *use* each other," Sadaf said, her voice breaking with hurt. "We don't even really know you . . ."

"Please, I can explain—" I began, but she turned away from me.

"Haya, let's go," she said, taking her sister's hand. Haya was silent as they left, but she looked over her shoulder, meeting my eyes, sadness spilling across her face. Sadaf pulled her along, and I wanted to cry, but Zayn was still standing there, waiting awkwardly. He was very fascinated by his shoes.

"Okay, let's talk," I said, clearing my throat. "We can go to the park."

"Okay."

We crossed the street and headed toward the park, walking along the pathway in silence until we reached a bench.

"Let's sit down," he said. I was glad for the reprieve. My legs were shaking. After we sat, he tilted his body to face me, but I couldn't look at him, I was so ashamed. "Is it something I did?" he asked, voice gentle. "I don't understand. Why did you run away?"

Wasn't that the big question.

"How did you find me?" I asked, then realized I knew. "Fareeha," we both said at the same time. I sighed and looked at him.

Zayn ran a hand through his hair. He looked so tired.

"Fareeha called me a few weeks ago saying she'd seen you," he said. "Which was strange, because your parents said you were in London for the summer at some study-abroad program before starting college there in the fall."

So that was what they had said. My cover story. Of course, they wouldn't have said I had run away.

"I guessed you were hiding out for some reason," he said. He shrugged. "And I figured since it was right before our nikkah, maybe that was it? But I don't understand why you didn't just tell me. Nobody would have forced you. I thought this was what you wanted."

He was confused and hurt. But he was being so nice about the entire thing that I wanted to cry. Why couldn't he yell at me? Tell me I was selfish and awful and cruel? I deserved to be punished.

"No, it wasn't you, I swear," I told him, trying to keep my

voice steady. I took a deep breath, looking into his dark eyes. He deserved an apology. I had run away from him too, but it had never been about him. The marriage was just another thing I couldn't handle on top of everything else. "I'm so sorry to leave like that," I said, "but it was . . . everything. It was all too much, so I . . . I ran."

"Oh . . . okay," he said, nodding to himself. He looked relieved. "Well, I'm glad it wasn't anything I did. I would have hated to have done anything to upset you."

He really was sweet. He deserved so much.

"Zayn, thank you for being so understanding," I told him. "You deserve the world, and I hope you find true happiness. I've just got so much shit going on in my head and my heart that I couldn't handle anyone or anything."

He nodded, taking that in. He sat back against the bench, releasing a long breath. I did the same. We sat in silence for a little bit until he spoke again.

"You deserve the world too, you know," he said. "You deserve happiness; you deserve peace. I pray to Allah that He grants it to you, and soon."

I don't know about that. I shook my head. "Ameen. Thank you for saying that."

Silence fell over us again. This had been so simple. I should have reached out to Zayn earlier to apologize and explain. But I hadn't even been thinking of him. I'd forgotten all about him until he showed up here today.

"All right, well, I guess I'll get going," he said, standing. "My sister will be waiting. But I'm glad we cleared that up."

"Wait!" I said suddenly, standing as well. "Can you tell me . . . How are my parents?"

"Last I saw them, they were doing okay," he told me, scratching the back of his neck. "They just looked worried. And sad."

The thought gutted me.

"And . . . Ahsen?"

Zayn shrugged. "Sorry, I don't really know—I haven't seen him. I heard he got into a few fights, but otherwise, I think he's doing fine?" He shook his head. "Honestly, I don't know."

"Oh . . . okay, thank you," I said, biting my bottom lip. "And . . . could you not tell them about this? I know it's a lot to ask, but . . . I need some more time. I promise I'll tell them myself."

"Yeah, no problem," he said, holding up his hands. "It's none of my business—you do you."

"Thank you, Zayn. Khudahafiz."

"Khudahafiz, Zahra."

He left, and I sat back down on the bench, watching him go. I released a long breath, my head dropping into my hands. As far as confrontations went, it hadn't been bad.

But while Zayn hadn't blamed me, I blamed myself. I had royally screwed up, running away from our nikkah and not telling him anything. And then I remembered Haya's and Sadaf's faces when Zayn told them.

They had taken me in, supported me, trusted me, and what had I done? Lied to them, used them, betrayed them. *Who are you?* Haya's hurt voice asked in my head. Tears filled my eyes and flowed over my cheeks. I gasped for breath, quickly brushing them away. My hands were soaked in a minute, but still, I wiped my cheeks, trying to stop crying.

But I couldn't stop. I pulled my knees into my chest and sat there on the bench for a long time, crying into my legs.

By the time I finally got up and went back to my apartment, it was dark out. I was exhausted beyond belief. I collapsed onto my bed, but not before pulling out my phone and ringing Haya.

I waited.

And waited.

But she didn't pick up.

I called Sadaf next, but no answer.

Bile filled my throat. I wanted to vomit. In such a short time, they had become family to me, and now I had ruined that too.

With a heavy sigh, I grabbed my pillow and hugged it to my chest, letting sleep and dreams take over.

Chapter 21

11:00 p.m. After curfew. We were playing poker, the six of us. Two girls, four boys. Blond hair and blue eyes, light-brown hair and green eyes, chestnut hair and hazel eyes—hijab and black eyes. No hair, not yet, though it was peeking out from my untied scarf, little wisps escaping. I knew how they framed my face, knew how effortlessly pretty it made me look. I did not push the hair back. Instead, I threw my head back, laughing as I won again.

12:00 a.m. Getting late now. I didn't want the night to be over now. We settled into the sofa and watched a movie. Knees pressed together. Tummy full of knots. Just two layers of sweatpants separating skin. One dimpled half smile. Blue eyes. Why did I love blue eyes so damn much?

2:00 a.m. Later than late. Movie finished. Time to sleep. We were leaving for home in six hours. The long weekend was over. Vacation done. Bottle up this feeling and these memories and that dimpled smile because your time is up, it's finished, say goodbye. Back to college applications and back to crying once the lights switched off. Back to life. Thoughts and thoughts and thoughts in a whirlwind.

Wait. My voice. Everyone else was gone. Just the two of us left. Blond hair close enough it really did look like sunshine. He was so tall. So strong. Carry me for a while, I wanted to say. But we didn't say a word. I bit my lip. How did this go? I wasn't sure.

Beige walls. Yellow lights. *Shhh.* Everyone's asleep. A stifled giggle. The key sliding in. A warm hand in mine. This was innocent. This was fun. Nothing bad, nothing wrong. I choose this. Just a little relaxing. Just a few more moments, then I'll stop. Promise. This will make everything better.

I don't think about the consequences, only the present.

Then all at once: everything. *Are you sure?* I can stop it, but I don't. *Yes.* I want this. Cold air on my ears and neck, then my hair, cascading down, black and seemingly infinite. Lips on lips. Lips on skin. Skin on skin. Sudden pain. A gasp. Time disappearing. Lips. Skin. Pain. Hands. Legs. Cold fingers. Nothingness. Quiet. Emptiness. Silence.

My heart, oh, my heart.

When I woke up, my skin burned from the sensation.

I screamed.

It was the first time that night had come back to me as a full memory. There was no relief in waking, no sanctuary because my memory was stronger, more alive. I thought I felt a hand on my leg, and I screamed again, pushing it away. The bed was too soft, too much like that bed. I fell to the ground. The floor brought me comfort, forced me to focus on this cold, focus on the solidness.

Hot breath. Hair on neck. My fingers spasmed and seized and ripped through my hair. I saw the strands between my fingers, black and infinite.

"No," I sobbed, in pieces. *This was your choice*, my mind told me, punching me in my gut. *You chose this.* I *had* chosen it. I hadn't known what it would be like after: the shame, the guilt.

I dug my nails into my arm and watched it bleed, but it wasn't mine—not my arm or my blood. I felt nothing, just saw the gorgeous, grotesque shade of maroon.

Everything was distant; everything was quiet. No words, no thoughts, simply blurry sights and a blurry mind and a blurry heart. Smudged, like a painting ruined. *Ruined.*

I heard knocking on the door and Haya's voice. *Who is she looking for? There's nobody here.* I heard my body retching up air from my empty stomach, but the guilt did not leave. Nothing left. It all stayed, swirling inside me, in my veins, in my gut, in every single one of my cells. And I lay there, thirsty and hungry, crying and dying.

What you did was unforgivable, my mind reminded me. *You deserve this pain. Suffer. Hate yourself, no one else. Do not detach from this body because it is yours, wasted and used. Suffer. Cry. Hate.*

I wanted to be home, to be in Mama's arms, to see Ahsen smile, to hear Baba's laugh. I wanted to hug Nano, to smell Nana Abu, to kiss my little cousins. I wanted to eat snicker-doodles, to feel sunlight. I wanted somebody to say my name. I wanted my home and my life and my people and my things and me from before, *from before*.

Most of all, I wanted her—*me*—back. I wanted to stop her and kill her and save her and hug her and hold her face in my hands and love her.

But there was nothing but the cold, dirty floor.

Chapter 22

I realized I wasn't dead when I saw Haya.

"Thank God you opened the door. Are you out of your *mind*?" she cried. Her tear-stained face was as pink as her glasses. "I thought you were hurt!"

There wasn't anger but hysteria and worry, then finally, relief in Haya's voice. She threw her arms around me.

"I thought something happened to you," she sobbed into my neck. I hadn't realized we were hugging until then. It wasn't a hug though, not really. I was limp in her arms, eyes half-closed.

It was halfway into the next day, and I had no idea where the time had gone. We stood in the doorway of my apartment. I felt numb. Separate from my body and myself.

"Zahra," she said, pulling away from me. She closed the door behind her. Putting her hands on my shoulders, she steadied me. "Zahra, I've been out there all morning, banging on the door. I called you like a hundred times. Zahra, talk to me."

But all I said, over and over in a whisper, was this:

"I'm sorry, I shouldn't have. I'm sorry, please forgive me. I'm so, so sorry."

"Zahra." Haya pulled my face into her gentle hands. I didn't have the energy to lift my head any longer, but she was so strong.

This was the girl I wished I could be: gentle and kind and pure—radiating light. *I am nothing but poison, nothing but shame.*

"Talk to me. What's going on?" she whispered. "Let's sit." She pulled me along, but I could barely move. I leaned a hand against the cool wall, then slid down to the floor, tilting my head back. Haya sat beside me. "Talk to me," she said, voice gentle. "Please."

"I did something."

The words were a shadow during sunset, near gone. Haya heard me anyway; she always did. How did she do that?

"Something bad?" she asked, voice soothing as sunshine. I nodded. I couldn't speak. A wretched little creature had stolen my voice and refused to give it back.

I didn't look at her. I focused on the empty glass on the table across from me, the pink lipstick stain on the rim. *I need to wash that.*

"Zahra, love, if Allah created us perfect, we would have been angels," she told me. "But He knew we would screw up. He knew we would err again and again and again; that's how He made us. So it's okay. Accept your mistakes and ask for forgiveness. He is the Most Merciful, after all."

"What if He doesn't forgive me?"

"Oh, hon, of course He will, of course He will." Haya took my hand in hers. Starved, I grasped her fingers, gripping them tight. Haya didn't flinch. "No matter how big it was, no matter how terrible. You think your Creator doesn't love you enough to forgive you?"

"My own mother doesn't love me enough to forgive me."

"Do you think your mother loves you more than Allah? The One who bathed your soul in light upon your inception? The One who orders your heart to beat every instant of every hour? The One who commands your lungs to breathe? He is the One who created your mother, who created *you*— who loves you more than you can imagine. You think He would not forgive you if you just asked?"

Tears welled in my eyes. "I can't—*I can't.*"

"Why not?"

"I should be punished."

In that moment, I wanted to be. I wanted to suffer physical pain if only to alleviate this intangible suffering within.

"Talk to me, Zahra. What happened?"

"My parents aren't dead," I told her, crying. "I'm not going to NYU. I ran away from home. Do you still want to know? Even though I've been lying to you this whole time?"

"Zahra," Haya said. "*Of course* I still want to know. You're my best friend."

"But I thought you were angry with me. Sadaf too."

Haya sighed. "No. I was just shocked, Zahra. It was a lot of information. And Sadaf is quick to get angry but just as quick to get over it. We love you. Just because we were upset with you doesn't mean we don't love you."

"Oh."

"Talk to me, Zahra. I'm a good listener, I promise. Sometimes talking about it makes it easier."

So I vomited the words onto her, but she did not care about the mess they made, did not tell me to stop. I continued until I was retching, nothing left to heave but fragments of words.

Even then, she listened.

It began as most stories did:

Once upon a time there was a girl and there was a boy.

He was cute, of course. In what world was the boy not cute?

You've heard this story before, haven't you? But no, I don't think you have. They never told stories about hijabis or Muslim girls or Pakistani girls. They never told stories about girls with limits and girls with hard lines that Could Not Be Crossed.

This was my story.

Of course, he fell for me. Why wouldn't he? Didn't I know that I smelled like lavender? Didn't I know how lovely I was when I batted my eyelashes? I knew it all—how cute I could be when I tried, how intriguing and fun.

I couldn't quite figure out why I had done it. Perhaps it was the illicit thrill that shivered through my body. That's all it was—adrenaline, pumps of glittery sunshine after so many cloudy nights. Finally feeling something *good*.

It was five days.

The first time I was away from home, the first time

without my parents and older brother watching over me. It was a school trip, one I had to beg for months to get permission for. *Just a week, Mama, please, please let me go. I've never been skiing before, and I really want to go. Vermont is so pretty, I've heard. Everyone is going. Please let me go, Mama, please.*

It was five days.

So little time in one respect but so much in another. It was five days of infinite hours, stretched across the horizon. Five days. It was five days of stolen glances that turned into stares, of accidental bumps that turned into grazing shoulders, of finger brushes that turned into hand holding, of proximity and warmth in a frigid winter.

He was just some guy from my year, someone I had never paid attention to, but on that trip, I noticed him. He noticed me.

He warmed my hands between his in the middle of a snowstorm—how romantic was that? He told me I was different, that I was beautiful and smart. That I could get into any goddamn college in the world and leave home and my parents behind—that I could forge my own path.

How do you know? I asked, and he said it was because he knew me. He could look into my eyes and see my soul, the way it shimmered and sparkled.

I was such an idiot, and I knew it, deep down. I did. I knew what he actually wanted, and it was the same for me. It was all an act, but I told myself it wasn't and fooled myself just long enough. Was it a lie if you believed it? I believed my lies, so they turned into truth. He saw *me*.

But really, it wasn't that deep, in the end. Not that emotional. I just wanted to forget—who I was, what I was responsible for, everything that was dictated to and expected from me. The mess of uncertainty that was my future and the stress and the anxiety that came with it. I just wanted to forget.

As if I could be saved by a touch, a kiss. Wasn't it supposed to work like that? I just wanted to forget.

So I did.

But some things you never forget.

I could feel again how my heart seemed to explode from my chest when the two of us slipped away the very last night. I could smell his cologne, see the beads of melted snow on the back of his neck, feel his warm fingers in mine. I could nearly taste him, right now: the candy cane and the hot chocolate and the confident laugher.

Would I ever forget the sudden cold on my ears when my scarf unraveled? The feel of skin on skin and sloppy kisses and hands roaming everywhere that could be explored? Would I ever forget how easy it was? How one thing had so quickly led to another, and another, and another? I could have stopped it, but I didn't want to. I wanted to see it through.

Would I ever forget the humiliation and vulnerability of being naked? Would I ever forget the raindrop stain on the white ceiling? The sudden pain between my legs and the tears in my eyes and then the vast hollowness in my chest as if I was dead? As if none of it was real? Even though I wanted to go through with it, all of it. I was aware of what was happening throughout the entire encounter, but I didn't realize it would only make me feel worse.

And then the sleep, and the messy collection of my things, the redressing and the ugly bruises, and the walk back to my room. The physical pain of it, the mental shame of it, the emotional emptiness of it.

Afterward, I knew I was damaged goods because I—

"It's okay," Haya told me, squeezing my hand. Her hands were so warm, where mine were cold. "You can say it aloud. Stop burying it in your heart."

My voice was a whisper when I finally said, "I had sex."

Even saying it gave me shame. The word was so stigmatized, covered in layers and layers of disgust, when it was simply a natural act—an act that created life. So why was it deemed so terrible?

Why was it that just the word, the three letters squished together, made my cheeks burn? It was not a word to be spoken, let alone an act to be carried out. It was the worst thing I could have done as an unmarried girl: with one single action, I had shed the single most important part of me—my honor.

Maybe I was tired. Maybe I was sick of carrying the golden weights of my virginity and my reputation and my family name. Maybe the weights of my future marriage and my modesty were too heavy. Maybe I had finally been crushed beneath the impression others had of me and what my parents thought of me and the only way to rid myself of the burden was to do the one thing that was forbidden, perform the one single act of defiance that could undo all expectations.

"I wasn't really thinking," I said, and I knew it was true. When I thought back, the memories were a murky, muddy pond where no creatures of logic lived. "I mean, I didn't plan it. I was so lonely. I was so scared—about college and the future and life and how it was all coming at me so fast. I just wanted to be held for a little while. I just wanted somebody to cup my face in their hands and tell me everything would be all right. And then one thing led to another, and I didn't want to stop it."

The words hissed out of my mouth, popping and cracking like burning firewood, leaving my mouth in smoke. Giving words to the memories made them more real.

I wanted to forget, but I couldn't. I could never forget the feel of his skin, the scent of his cologne.

I let go of Haya's hand, pulling a lock of hair in front of my face to hide behind. I tugged on the hair until pain pinched my scalp. Gently, Haya took my hand and placed it in my lap. There was dried blood under my fingernails.

I focused on my hands. I was frozen, barely containing everything within. The instant I let go, I would shatter into a thousand little pieces, and I would never get back together again.

"I don't know why it's been so hard," I said, voice quiet. "I wanted this. I chose it. I knew what was happening the entire time. But still, I feel so . . . so . . ."

"Having sex can be traumatizing even if it's consensual. It's a big thing to go through, emotionally, mentally, and especially physically," Haya told me. "Don't invalidate how you feel."

"In school he acted like he didn't even know me, which is typical of high school guys, I guess, but it was weird for me. Good, in a way, because I definitely didn't want it to happen again, nor did I want him to bring it up. But weird, still, because sometimes I thought it didn't happen. But I always remembered, every night when I laid down in bed to sleep. For a month afterward, I slept on the floor. I felt so guilty and dirty and stained and used. I knew it was the end of me. Even if nobody found out, it was the end of me. I knew, and he knew, and *He* knew.

"I lost my voice. I didn't want to speak . . . I just cried all the time. I was so scared. I had nightmares nearly every other night, so of course Mama noticed. She noticed how I stopped eating and slept too much and how sometimes I forgot to shower.

"She thought it was stress, so she told me to stop being ungrateful—tough love. She thought I was angry with her for something, but it wasn't about her. It was about *me*. I just—I didn't understand anything. I couldn't speak to anyone or say anything at all. It was just silence, just a vast emptiness in my mind.

"No words, simply sensations, sensory memories that made me want to rip my mouth off my face sometimes. And I got angrier and angrier. Ammi did too. She hated me for not opening up to her about anything, for being sad and ungrateful and anything but the picture of perfection and happiness.

"But I guess . . . maybe she was apprehensive because of college acceptances, and she was scared I would leave home like Ahsen did and never come back. She must have been worried about what happened to me. So, it was my fault, really. It was all my fault. Of course Mama would find out. Of course she would.

"She read my texts one random day when I was asleep. I had only told one person—my roommate from the trip—because I wanted to talk about it. I didn't know how to deal with it. I thought— Anyway, when she found out, I didn't know right away that she knew. It was a Friday night, I remember. I went out with my friend. We got coffee, and it was a good day after a long gray spell. I thought things would be okay. When I got home, Mama was in bed. She said she was sick, and she looked it—face swollen, eyes red, voice raw."

The image was burned into my mind. Every time I blinked, I saw it. My heart knocked against my rib cage, screaming and begging to be released. The memory choked me, resurfacing, but I didn't want it all to come back.

It was so many months ago, why couldn't I just forget?

"Haya, I can't—" I cried. I couldn't breathe. "I can't."

Haya took my hands in hers, squeezing tight.

"Try to breathe," she told me.

Inhale for seven, hold for six. Exhale for eight.

My mouth tasted like vomit, but I continued. Haya didn't pressure me to, but I knew I had to. She was right; talking about it did make it easier.

Already, I felt a weight being lifted from me. I had been wanting to talk to somebody for so long about this. Now, I finally was.

"She said she was sick. I remember going to her room that evening with chai and a sandwich in case she was hungry. I remember being happy because I had had a good day. I remember laughing and telling Mama about something, and she didn't respond. I thought she was sick, so I said goodnight. I asked her if she needed anything, and she shook her head. She hadn't even touched the chai or sandwich yet. I thought she was sick."

The memory made me want to puke. It was so embarrassing, how naive I was, how happy I had been. How much angrier it must have made her, to see me laugh when all I had done was cause her pain.

"Until I had one foot out the door and she spoke. 'Ab khush ho?' she asked. I didn't understand, but already dread was filling my lungs. I turned around and her eyes were like daggers. I felt them pierce through me with hatred. I didn't even recognize her, the pure rage and disgust in her eyes. 'Tumhe patta hai ke tumne kya kiya hai,' she said."

I wished I could forget.

"I guessed then that she had read my messages. It was only a few lines in one message, but in some way, the lack of detail made it worse. It left space for her to imagine things that were not true. I didn't say anything. I didn't know what to say, what to do. I remember fidgeting with my fingers. Then, she began to yell.

"She was across the room but it felt like rounds of artillery pounding into me. She screamed, 'I am so disappointed in you. How could you do this? Sharam nahi ayee? Your father would be devastated if I told him, but I won't. I won't break his heart as you broke mine. Don't you know how much he loves you? His perfect daughter? Besharam. *You're a slut.*'"

I flinched at my own voice because it sounded so much like hers now. I began to shake, and fresh tears bubbled in my eyes, boiling and spilling over my cheeks.

"It didn't seem real, but it was. It was. She said, 'You're nothing but a whore. How could you? Beghairat. You have broken my heart, Zahra. This is unforgivable. What if I told your nano? She thinks you're perfect . . .' And that was worse, the threat of her telling my father or my grandparents. It was worse than everything."

I just wanted to be perfect forever. I wanted them to love me forever.

"I remember tears streaming down my face. 'Don't you dare cry,' she snapped, and she was crying too by then. 'I can't even look at you,' she said. My mouth was wide open in shock. I didn't understand. It was like watching a movie, but it was my life. I felt disowned, as if the link connecting this daughter to mother had been permanently severed. She looked as if she wanted to kill me. She threw pillows at me from her bed."

My fingers absentmindedly traced the faded scars on my wrist, the jagged shapes they made. She hadn't hurt me that night, but I had.

"She didn't even flinch. When I wiped my tears away, she said to stop pretending. She wouldn't pity me. I deserved it. Then she told me to leave, leave before she killed me because my father would never forgive her if she did. 'Dhafa ho jao yahan se,' she spat at me."

Haya squeezed my hand, but I pulled it away to wipe the tears from my face. I held my face in my hands, pressing my fingers into my temples to stop my head from pounding.

I stared ahead, eyes unfocused.

"After that, I went quiet. I couldn't disagree with anything she said. Any time I tried, she would bring up my shame once more. I had to grovel and apologize over and over, try even harder to be perfect. I wasn't allowed out to see friends because she didn't trust that I wasn't going to see him."

"As if I wanted to see him." I shook my head. "I had used him as much as he had used me, just for different reasons. I wasn't allowed to be sad because it would be ungrateful. I wasn't allowed to be happy because I should feel guilty. So I walked on eggshells, gauging Ammi's mood and what she wanted me to be at any given moment, and then she gave me a choice.

"Around March she told me I had two options—become a doctor or get married. To her, it seemed reasonable—invest in the future and forget the past. But I hadn't wanted to do either. I didn't know what I wanted to study, who I wanted to be. I barely knew who I was. In the end, I chose to get married because it would get me out of that godforsaken house. I just wanted to leave.

"The worst part was, I had to convince Baba. Ammi didn't tell him about our deal, so I had to act like it was my idea, like I wanted it. Baba wasn't sure, so I had to get him on board.

"When Baba finally agreed, Ammi told me to act ecstatic or he would worry. It killed me every time I smiled. I just wanted to die by then. I wanted to flicker out of existence. To sleep forever, until one day I could wake up and everything would be all right again.

"So I ran. I couldn't face it. Any of it or any of them. So I ran."

I could feel it as a physical sensation, the blood pumping from my heart to my legs, the quick strides of a sprint, the blur of the landscape before my eyes as I passed everything by. Everything was a mess of memories and people and things and the past and my life, all my life just fading into incoherence.

"You're still running," Haya told me, voice soft.

I didn't think it was true, but it was. I was still running, still paranoid and afraid and depressed and not forgiving myself or letting myself be forgiven.

"I'm being unfair," I said, shaking my head. "You've only heard my side so far. I know why Mama reacted the way she did. I broke her heart. I was so scared of her for a while, always flinching whenever she came near, and one day she said, with surprising kindness, 'I said those things because they are true.

"'I am cruel because the world is cruel. You must learn the lesson in this and never do anything like it ever again,' she told me. 'When I was seventeen, I met a boy in our garden and when my ammi found out, she slapped me so hard I saw stars. I remember how much it hurt, so don't think I don't know how much my words hurt you. I wasn't allowed out in the garden anymore, and *I learned my lesson.* In the same way, you must.'"

Have I learned my lesson? Maybe I had. But my duty was to my family, wasn't it? And I left.

"You know that you have a duty to yourself too, Zahra, not only to your family," Haya said, reading my mind. "That environment was killing you. You had to leave."

"No." I sobbed, hands dropping from my face to clutch my arms. My nails bit into my skin. "I'm a coward," I whispered.

"Oh, love," said Haya, her voice as broken as mine. "You're not. You are so, so brave."

I didn't believe her, and she knew it. She knew I wouldn't believe a word she said, so she put her hands on my shoulders. I shook as I bit back cries. I would not let her see me sob. I didn't want her pity or her worry or her love.

"Please go, Haya," I whispered, closing my eyes so I wouldn't have to look at her kind face. "I want to be alone."

She released a breath, hesitating. Then finally, she let me go. The air shifted as she stood.

"You need to help yourself, Zahra," she said. "You can do it. Stop fighting yourself, love. Stop suppressing yourself. You're drowning and only you can swim to the shore. Please, talk to Allah if you don't want to talk to me anymore."

I nodded.

I wanted her to go, and finally she did.

I opened my eyes in time to see her make it to the door. She looked over her shoulder, giving me a final glance filled with worry, despair, hope. I saw her lips move in a prayer.

Then she was gone, and I was alone again.

Just my demons and me.

Chapter 23

I was afraid. God, I was so afraid. I didn't want to do anything but sleep for an eternity, but that was all I had been doing, and it wasn't working, so maybe it was time to try something new. To take Haya's advice and talk to Allah.

How does this work?

I went to the bathroom and made wudu, washing away the hot tears with cool water, cleaning the blood. I changed into fresh clothes and wrapped a scarf around my head. I stood on my janamaz, facing the qibla. I said Allah hu Akbar, and I prayed.

But nothing happened—there was no epiphany nor sudden rush of peace.

I cried. Through the words of the salah and around its motions. I cried and I felt nothing but my usual despair until I reached the final sajdah. My forehead was pressed against the ground in prostration and I just—stopped. I took a breath, and I stayed in that position until I felt the weight of the world slip from my shoulders.

Then I began to sob.

I pleaded, "Ya Allah, please forgive me," over and over and over again, until I felt my heart stretch awake inside me. "Forgive me, please, forgive me."

I sat back up and finished my prayer. I said salaam over my right shoulder, then over my left. I took a deep breath. Exhaled. Then took another breath.

This is the beginning.

My faith was still intact, but I had to work on it before I could get to where I wanted to be. I could feel myself on the edge, life precarious, but I realized it was okay.

I was getting there. One day this would be a small hurdle I had to conquer to become who I was meant to be.

I felt okay. I could breathe. I could see. I felt my pulse in my neck, felt my heartbeat against my chest.

I am alive.

I made myself something to eat, comforted by the motions of cooking. I took a long, hot shower and thought about how sometimes I was the happiest person in the world. Sometimes I was the saddest. That was okay too.

In that moment, there was peace. My apartment was quiet, the town was asleep. It was just me and the milky moonlight streaming into my room. *This is enough.* You *are enough.*

Everything was okay, in truth. It was foolish of me to have been focusing on only the bad, underscoring only the pain within myself. It was all I had thought about for so long—the gray staining my soul.

But what about the color? The color that Allah had put within me and my life. It had been there all along—I just hadn't noticed it.

It's just . . . things were okay. And I had been so blind to it. I would try to start looking for the color now. I was tired of being sad.

I wanted it to be gone, the endless ache in my chest.

Chapter 24

The next day, I woke up and searched for the strength to get out of bed. I would be better, I promised myself. I wasn't the problem. I wasn't too sensitive.

I could push forward. I could do it.

I got dressed then walked to the closest bus stop, taking deep breaths to calm myself. The sun was warm upon my back. I kept my hands at my sides, trying to stop myself from fidgeting. The entire ride to the masjid, I recited adhkar under my breath, trying to hold on.

I walked from the bus stop to the masjid, eyes on my feet. I placed one foot in front of the other. One step at a time. Finally, I made it to the masjid. It was Wednesday, so I was volunteering for the day camp in the morning, then Zuhr, then Youth Group. *I can do this.* I repeated the words to myself as if they could overwrite how fragile I felt.

I took my shoes off at the doors and walked to the women's area, where the kids were all separating into their classes for the day. Camp hadn't started yet, so I sought out Haya, whom I found immediately, standing off to the side, chatting with Mawa.

"Zahra!" she called, coming over. We met halfway, and I cleared my throat, finding my voice.

"Haya." I tried to keep my voice strong, but it broke anyway.

"How are you?" she asked, worried and hopeful. Around us, volunteers were ushering kids to their classes, sitting them by their desks, and having them pull out their books. The younger kids were being guided to the babysitting room, where Mawa and I were in charge.

"I'm ... okay." I meant it. I flashed her a smile, and her eyes lit up like a thousand lamps. I wondered if I looked visibly different, because everything inside me had changed. I was loosely put together, the parts of me gingerly aligned, but it was together nonetheless.

I *was* okay.

Haya threw her arms around me, and I couldn't breathe, she was hugging me so fiercely. It was the best sensation in the world. Arms tight, we clutched one another, and this time when I cried, it wasn't sadness but relief that this girl was my sister.

We pulled apart, and Haya squeezed my hand. Before I could say anything else, I was attacked with a hug from the side. Not unlike the first time I had met her, Sadaf squeezed me, without warning, to her.

She pulled away then looked into my eyes, her face sincere.

"Zahra, I'm so sorry I was such a bitch," she said, eyes hooded with guilt. Her voice was soft. "My mind automatically thought the worst, and I lashed out. Please forgive me?"

"It's okay," I told her, squeezing her hand. "You're forgiven."

And sometimes, it is that simple.

"Oh, thank God," Sadaf said. "I guess I got these donuts for nothing?" She grinned, holding up a bag from the donut shop we loved.

"I will always accept apologies in donuts," I said, laughing. We chatted for a minute, but then an announcement was made for classes to begin, so I went to the babysitting room, where Mawa was waiting for me. I spent the next few hours with the kids, and after, I prayed Zuhr beside the others in jamaat.

The students left but the volunteers who were part of Youth Group stuck around, waiting for the meeting to start.

"Zahra!" Madiha called, beckoning me over. I went and stood with her and Imaan, who told us about this *Teen Vogue* article she'd recently read about desi girls in media. As usual, Imaan was wearing something trendy and super cute.

"Ohmygod, I love the print of your scarf, where'd you get it from?" Imaan said, reaching over and touching the fabric. I smiled, and we all talked for a bit before Haya pulled me aside to whisper a secret to me.

"Carlos told me he likes me," she said, eyes wide. "And I said that I like him too." I squealed, grabbing her arm.

Tears pricked my eyes. It was dramatic of me, but I couldn't help it—I was so genuinely happy for her. It was the first time

I had ever cried of happiness. I was filled with a bubbling feeling of both joy and sadness. I wrapped my arms around Haya and bounced her.

"This is. So. Exciting."

Haya laughed, pulling back. "You're so funny. We basically agreed to talk now—it doesn't actually mean anything!"

"But it could! And whatever the case, you deserve infinite love," I said, clutching her hands. "So, if there's hope for that here, of course I'm excited!"

"It might not work out—" she started to stress, but I squeezed her.

"There's no rush. You'll figure it out," I assured her. "I'm here if you need me. Always."

She took a deep breath, and when she let it out, she smiled.

"You're right," she said, this time grinning. "The other day, he called me 'cariña'—how cute is that? And then he got all flustered about it. I think I had a heart attack and died right there. But then I was like, I have to come back to life so I can tell Zahra about this."

We both swooned. I laughed, feeling every movement in my body, the tightening of muscles in my belly and in my cheeks. I was so beyond happy for my best friend, and for once, it felt nice to not be stuck in my own bubble and notice that Haya was a person too. That she had problems and fears too.

I told myself I would notice more, be more attentive and considerate like Haya was to me. I hugged her again.

"Thank you," I said, voice thick as I pulled back. "You're

the best friend I could have ever asked for. It's like Allah sent you straight to me. Thank you."

Haya smiled at me.

"Aw," she said. "I'm always here for you, love. I only wish happiness for you."

"And I for you," I said. "Without you, I would have never turned back to Allah given what I had done." The allusion was enough, but I didn't want to be afraid of the word anymore, so I started again. "I asked forgiveness for having sex, and I think things will be okay."

"Oh." Someone said behind me, startled. My heart stopped. I turned and saw Imaan, her face shocked. "Sorry, I didn't mean to eavesdrop—" She looked away, cheeks red. She had heard. She was embarrassed about what I had said. *Oh God.* "Uroosa's calling the meeting to start, so I came to get you guys," she finished.

"Imaan, I—" I started, but my mouth dried, and I didn't know what to say. How would I explain it to her? One of these younger girls in the Youth Group, in this community I was stitching myself into?

"No, no, you don't have to say anything," she said quickly, still not meeting my eyes. She looked ashamed of me. Disgusted. "I'm gonna go sit."

She quickly walked away, and my chest tightened.

It was like the pillars had been kicked out from within me, and I watched as the blocks of my body came crumbling down.

How had I been smiling not five minutes ago? I saw Madiha and Sadaf turn to watch Imaan walk away from me, the other girls turning with them, as if everyone had heard. As if they were now watching the shame on my face. I saw their arched brows and the curious eyes and pursed lips.

I will bring this community nothing but shame.

It was as though the words had pulled a loose end from the knot within me and the weak bundle of strings came loose, everything unraveling and coming undone.

Nothing but shame.

I ran.

Chapter 25

I was running and running and running.

It seemed that was all I knew how to do. Maybe if I pushed myself hard enough, ran far enough, I could get their voices out of my mind.

I ran, squeezing my eyes shut to quiet the world, quiet these sensations. All I wanted was the pain in my feet to trump everything else, because it would hurt less for my toes and muscles to strain than for my heart to tear.

I closed my eyes hoping for everything to fall away, but it always came back. All I could hear in my mind was Ammi's voice, broken and raw, yelling, *How could you? How could you?* Over and over, and it made me want to rip my heart out of my chest, knowing that I caused her that pain, knowing those tears were because of me, knowing that anger in her eyes was directed at me.

How could I? How could I?

Besharam. How could you do this? Sharam nahi ayee? Your father would be devastated if I told him—but I won't. I won't break his heart as you broke mine. Beghairat. You're a slut. How could you? You're nothing but a whore. Besharam.

How could you? I cried to myself.

How could you do this to me?

I ran and I sobbed, and everything was a gorgeous, grotesque shade of maroon.

Chapter 26

$\mathcal{I}$ sat at the beach, watching the waves.

The ocean was so vast, extending to infinity, off the horizon, and here I was—on the edge of the world—water lapping over my bare feet. If I ran into the ocean, I would be swallowed by oblivion, would become part of the sea, just another drop in the abyss of water.

But I didn't want to jump. I was okay here, watching the waves perpetually crashing along the shoreline, high for a moment, an infinitesimal moment, when the world was theirs to take. But then gravity—a force that could not be resisted—took over, and the waves tumbled down, and they dissolved once again to be pulled back into the tide.

What was this life, truly?

It was fluid, a never-ending ocean, perpetual, infinite. I swam in time, and I told myself I was swimming of my own accord, but I never realized that I was drowning too, beneath it all. I realized it then, staring out to the horizon—and realizing it was the first step to saving myself.

So I pushed, through the black waters up toward the sunlight and finally, finally, I emerged.

I took a deep breath, and Allah spoke to me.

In my thoughts, He gave me comfort. He told me what I needed to hear. I had always thought that inside myself was just *me*, just Zahra, but I never realized He was there too. He was in my heart, in my veins, in my pulse.

Finally, I realized this, and from there, everything fell into place.

I breathed, and Allah spoke to me. This time, I listened.

It was so quiet, on the tip of the continent, right on the water. The beaches here on North Shore were rockier than I was used to in California, the water more gray than blue, but the water was calmer, not as chaotic. I was a continent away from the ocean I had always known, but the waters were all connected.

Everything was murky and bleak, the sky cloudy, no sun visible. But the ceiling of the sky looked like a great blanket of gray feathers covering the whole world, and everyone on earth was under it, snuggled in tight, sort of like a snow globe. We were all in this magical land within that snow globe, and everything was okay because I was not alone.

It was bitter cold and wet, so at first, it seemed awful. But when I took a deep breath of chilly ocean air, really felt it go down my throat, I shivered. My toes felt just about ready to be amputated. I rubbed my fingers together, and my nose and my ears were little icicles—it was an incredible feeling.

I focused on it and let light crack through my heart. I relished the quiet—I sat and I thought. It was just me and Allah and that was all I needed, so I spoke to Him.

I said, "Ya Allah, my heart hurts, and it's been hurting for so long. There's so much I want to say, and I hope I can—I hope I can purge it all from within me and feel better."

It seemed silly to speak aloud when nobody was there, but He was there, so I continued. I was already on the brink of tears, and it wasn't sadness, per se. It was just the thoughts, leaking out. There was so much to be released from within me, and I didn't know where to start.

I didn't feel like talking, not really, but I knew that if I let everything sit within me, it would soon devour me whole. It had already engulfed enough of me, and I didn't want that anymore.

My mind went blank but there was so much inside me. I felt it, just below the surface, like blood beneath a scab—I was picking at it and picking at it, hoping for the poison to be released so the wound could finally heal. So I spoke.

"Ya Allah, I'm at a crossroads—or no. Maybe I'm just on a road, but I don't know where it's going, and there are about a hundred different routes I can take, which scares me so much I freeze, choosing none of them. I don't know what's best, or what each path will bring, and I'm terrified of making the wrong choice. And I've got loads of questions that need answering—Who am I? Who do I want to be? How can I close the gap between the two?

"Who am I? It's a good question, right? One I've been contemplating since I was thirteen, I think, when this all began. By 'this,' I guess I mean the sadness I feel, the hollow feeling of emptiness, sort of like depression, but I don't know enough to self-diagnose. Thinking about it makes me feel so . . . pathetic. Like, there are so many others who have it far worse, and here I am . . . You know, though. You know everything, I know, but it's helping me to say it aloud, so just bear with me while I try to figure it out, okay?

"I don't know if there's *actually* anything wrong or if it's all in my head. And who am I, really? In truth, in essence, stripped of all my pretenses and stripped of all the people around me. Who am I in the darkest hour of the night, in the deepest corner of my dreams and my hopes? *Who am I?*

"I can't seem to figure it out. I really wish somebody could tell me, but to be fair, I don't think anyone knows me as well as I know myself, right? So, I guess it's up to me. I've got to dig deep and search for the answers only I have, don't I? Sometimes I wish I could lie down in somebody's arms and say, 'Here, you take care of me for a while now, I'm tired.' And I know it's a laziness in me and I shouldn't indulge it. I have to be independent; I have to take control over myself. I have to be okay on my own.

"Because people are busy and transient and not there for me as much as I should be for myself, if that makes sense.

What I mean is, whenever I am sad, I am here, like I'm two people sort of. There is the one who crumbles and the one who lifts my chin and says everything will be all right.

"I still cry, but I'm learning to love myself, and that is a blessing, Alhamdulillah, but I'm not enough yet. I'm not trying to complain, I'm just trying to figure it out, okay? Because that sadness . . . it's always there, so easily aroused, a beast so easily awakened. And I don't want to be like that, so moody—fine one moment and sobbing the next. I want to be okay."

I began to cry then. Warm tears slid down my cheeks, water wrung from my heart. It hurt, but my heart felt soft, malleable, and I knew that I could mold it whichever way I pleased.

"And I guess, another question is, who do I want to be?

"Well, I want to be modest and beautiful. I want to make Mama and Baba proud. I want to be confident and cool, never awkward or unsure. I want to be happy. I want . . . to make Mama and Baba proud."

Be smart, be kind, be generous, be beautiful, be thin, be obedient, be religious. Smile. Don't talk back. Voice your opinion, but not that one. Be quiet, but don't be mute. Don't talk too much, don't talk too little. Just be yourself. Don't pretend. Don't lie. Be perfect.

"I want to be perfect."

And that was a big chunk of it. There was depression in me and trauma from having sex and the aftermath and the need to define my life, but the perfectionism was something I hadn't truly acknowledged until that moment.

"Perfection is the goal," Ammi would always say, and the

thought behind it was that if you aimed for perfection and missed, there was a decent chance you would end up at least somewhere close.

But nobody and nothing was perfect, so I had to stop trying to be.

For now, that was a step in the right direction.

It was time to go home.

As I took the bus back, I checked my phone. I had loads of missed calls and messages from Haya and Sadaf, but it was the few from Imaan that stuck out to me. I took a deep breath and called her back. I would resolve this now. I wouldn't let it haunt me.

"Zahra, salaam!" Imaan said, picking up immediately. "You left so quickly, I really, really hope you weren't—*aren't*—upset because I accidentally heard what you said to Haya. I'm so, so sorry. I really didn't mean to overhear. Can you please forgive me?" The words rushed out, and she sounded on the verge of tears.

I realized I had projected my own insecurities onto her, that I had imagined the shame and disgust on her face because that was what I was afraid of seeing if people found out. But now I realized that I couldn't control how people reacted; I could only control myself.

"Imaan, don't worry about it, seriously," I said, voice steady. I meant it. She released a breath.

"Are you sure? I really, really didn't mean to overhear."

"Yes, don't worry at all! Please. It's cool." I added a little laugh so she would feel better.

"Okay. Don't even worry because I'm literally going to pretend like it didn't happen. Hear something? What? I didn't hear anything!"

This time I laughed in earnest. "Thanks . . . You didn't tell anyone, did you?"

"No, no, no! Ohmygod, no! Not even Madiha, and she's my best friend, you know that. I didn't say a thing. Sadaf asked me why you ran off, but I said I didn't know."

"Okay, thanks. I appreciate it."

"Like I said, I didn't hear anything."

"Thanks, Imaan."

I said goodbye, my heart feeling more at ease. I was glad to have talked this through immediately, rather than wondering and worrying. And I was glad Imaan wouldn't mention it.

The rest of the bus ride passed in silence, and I gazed outside my window, watching the buildings and lights pass by. I got off at the right stop, then walked the rest of the way.

When I finally arrived and knocked on the door to the Chaudrys' house, Haya answered. Before I could register her reaction, she engulfed me in her arms.

"I thought you were dead in a ditch somewhere!" she shrieked, hysterical. From inside the house, I heard Sadaf run down the stairs. She latched onto us as well.

"Zahra!" she screeched. "You lunatic! We were worried *sick*!"

"Zahra? Beti?" This time Nabila Auntie, followed by Umar Uncle.

"Acha, acha, bas," Uncle said, peeling his daughters off me.

Fresh air flooded my lungs and for some reason, I laughed. "Let her in, will you."

I entered their home and Nabila Auntie held my face between her hands.

"Are you all right, jaan?" she asked, searching my eyes. I nodded, and it wasn't a lie. She knew, so she hugged me, just tight enough to fuse my pieces together with the scent of powder. Umar Uncle placed a hand on my head and smiled.

"Teek?" he said. I nodded, inhaling the familiar scent of cigarettes.

"What's this! You've been bleeding!" Haya grabbed my arm, and I looked at the scab.

"I fell while running and cut myself on a piece of broken glass," I said. It was the truth. I wouldn't hurt myself again, I vowed. "I'm a klutz, I know."

"Zahra, don't *do* that to us." Sadaf clutched her heart. "I probably have high blood pressure, and my old soul can't handle this sort of excitement." A near-smile touched her face.

"Ooh, sorry, Dadi," I said, laughing. Finally, Haya smiled.

"Goodness, what a wild few days," she said, shaking her head. Her eyes were still frazzled. "Let's all go and lie down. I'm drained. Mama Dearest, can you please make us chai?"

So we climbed into bed, limbs overlapping and radiating warmth. I was lying on a bed of sunlight, and at that moment, everything was all right. Everything was quiet inside me.

I felt . . . almost whole. I could feel light in my core, in my soul, the light Allah had placed there when He created me. It was time I stopped letting others—and myself—put it out.

My mouth split into a smile.

"Damn, girl, are you high?" Sadaf asked, looking at me. "What are you on? And can I have some?"

I laughed. "High on life, babe." I looked up at the ceiling and had the courage to speak.

"I'm sorry for worrying you, but I needed the quiet and the peace for a bit. I watched the ocean for a while and thought and talked and thought. I did my mental sorting and it's all very embarrassing how dramatic I was being earlier, but hey, I was a young soul then—young and naive. I'm much older now."

"You're crazypants," Haya told me, shaking her head. She studied my eyes. Seeing I was okay, she smiled. "Luckily for you, so are we." She held my hand, nestling into my side. Sadaf reached for my other hand and did the same.

"So, I guess we, like, sort of love you anyway," Sadaf said.

"Aw. I guess I sort of love you too," I said, and though it was directed mostly to Haya and Sadaf, it was directed toward myself too.

I love you.

Haya leaned her head on my shoulder, and I leaned mine on Sadaf's. We were a jumble of limbs and love, hearts and harmony.

Everything will be okay.

Chapter 27

Of course, it wasn't that easy.

I had taken the first step toward self-healing, but externally, I needed to lay better foundations for my life. Now that I no longer felt the urge to run, I could firmly plant both feet on the ground. I could put down roots and build a life.

To do that, I needed more money. Summer camp at the masjid would be ending soon, so I would have more time to work, which was good. I also needed a new place to stay. The lease on my studio was up at the end of August, and I needed to decide if I would renew it for the fall or look for something better.

I also wanted to save up and start seeing a therapist soon, ideally next month. I'd already looked into therapists—particularly women of color therapists—and I'd found one whose office wasn't too far.

It was a big step for me—considering therapy. It was something that had been so stigmatized my entire life that I had never even considered seeking professional help to deal with everything I was going through. Battling my perfectionism and rediscovering my faith were things I could learn to maneuver, but depression and trauma were way out of my league. I needed professional help to truly heal and move forward. Going to therapy did not mean I was broken. I was sick; this was medicine.

It was what I was thinking of one day as I worked a shift at Chai Shai, chopping up onions. I didn't say a word to anyone, lost in my thoughts, and after a little while, Yaseen came over to grab some unpeeled onions from my pile.

"Hey, have you done the new training?" Yaseen asked me. I stopped chopping to look at him.

"What new training?"

"It's something we all had to do, you know, the cannabis training," Yaseen continued, pointing to a massive bag of dried green stuff on a table across the kitchen.

"The . . . cannabis training?" I repeated.

"Yeah, the cannabis training," Yaseen said, dead serious.

"Um . . ."

I was so confused. Yaseen stared at me for a second before breaking out into laughter.

"Nah, I'm messing with you, it's dried mint," he told me.

"Ohmygod, you're the worst," I said, laughing with him. "I was actually worried for a second. I was like, what is going on?"

"My philosophy is that one laugh can make the whole day better," Yaseen said. He took a bow. "You're welcome."

Right then, Muzzamil stepped into the kitchen from outside with dirty dishes. Yaseen turned to his older brother.

"Hey, Muzz Bhai, did you do the cannabis training?" Yaseen asked, pointing to the dried mint. Muzzamil gave him an unimpressed look.

"There's no way you think I'm falling for that," he replied, carrying the dishes over to the sink. "I mean, how stupid do you think I am? I'm insulted."

I let out an offended sound. "I think it's a reasonable thing to fall for!"

Muzzamil looked at me, then realized what had happened. He shook his head. "Zahra, Zahra, no! Don't tell me you fell for this goon! Come on! I thought you were smarter than that."

"His face was so serious!"

"That man is the most unserious man I've ever met!"

"Hey! I'm right here!" Yaseen objected.

The teasing was good-natured, and we all laughed. I enjoyed the brothers' company, and at the restaurant, it was usually them I spent the most time with. I basically worked from opening to closing, and so did Yaseen, since he was on summer break from college.

Working at Chai Shai was my favorite job. I also worked at the mall and tutored. While the latter was nice because I could interact with kids, the mall was majorly boring and tiring. At Chai Shai, I actually had fun. And it wasn't just that Lubna Auntie was a sweetheart or that Yaseen was goofy or that Muzzamil was nice—it was the cooking. I really enjoyed it.

Which was why later that weekend, when Sadaf and Haya invited me over for dinner, I offered to make a dish of chicken pulao. I had made it with Mama once—last year. I didn't remember the recipe entirely, but it was one of those comfort foods I had missed these weeks in New York.

So I looked up a recipe and bought ingredients and spices and attempted it at my studio. The smell of browned onions and garam masala immediately brought me comfort, and I poured my heart into cooking, losing myself in the stirring of the chicken and the rinsing of rice.

When it was done, it smelled amazing, and after taking a bite, I felt so accomplished and proud of myself. *I made that!*

Haya came to pick me up. I carried the dish into the car and set it on my lap on a towel. She took a deep breath.

"Ohmygod that smells *sooo* good," Haya said. She reached over to open the lid, but I swatted her hand away.

"No peeking!"

I was proud of the soft brown color of the rice, and I wanted to make a big reveal.

"Okay, okay, sheesh." Haya laughed. We chatted and drove to her house.

"Welcome, welcome!" Sadaf hugged me hello at the door, then ushered me inside. I set my pulao on the dining table, saying salaam to Naadia and Humaira, who were there too. I saw that Naadia had brought a tray of brownies, while Humaira had brought homemade chocolate croissants.

It was a casual night in. After eating, we planned on watching a rom-com. Naadia was dressed in sweatpants and a long-sleeved T-shirt, while Humaira wore a cute baby-blue matching set.

"I told Baba to stay upstairs, so you guys can take your scarves off," Sadaf informed us. Naadia, Humaira, and I slipped out of our scarves. Naadia's hair was up in a messy bun, while Humaira's was perfectly blow-dried and bouncy.

"She's such a try-hard," Naadia joked, ruffling her sister's hair. Humaira pushed her sister's hand away, smoothing her hair back into place.

"It isn't a crime to look nice!" Humaira said. "You're just jealous."

Naadia stuck out her tongue, and we laughed. "No, I'm just *exhausted* from medical school applications. Which I should theoretically be working on now."

"No, no, you need a break," Sadaf said, bringing a dish of mac and cheese to the table, while Haya brought over a basket of bread. "Now, let's eat!"

I pulled the lid off the pulao, which was still hot, and steam rose from the rice. The girls all took in a breath, sighing at the smell.

"I'm going to eat all of this," Naadia declared, heaping a serving onto her plate. "I haven't had good pulao since forever." We all filled our plates and dug in. I was proud of how the dish had come out—not *just* like Mama's, but pretty close.

"This is divine," Humaira informed me, between mouthfuls of brothy rice. "Truly."

"How come our cooking auntie never makes it this good?" Naadia asked Humaira.

"Your cooking auntie?" I asked.

"Yes, usually it's my phuppo who cooks, but she's a doctor, so when she's busy or not up to it, we order from this auntie who lives by us and caters out of her house," Naadia explained. Haya had mentioned that the Mirza girls' mother passed away some years ago and that their young phuppo had come to live with and help take care of them.

"Zahra!" Sadaf exclaimed, dropping down her spoon. "You should be a cooking auntie!"

"Ohmygod, *yesss*," Naadia said, looking at me. "You're such a good cook, you should also cater like that auntie does! She's a single mom and literally makes enough to sustain herself."

"Really? You guys think the food is that good?"

"Yes, absolutely," Humaira said. "I would have no qualms paying for a tray of this, or anything else you made. You have zaiqa in your hands."

"Aw." I was touched. I liked cooking, and found satisfaction in bringing people joy through food, but I never thought of making a business out of it.

"Wait, that's actually such a good idea," Haya said, getting excited. "Zahra, you could totally sell loads of food at school too! Sadaf's always complaining about how much the dining hall food sucks."

"Oh, it for sure sucks," Sadaf said.

"Agreed," Naadia added. "Whenever I don't bring anything from home, I simply suffer."

"Thanks for the idea, guys," I said. "I could make a large batch of something like this, then sell portions for lunch and dinner, right? You think people would actually be interested in that?"

"Yes, definitely!" Sadaf said. "And we'll promote you, don't worry."

"Aw, thanks. I'll definitely think about it."

It did sound fun. Plus, it would be a good way to earn money. Making one pot of pulao didn't cost me much, and if I divided it into portions and priced them anywhere from eight to twelve dollars, it was a pretty good profit margin.

"University business aside, you've already got a confirmed client in us," Humaira said. "Honestly. I'm going to order from you regularly."

"But, Humaira, you're such a good cook yourself," I said, feeling bashful. I held up my half-eaten chocolate croissant. "I mean, these are amazing!"

Humaira waved a delicate hand. "I love baking, I do, but with school, cooking proper food every day for the whole family is too much. I'd rather order from you!"

"Okay, sure." There was one client!

I felt excited at the prospect of making cooking a career. And it would definitely bolster my weekly income. If I did a few orders for the Mirza girls soon, I might even be able to start therapy sooner than expected!

"Literally great teamwork, girls," Sadaf said. "Now let's watch a movie!"

We took the tray of brownies into the living room, which

was set up with blankets and pillows. Haya brought popcorn and Sadaf flipped through Netflix, looking for something to watch.

"Let's watch a period drama!" Humaira suggested. Naadia hit her with a pillow.

"Period drama ki chachi!" Naadia said. "You do not need to watch another period drama and thirst over a man's exposed neck in the brief moment he's not wearing his cravat."

Humaira sighed dreamily. "But that's the best part!"

We all laughed, settling in, and it was a wonderful night. I was closest with Haya, then Sadaf—I had even told Sadaf a condensed version of why I had run away and explained the situation with Zayn—but it was nice to be friends with other people too. Like Naadia and Humaira. And Madiha and Imaan. And Yaseen and Muzzamil. And the other Youth Group girls.

Even if I wasn't *as* close with them as I was with the Chaudrys, it was still nice to be a part of a community, to know these people and to be known by them.

And of course, knowing people helped me build my life. I got some new students to tutor through Nabila Auntie and people she knew. I was able to start my catering business and get more clients through both the Chaudry sisters' and the Mirza sisters' word of mouth. Because I had Youth Group and volunteering at the masjid, life wasn't only work.

But of course, summer had to end. Which meant camp was ending, and so was my apartment lease.

"I'm thinking of renewing my lease," I mentioned to Haya, while we were out for coffee one day.

"Hmm," she murmured in response, her eyes on her phone. Suddenly, she lit up. "Oh!" She looked at me. "Don't renew."

"What?" I gave her a funny look. "Why?"

"I was waiting to be certain before mentioning it to you," she said, taking a sip of her iced latte, "but basically a few weeks ago, my school emailed me to say that the renovations on one of the dorm buildings won't be completed for the fall semester so they're overbooked, and that if we rescinded our dorm slot, we would be fully refunded."

"Wait, that sucks!" I said. "They told you so late!"

"I know, it was majorly annoying," she continued. "They sent a list of apartments near campus for students to look into, but I was like, I don't know, maybe I'll commute. But then like two weeks ago you mentioned how you were wondering whether to renew your lease or not, so I was like, ohmygod, why don't Zahra and I get a place together?"

"Ohmygod—and?" I asked, getting excited at the prospect.

"Just listen! I didn't tell you before because I didn't want you to *not* renew and then have me not even get a place! Anyway, I started scoping out the apartments and they were pretty nice! So I sent in an application to my school, and I literally just now got an email that there's one available for me if I want it!" She squealed. "It's a two-bedroom, and it would be perfect for us, especially you! You could focus more on catering and take deliveries straight to campus! And we could be roomies!"

"Ohmygod!" I squealed with her. "That literally sounds like a dream."

"So, you want to?" she asked. "I mean, should I tell them yes, I do want it?"

"Yes, yes! Of course I want to live with my best friend and not alone in some tiny studio! Tell them yes immediately!"

"Ah, ohmygod, this is going to be *so fun*—it's literally going to be like a sleepover every night! Sadaf is going to be so jealous! We can do face masks, and watch rom-coms, and . . ."

We were both buzzing with excitement, and I took a moment to whisper alhamdulillah. This was all from Allah. He was looking after me. He was taking care of me. He was helping me not only survive here but *thrive*. Making life not only livable but beautiful.

So the pieces of my life kept falling into place.

Chapter 28

I awoke before dawn to pray Fajr.

It was the first prayer of the day and my favorite. My skin felt cool and fresh from wudu, the cleansing process. My mouth was minty from toothpaste. My muscles were keen to stretch and bend.

Best of all, my mind was clear. No thoughts or worries of the day had yet plagued my mind; there were no distractions to hinder my spiritual availability. There was hope in my heart—a new dawn was a new beginning.

I prayed, letting the Arabic flow from my tongue, the letters soothing my mouth and throat in sounds the English language did not contain. When the last sajdah came, I pressed my forehead to the ground in prostration and breathed. I exalted my Lord, the Most High, and repented sincerely in my heart.

I stayed there for a long time, praying.

Afterward, I raised my head and folded my legs, staying on the prayer mat to make dua. Across from me, the sky was changing color through my window. Sunshine spilled across the horizon like golden rain. The darkness was usurped by the sunrise, black evaporating into pink and yellow tufts, until all the world was one fluid shade of baby blue.

I cracked the window and took a deep breath of cool air. New York was freezing at the end of December, but it reminded me of all the warmth I had inside me. Nature's melody filled the air—the wind whistling, the leaves rustling.

Closing the window, I floated through the apartment, tidying and admiring. It was mine and Haya's, and living with my best friend was every bit the dream come true I imagined it would be.

It was a two-bedroom apartment close to Haya's campus, and we had done our best to make it home. The place was small—smaller still when Sadaf came by, as she often did—but it was cozy.

My fingers danced across stacks of books. I inhaled the scent of roses from the bouquet of flowers sitting on the dining table. I touched the petals, taking in the sight of our living room littered with soft blankets and cozy pillows. Then I went to the kitchen, where there was always cookie dough in the freezer and fresh fruit on the counter. I watered my little garden of potted herbs that I used for cooking.

Sunlight tinged the kitchen gold, and dust danced through patches of sunlight in mesmerizing swirls. I watched the dust shift with every breath.

Inhale. Exhale.

I breathed, closing my eyes to focus on this wonder of a

body, this glory of synapses and nerves. I touched the pulse in my neck—the rhythm told me with each beat that I was alive, that this life was truly mine.

Alhamdulillah. I thanked Allah for this peaceful morning, thanked Him for my intimate apartment, thanked Him for love. But most of all I thanked Him for this clarity within me, this appreciation and this sight that could cherish all the abundances my life was overflowing with. Not always did I have this sight, these eyes that saw Technicolor and light.

A few months ago, things were so different. I thanked Him for this peace and began my day.

I went for a walk, and the world was a spectrum of colors—a red cardinal flying through the bright-blue sky, past evergreen trees. My life was vibrant, a gamut of shades, an entire rainbow. There was no gray, not anymore.

Those gray days, those weeks, those months—how awful they had been. Then finally, days that weren't gray, and the shift between the two.

Summer had aged into autumn. The world was the same as every year when things turned golden, burgundy, and bronze. There were still apple desserts and cinnamon lattes. The chilly air still bit my uncovered wrists. The leaves still crunched beneath my boots. There were shorter days, warm sun, cold air. Then autumn shivered into winter, into hot chocolate and mint and oversized sweaters and fuzzy socks.

The world was the same, but I was different now.

Five months ago, I stopped drowning and learned how to swim.

Who am I? Who do I want to be? For so long, these had been the sole two questions in my mind, and deep down, I think, I had always known the answers.

Who am I? Imperfect. *Who do I want to be?* Perfect.

But it was unrealistic and impossibly cruel toward myself to aspire to perfection when nothing in life is perfect.

Life is messy. By trying to define myself, I was confining myself. Definitions created little boxes. You had to color in the lines. But life didn't give you crayons to simply color within a set little rectangle on your sheet. Life gave you wondrous glitter and paint and charcoal to draw wherever the hell you wanted, to create your own picture of beauty.

So I learned to draw outside the lines. I learned to love being imperfect because it meant that I was no longer suffocating within my own confinements. It was so unbelievably cruel to try and force answers to such broad questions as "who am I?"

There were no singular answers, no definitive solutions. Identity was not a singular branch—it was an entire tree, with vines and leaves and branches jutting out in all directions, some blossoming and thriving while others shriveled and died.

Humans were constantly evolving. Each bit of knowledge learned was like a brushstroke on the canvas of your existence. The more you learned, the more breathtaking the painting became. And if you learned nothing more, you remained incomplete.

I loved myself much more now than I ever had before.

Even more than the pure, innocent love I had felt before I learned to hate. And I think it was because I learned to love myself despite all the flaws, despite all the cracks and bruises. I loved my whole self.

I was unapologetically me.

I was not in this world for my brother or my father or my husband, as my mother had always taught me. They would have a place in my heart, yes, but they would not define me. They would not be the batteries in my engine, the sole reason I could and did live. I was not on this earth for men. It was not my duty to serve them.

I was allowed to have an opinion, to have fun, to breathe without worrying what others would think. I should not have been stifled just because I was a girl.

I was allowed to live.

Yes, I had had sex. Yes, I had sinned. But that gave nobody the right to ostracize or shame me. My life was mine; I was done having others tell me how to live it.

So I lived.

When I got back from my walk around the quiet neighborhood, I changed and wore a warm, soft sweater and fuzzy socks to ward off the cold. I wrapped my arms around my body, hugging myself, feeling the blood and bone of me.

Over the past few months, I'd gained a bit of weight, and for the first time in my life, I was glad for it. My face was fuller, my cheeks chubbier, and my body was softer in the way that it used to be. I looked more like myself, the way I did when I was younger.

And it felt good. It felt healthy. I was no longer starving myself as punishment. I was no longer aiming to be thin. I was simply living. Eating well and trying to be healthy but allowing myself indulgences too.

"You are so beautiful," I told the girl in the mirror. A smile curved her lips upward. I made my way to the kitchen for breakfast. I made myself coffee and popped a bagel in the toaster. (I was really getting used to New York bagels.)

After breakfast, I had to send a fresh batch of boxed lunches with Haya to her college for some students. So I began to cook just as I had been doing every week of the semester, infusing the food with the love I could remember tasting in all my meals growing up.

There was comfort in cooking—in quickly chopping coriander and garlic, in the aroma of fried ginger and onions, in the explosion of flavors on my tongue, and the meditative relief that came from just stirring and stirring.

After the food was cooked and boxed and fitted with little cards for all my customers, I finished getting ready, making sure to apply a pretty lipstick and be happy with my appearance but comfortable too. I pulled my long hair into a bun and wrapped a scarf around my head.

The mornings were always quiet and rosy, spent in solitude, which I didn't mind at all. I was usually out before Haya was up—she had late classes, studied late, and woke up late. Even though I didn't see her for most of the day, I knew she would be home when I came back.

I took the bus and walked to Chai Shai. More people

were hitting the streets and the air filled with chatter. But the winter winds carried silence too, though not one that made me feel empty.

When I entered the restaurant, it was quiet, before opening. I saw the older woman behind the counter.

"Salaam, Lubna Auntie," I said. She gave me a warm hug and smile.

"Hai, bachi, your cheeks are so cold!" she fussed, putting a hand on my face. "Where is your scarf? And gloves?"

"Auntie, it's not even that cold!" I said, laughing, but she tsked.

"You kids," she said. "Yaseen said the same thing, and go see what he is wearing—a short-sleeved shirt! When you catch colds, don't come crying to me to make you all soup."

"But, Mama, your soup is the best part of getting sick," Yaseen said, entering from the back and hugging his mother from behind. She swatted his arm.

"Mmhh," she huffed. "Enough laadh-pyaar. Go work."

She shooed us off to the kitchen.

"You should have seen that one coming with the short sleeves," I told Yaseen. I took my coat off and hung it in the office before joining him in the kitchen. He shook his head, laughing.

"It gets so hot in here! Woman works me like a servant and won't even let me dress how I want," he said. I snorted, and we both began cutting vegetables for the cooks.

"Okay, Drama Queen. Tell me you at least wore a coat," I said. "Don't you have class after this?"

"He wore a hoodie," Muzammil said, joining us in the kitchen. "All these years and he still hasn't learned."

I laughed and felt at ease in the restaurant where I spent so much of my time. We continued prepping and cleaning and cooking for opening, and when lunchtime hit, the regulars started coming. I spent more time after that serving with Lubna Auntie, while the guys handled the cooking.

I preferred watching humanity's machinations, all the people, of different shapes and facets, but all so raw, so beautiful and human. There were always couples falling in love or mothers feeding little children or grandparents sipping chai and sitting in silence.

I felt alive—seeing all these people, observing them.

Afterward, when my shift was over, I tossed together something to eat from the leftovers in the kitchen.

"Ooh, whatcha making?" Yaseen asked, peering over my shoulder. His shift was over too. He had class soon.

"I'm putting this leftover raan roast on bread with mayo and butter, then throwing in some shredded cheese," I told him, moving over so he could stand next to me and see. I finished making the sandwich, which smelled amazing, then cut it in half, offering it to him.

"Yes, please," he said, greedily taking the sandwich. "You know I can never say no to your concoctions."

"Let's hope it's good," I said. It was my first time trying this combination. We raised our sandwich halves in a toast, then took a bite at the same time. Yaseen let out a pleased sound.

"Yooo, this is so good," he said, taking another huge bite. "You never disappoint."

It really was delicious. "Thank you, thank you, I'll be here all week." I did a mock-bow.

"Seriously, you should apply to culinary school or something," Yaseen said, finishing off his sandwich. He pulled the ingredients out again to make another one.

"Culinary school?" I repeated. I had never considered that.

"Yeah," he said. "You do all that catering, right? And you love cooking. Plus, you're always trying new shit like this, which ends up amazing. Whenever I try mixing something up, it always ends up tasting like crap."

"Hmm," I said thoughtfully. "I'll look into it."

"Def do," he said. "And remember, we get dibs on you when you're a successful chef, okay? No running off to Paris or somewhere fancy."

I laughed. "Don't worry, I'm not going anywhere." Watching him try to replicate my sandwich, I shook my head. "Let me do it. I'm taking half, and I don't want it tasting like crap, thank you very much."

"Thank God," he said, eyes full of mischief. "I was waiting for you to take over." As I finished making the sandwich, he went and grabbed my coat. "And don't worry, as thanks, I'll drive you wherever you're off to next. You have tutoring, right?"

"Aw, thanks," I said. "And yes, I'll show you the way."

"Aight, let's head out. We can eat these in the car."

We said Allah hafiz to Lubna Auntie, then headed out,

where a cold gust of air immediately blasted us. Yaseen groaned, shivering.

"Ugh, it's brick out."

I feigned surprise. "Yaseen? Admitting it's cold?" I said dramatically. "I might just die of shock."

"Hey, not all of us are from sunny California and throw on three sweaters once it hits the fifties," he replied, laughing. We walked over to his car. "*Some* of us were born with this thing called tolerance to the cold."

"Oh, really? And how's that working out for you?"

He was currently bounce-walking to keep warm, hood up, so he knew he was beat. "You still want a ride or not? Keep roasting me and I'm taking back my offer."

"Okay, okay, I'll stop. Yes, I want a ride. I'm from sunny California and can't handle this cold."

We made it to his car and immediately got in. Once the car started, I put my fingers in front of the vent, waiting for the air to get hot.

"So, how's school been?" I asked, as he pulled out of the parking lot. "Are you any closer to revolutionizing Chai Shai for the modern world?"

Yaseen was majoring in restaurant management, which Lubna Auntie was ecstatic about. Every time he left the restaurant to go to school, she beamed with pride.

"Ah, not quite," he said, running a hand through his long hair. "First, I gotta conquer managerial accounting."

"Yuck. But at least Auntie's duas are with you," I said. "You know sometimes she'll grab me for an impromptu prayer circle and she's like, *Ya Allah, please help my Yaseen pass his classes. I know he's not that smart, but please just have him pass.*"

"Quit playing," he said, and we both laughed. "For real though, having Mama's support really keeps me going. And you know, at first, I didn't even want to go into management because it was expected of me? Like, that old spitefulness kicked in where if someone tells you to do something, you just won't. But then I realized, I kinda loved it. Why let spite get in the way?"

"You know, I think I was the same way with cooking, in the beginning," I said. "Mama would always make me cook, and it annoyed me. Like, she just expected me to cook since I was a girl, and she never made my brother do it. But then I realized, I kind of love it."

"Maybe it wasn't a guy-girl thing," Yaseen said, shrugging. "Maybe your mom just wanted to spend more time with you. I mean, my mom taught me loads of cooking stuff she didn't teach Muzz Bhai, but that was because I was mad quiet and wouldn't chill with her otherwise."

"Hmm," I said. "I've never thought about that." I turned in my seat to look at him, to really look at him. Something warm and soft came over me.

"Well, that's because you're not as smart as I am," he said.

"Shut up, you goon."

"Aye, look who's picking up the lingo!"

He turned to look at me, one hand on the wheel, and smiled. It might have been freezing outside, but here, the look in his eyes was enough to warm me from my teeth to my toes.

Yaseen dropped me off and waited for me to enter the house before driving off. As my student's mother opened the door, I looked back at him and waved. He grinned, raising a hand.

My heart felt a little nudge.

"Zahra!" Yusra said, running to meet me at the front door. "I got my math test back!"

"Hey, beautiful!" I said, giving her a hug. "Let me guess." I pretended to think. "You did amazing!"

Yusra hugged her paper to her chest before turning it over to show me a big 100.

"Wow!" I cheered. "You're the smartest six-year-old I know."

She grinned, holding my hand and leading me to the table where her homework was set out. I tutored her in various subjects throughout the week.

We cracked open her books, and between lessons she told me stories about her friends and how her grandparents were going to visit from Bangladesh soon. I smiled, was patient and kind. I tried to be a source of light in this little girl's life because she was such a source of warmth in mine. Before I left, I held her chubby face in my hands, feeling her grin in my palms.

"I adore you, Yusra," I told her, just as my mother had told me all those years ago.

And such was life. All these little moments and all these people and this joy that filled my life to the brim with warmth and happiness and vibrancy. Everything felt whole and full. I was alive. I was *living*.

But I wasn't forgetting.

Which was where Eya, my therapist, came in.

Therapy was the last stop for the day. I had been going for nearly three months now, and it had changed my life.

"I'm so content, but I feel like something is missing," I told Eya that afternoon. She was a soft-spoken Nigerian woman with a kind face.

She sat in front of me, on one of the sofas piled with pillows of varying sizes. Her office smelled like lemon and felt safe, comfortable.

"I've been thinking about my family a lot," I continued. "About how much I miss them. Even though they hurt me, and I hurt them. I miss them."

What a complicated thing it was, family. I didn't blame my mother anymore. Not for her mindset, because she grew up in a world different from mine. She grew up in a world of suffocating cultural expectations underneath the guise of religious accuracy.

Change was so difficult. It didn't excuse my parents' behavior, but it softened my heart. It made me want to forgive them because in truth, I did love them. My family. My blood.

I knew, deep down, that my mother's tyranny over me was the exact same tyranny that she had experienced from the women in her life, reinforced by the culture around them. It didn't make it okay, but it made it easier for me to begin to forgive her once I understood her.

And in the end, wasn't that what everyone wanted? To be understood?

"Why do you think you've been thinking about them so much if you are content with your life here?" Eya asked me.

"I still love them," I told her. "But I didn't love them six months ago when I ran away, and I don't think they loved me anymore, either."

"Do you think now that you've had some time and distance, you can see things more clearly?" she asked gently.

"I think so," I said, nodding. I hadn't been able to before. It had been too painful. But now, I could see the months leading up to running away. In March, when I had made the decision to get married, it had been my last. April, May, June . . . the months were smeared together in a haze. I'd made no decisions, done nothing but hurt myself emotionally and physically.

And I had blamed it all on my family when it was no one person's fault.

Family was so complex, so contradictory and confusing. Sometimes it killed me how mercurial family could be. Why couldn't things be black or white, cut and dried, you loved me or hated me? It was so beautiful and terrible, family.

There was an inexplicable bond between us all, a bond that transcended blood and life and memories. It was a bond that extended into the cores of who we were, into our very souls.

"Why do you think you stopped loving each other?" Eya asked me.

I thought back to the blur of my past. It was a year and a lifetime ago.

"Well . . . I think . . . since forever, we loved each other unconditionally. And maybe that was the root of how we could be so cruel to one another, so awful. Because we knew that love would always remain. They would never leave me. They would always forgive me. They would always love me.

"It was all right to be a jerk sometimes because I knew they would forgive me anyway. They would forget and things would return to normal. Fighting one moment and laughing the next—ready to kill, then ready to love."

Eya nodded, absorbing my words. "What happened to a love like that?"

"What happened? I'm not sure. It had seemed infinite, then, unconditional and perfect. Then it was all gone."

"Do you think it left all at once? Or gradually?"

"I think . . . gradually," I told her, starting to realize as I spoke. "Bit by bit, drop by drop until suddenly the well was dry and I was dying of thirst. Because it hurt, the inconsistency of it all. And it hurt more than the little bruises or cuts. Sometimes it felt like gunshots and broken ribs and shredded hearts, and it got harder to bounce back into love."

And, I think, each time you hurt somebody, they love you a little less. I kept hurting and hurting, so bit by bit, the love began vanishing until there was nothing left. So I fled. I didn't want to live in a world where I didn't love my family anymore.

"Do you think that's why you ran?" she asked. "Because you felt you were no longer loved?"

"Yes . . . yes, I think so."

"The way you have spoken about your family and the love you feel for them, a love that immense and strong . . . do you think something like that can ever return?"

It made me think. About my mother and my father and my brother and me. About my family and my life and if I would ever go back to California. Would that love ever come back to me?

And I knew.

"It already has."

Chapter 29

When I got home, my best friend in the whole world was waiting for me. Somehow, even though we lived together and I saw her every day, I wasn't tired of her.

"You're home!" Haya announced. She was sitting on the couch, but when I entered she came to greet me and enveloped me in a tight hug. Behind her, I saw Sadaf get up to do the same.

"Finally!" Sadaf joined in.

"Sadaf! You're here too!" I said, hugging her.

"She just couldn't stay away," Haya said, shaking her head. "I mean, honestly, she should pay rent at this point."

I was bone tired from a long day, but they made it instantly better. As we walked to the table, I saw Sadaf had brought takeout and flowers.

"Ooh, what's the occasion?" I asked, pulling off my scarf. I went to the bathroom to wash my hands and heard Sadaf pouring drinks for all of us. When I came back to the table, Haya and I sat down, but Sadaf stayed standing.

"Hear ye, hear ye!" Sadaf said, raising her iced tea in a wine glass. "I've got news!"

Haya and I exchanged a glance.

"I got a job for after graduation! A real-life adult job!"

"What!"

"Ohmygod!"

"I know! It's at a day care for special needs children," she told us. "And I'm so thrilled but scared too, because I don't want to make things worse for them. But really, it's my job to do fun activities and exercises with them, to sort of remind them what it means to be a kid. Which I know I can do."

"That's incredible!" I screamed. "Truly. I'm so happy for you."

We ate the warm Thai food and discussed the frightening, exciting prospect of Sadaf being a working adult in the real world—even if it was just for a gap year before her master's. The chill of winter had reached the windows, so after dinner, I pulled cookie dough out of the freezer for a celebratory treat. As the cookies were baking, I looked out the kitchen window at the sky and saw shimmering lights in the night.

"Let's look at the stars," I said. "The sky's so clear tonight, and I'll make hot chocolate to keep us warm."

"Ooh yesss, I feel like we haven't sat outside in a while," Haya said. Our apartment adjoined a house, and by the entrance there was a little garden area.

I whipped up the hot chocolate as the cookies finished

baking. We grabbed blankets and pillows and piled onto the bench outside. I sat in the middle, leaning against Haya, letting Sadaf stretch her legs across my lap.

It was chilly, as December nights were, but it wasn't the coldest night. Wrapped up in blankets and each other, with mugs of hot chocolate steaming in our hands and cookies melting in our mouths, we were warm. We tipped our heads back to look up at the clear, dark sky, the expanse of sugary stars that floated in the inky night.

There were so many, floating in the rich, cloudless sky. I felt like I could just drink it all up, like I could reach out and catch the stars like fireflies. I knew now what it was like to have perpetual light inside me—knew now what it was like to fly.

SubhanAllah. *This is peace.*

"Therapy was good today," I told them, after some time in silence and a few burned tongues. "I realized how much I love my family and that I think I forgive them."

Forgiveness was so hard, especially when it seemed history was on repeat—the same agitations, the same grievances and the same reactions and little pricks in your heart because people didn't change easily. You had to be patient. You had to love more than you hated, and even that was difficult. Maybe that was why it had taken so long—but it was true now.

I had needed some time for the love to come back, and it had.

I loved my family. Despite everything. Despite all the tears and pain and neglect. Despite all the shame and hatred and despair. I loved them and didn't want to lose them. Because I could picture so clearly the good times, the times when nobody was arguing and it was the four of us all together, sitting around the dinner table, and there were no fights, just laughter and love.

I could so easily remember my mother's laugh and my father's jokes and Ahsen's half smile—they were imprinted on my soul; they were the fingerprints on my heart. My family was a part of me, for better or for worse.

"I love them," I told my best friends. "And I don't want to lose them forever. I don't want to lose my entire past. All the family friends and cousins and my grandparents and my roots and my world. I had to run from them, and I know why. Going back doesn't mean I'll be the same person. I won't let them hurt me anymore or take advantage of me. I just—I forgive them."

In all the studying of this religion of mine, if there was one lesson I had learned it was this: *be kind*. Across the board, that was the conclusion: to treat others with respect and dignity, and to uphold their rights as individuals.

So I wanted to treat my family right. I hadn't, by running away. Everybody had the right to know when somebody would be walking out of their life. It was unfair to disappear.

Though in Islam, it was okay to take space from toxic people in your life, even if they were your own family members. The story of the Prophet Ibrahim taught us that—he loved his father deeply, but he needed space from him, so he left with the intention to one day return. It didn't mean he didn't care for his father. It didn't mean he didn't love him. It just meant Prophet Ibrahim had to do what was best for himself at that point.

In a way, I had done that. And now I was ready to go back. I wanted to apologize outright for leaving. I wanted to heal and move forward together. If such a thing was possible.

"They're your family," Haya said, smiling softly. She leaned her head against my shoulder.

"Does this mean you're going back to California?" Sadaf asked me. Her mouth was full of cookies.

"I want to," I said, realizing it was true. "I'm sort of scared."

"Look, you have to do your best, at the end of the day," Haya said. "Tie your camel and leave the rest up to Allah."

"Exactly," Sadaf agreed. "If it feels right to go back and reconcile, then that's what you should do. And if it doesn't work out, it wasn't meant to be, and at least you tried."

I nodded. "Allah is the Best of Planners. I trust Him." I bit my lip, nervous. "But what if they don't want to see me?"

The sisters exchanged a glance. Haya adjusted her glasses. "Um, I think they will want to see you," she squeaked.

"How do you know?"

"Sadaf?" Haya said. I turned to Sadaf, confused.

"Ahsen was here. He found you," she said.

"*What?*" I couldn't believe it. "Repeat that, please."

"Ahsen was here," Haya said. "I mean, I didn't see him, but Sadaf did."

My mind whirred with questions. "When? Where? How? *When?*" I needed more information.

"The night you ran to the ocean," Sadaf told me, a strange look on her face as she recalled the day. "He was at the masjid. I recognized him immediately—you guys look alike. He was asking for you, but you had just run off. You just missed each other." She released a deep breath.

"He was so gutted. I went and got coffee with him, to let him know you were okay, that you were building a life for yourself. He was glad. We talked for a while. He seemed . . . I don't know, different than you said he would be. He didn't seem like an ass or arrogant or immature. He just seemed sad. Heartbroken."

I had a sense there was more to that day than she was letting on, but Sadaf finished talking. There was something in her eyes I couldn't decipher, but I could tell it didn't have to do with me. Maybe that was her own story.

"He found me?" I asked. "How?"

Tears welled in my eyes, hot against the cold air. Haya nodded.

It was tragic, how close we had been yet how far apart we still were. The timing wasn't right—perhaps neither of us had been ready then. But he had looked for me. My brother, the man who I thought wouldn't even care if I left, who I thought would hate me.

He had searched for me, and he had found me. How had he done it? I felt beyond loved. I wanted to know the man my brother had become, the man who would look for me even after I had left him.

"He didn't tell me *how* he found you, and he went back

that same day," Sadaf continued. "He said not to tell you he was there unless I thought you wanted to hear it, and I talked it over with Haya. We thought you wouldn't be able to handle it back then. You had already been through a tough few days."

"And we're sorry if keeping it from you all this time was a bad idea," Haya jumped in. "But we didn't want to add to all your emotional turmoil."

"Yeah, exactly, but now—you're wondering if you think your family will even want to see you, and the answer is *yes*. At least, one person will. Which is why we're telling you now."

"I understand why you didn't tell me," I replied. "Really. I don't think I could have handled it back then, but you're right—I can handle it now. Thank you."

I looked up at the stars, up at the shining moon, which cast a white light all over us, and I felt something awaken inside of me.

And it was like Allah poking me, saying, *This is it. You're ready now.*

It was time to go home.

Chapter 30

$\mathcal{I}$ was back at the airport, back to the beginning.

So much had happened since I was last here. I could almost see the ghost of myself, arriving in New York. It made me sad to remember how broken I had been then. It had been the lowest low of my life, but I suppose things had to get worse before they got better.

And they did get better. I was at peace. I was content. I was happy.

So why is my tummy curdled with fear?

I was going home.

Home home. To Ahsen and Baba and Mama. If they would still have me.

Had six months been enough time for their anger to wear off into love? When Ahsen had come to find me, had it been on his own accord, or had Mama and Baba known too? I had no idea what I was getting into, and it scared me shitless, but I had to go.

Just enough time had passed. I was removed enough from the pain, but not so far removed as to not miss home. I wanted to go back to reconcile my past because everything else had fallen into place—I was in a good place spiritually, mentally, emotionally. I had laid the foundation for a good life; I had a good support system. But I didn't want to move further ahead without my family. They were still vital.

"Got everything?" Haya asked, sticking her hands in her pockets to ward off the cold night. It was four in the morning; my flight was at seven. We stood in front of Sadaf's car at the drop-off area at John F. Kennedy International Airport.

Around us, people were getting out of their cars, grabbing their luggage and their children. The sound of horns beeping was loud in the air.

"Yes, I have everything," I told Haya, gesturing to my wheeler and purse. Her eyebrows were knitted with worry.

"Are you sure?" Sadaf asked. She gave me a similar apprehensive look.

I was not the same as I had been six months ago. I hadn't had these girls then.

"Yes, yes, thank you," I told them. "Insha'Allah, I'll be okay. I have to do this."

"You do," Sadaf said, biting her lip. "And you *will* be okay. You're a badass bitch."

"I agree. I know you have to do this and that you can," Haya said, pulling me into a hug. "You're so, so unbelievably brave. You can do this. You will."

I internalized her words. When she pulled away, there were tears in all our eyes.

"I'll be back before you know it," I told them.

But even that I didn't know. Would I be back here in two days, kicked out of my home this time instead of running away? Would they even let me leave again? I was scared.

I was frightened too, that everything I had built in New York would fall apart while I was gone. Rent was paid for January, so I had a month, at least. And Lubna Auntie had understood me going home. Yaseen said he would cover for me while he was on break from university. The kids I tutored were on vacation too, and I didn't have much catering business anyway, since universities were on break. Hopefully, it would all be okay when I came back.

"Call me the instant you can," Haya told me.

"And keep us updated!" Sadaf added.

"And you guys keep *me* updated," I told her, forcing a smile. "Like if you start training for the new job!" I told Sadaf.

"Ew, I don't want to be an adult," she said, making a face. "I think I'll just be a potato for all eternity."

I laughed. "And, Haya, I wanna hear if anything new develops with Wonderboy Carlos," I told her.

Haya smiled a shy smile. "Of course, though probably nothing because we are taking things very, *very* slowly. I mean, he's still figuring his life out as a Muslim, and I'm too young to think about a serious relationship, and—" she rambled, until I gave her a look and she stopped. "Right. Sorry."

"Yes, please shut up," Sadaf said. "We've only been

following this saga for four months! He likes you, you like him, we get it."

"You shut up!" Haya smacked Sadaf. We laughed, piling into one final hug.

"Okay, bye for now," Haya said, voice hoarse when we pulled away.

"Bye for now," I said. Sadaf blew me a kiss, and I put my hand up in a wave as I walked toward the entrance of the airport.

From there, I was on my own. But I could face this.

I went through security, through all the nuances of air travel that I had to, but this time I kept my eyes open. I remembered why I loved airports so much when I saw little kids running into their grandparents' arms. I remembered when I saw an old man kiss his daughter's cheek, when I saw people from different cultures and countries and lives fuse and reconnect.

I hoped I would be welcomed home.

"Ya Allah, please facilitate whatever is best for me to happen," I prayed. "Ya Allah, give me strength. Give me infinite strength."

Over and over again as I waited at the gate. Over and over again as I watched the rain pitter-patter down the windows.

Give me strength, give me strength, give me strength.

I would need every ounce I could get.

I finally boarded and settled into my seat. I recited prayers for the journey, hoping for the best. A lanky boy came and sat beside me. He had white-blond hair and the bluest eyes, and for the first time in a long while, I could appreciate how cute he was without wanting to recoil.

I smiled at him politely, and he smiled back, and that was that.

He plugged in headphones to begin a movie, and I looked out to the lights shimmering in the night. It was raining, soaking the runway. There were planes landing and planes taking off, some adventures ending as others began.

Then it was our turn. We took off, soaring through the rain and the clouds. Everything went hazy for a while, so dark and blurry I couldn't see anything. But eventually we came out on top and left the stormy clouds far below. We traveled through the infinite sky to make our way home.

Chapter 31

Tired from waking up early to get to the airport, I slept through the entire flight, rousing only when the pilot announced we would be landing soon.

When I exited the plane, it was funny how clearly I recognized California. I could taste it in the air and feel it in the sunshine and see it in the people. This airport was familiar to me—I had traveled through it so many times—but this was my first time coming back alone. It was just me.

I saw families all around me, couples and little kids and teenagers. That's where I was going—to *my* family. But not yet. I still had a long way to go.

When I exited the arrivals area, there was nobody there to greet me. On my left, a young woman hugged her older parents, and on my right, I saw a middle-aged man kiss his wife.

Once, I had stood in this exact place, and my aunt and cousins and grandparents had welcomed me home. Another time, I had stood on the other side, welcoming my relatives home.

Today I was alone, and suddenly I was so sad. I wanted to go home to Haya and Sadaf.

I wanted to go home to Mama and Baba.

I pulled my wheeler along and sat in the seats by a Peet's Coffee. The aroma of coffee wafted to me. It had been forever since I had Peet's. So I got up and ordered some coffee and a pastry, and in that first sip, everything came back at once. This was familiar. This was normal. I slowed my breathing and took comfort in the chocolate and bread in my mouth.

I took a seat in the arrivals area, facing the parking lot. The walls were almost entirely windows, and I could see the clear sky outside. Winter in California. Nothing close to the winter in New York I had experienced this past month.

Here, there was more sunshine and a softer wind. It wasn't as cold. Here, I would seek out those patches of sunlight in the house and sit there all morning, shifting as the sun did, and I would drink our chai and watch old home videos on the television with my family. I always loved winter, even when the days were too short, and the sun disappeared, and the cold bit my nose. I was back. So close to those memories and everything I loved, but I couldn't bring myself to make that final hour-long journey home. *Should I grab a taxi or take the train?* But I didn't want to be alone anymore.

Should I call Ahsen? I wasn't sure.

He *had* come to find me, but I still wasn't sure if it had been out of love or anger.

I *really* didn't want to be alone anymore.

I dialed the number I still knew by heart and waited, phone cold against my cheek. It began to ring.

"Hello?"

It was his voice, thick and groggy from sleep, but it was him. My brother! I had woken him. It was early, and he was on break from college.

"Ahsen?" I hesitated but forced myself to carry through. "I'm in San Fran. Are you ... here? Or in Boston? Can you pick me up from the airport, please?"

"Yeah— Yeah, I'm here. I'm coming."

He sounded—I couldn't tell, actually. All I knew was that I hadn't heard his voice in so long, and I didn't realize how much I had missed it until then. How hearing his voice transported me to another time, how it struck a chord deep within me, a chord that had not been touched for months.

"Okay, thanks," I said, voice high. "See you soon."

Nerves squirmed in my gut.

For an hour, thoughts jumped around in my mind, worried and excited. I didn't know what I would say to him. Would he ask me why I ran? Did he hate me all these months? Would he forgive me for leaving and for leaving him to deal with the aftermath?

A thousand questions flurried through my mind like a blizzard. I played over what I would say to him, potential conversations and reactions, but when the time actually came, I froze.

I saw him enter through the doors, and then I had a

moment. That moment when you haven't seen somebody in a long while, and seeing them again is at once both foreign and familiar. Small things, you notice, have changed, such as articles of clothing you've never seen before, or weight, or height, or the way the person carries themself.

But overall, the mold of the person is still the same.

My brother.

"Zahra!"

My mouth split into a grin. *He's here!*

We reached each other, and there was the instantaneous question between the two of us as to whether we would hug—we never had been ones for physical affection. In the end, he hugged me.

Neither of us familiar with the act, the reunion hug was swift and gauche. My chin hit his tall shoulder, and he kicked my wheeler. We both laughed. I felt flowers blooming in my heart after a long, long winter.

"Someone's happy to see me," he said, smiling bright, dimples cutting into his cheeks behind his beard.

I smiled and took the time to look over his face, cataloging the things that had changed and the things that had stayed the same. I took in his dark-brown eyes—the same as mine—and the thick eyebrows. He used to wear earrings, but they were missing today. His beard had grown a little, but he had the same haircut—straight hair cut into a fade. And he had the same crooked, toothy smile, though I hadn't seen it much before.

I couldn't get over it. He seemed so different but the same.

I couldn't quite place it, but I knew I liked the change.

"Hot chocolate?" he offered. He reached out and took my wheeler before I could process. *That was thoughtful.*

"Perfect." It was unspoken, how neither of us wanted to go home yet.

I hardly reached his shoulders, but it was nice walking beside him. I had always thought him to be so much bigger, for some reason, but he was just a person like anyone else.

He seemed humbler, somehow. Less arrogant. Softer. Different. Just the way he was carrying himself and the way he spoke. He wasn't tense at all, as he usually was.

We grabbed our drinks and settled down where I had been sitting before.

"Oh, before anything else," he said, pulling something from his coat. "I've been carrying this around for the past few months, but it belongs to you."

He slid over a journal, and it took me a moment to recognize it. When I did, my eyes widened, eyebrows raised.

"Wow," I said, astonished. "I can't believe you found this. Where *did* you find it?"

"In your room," he said. "It was between the wall and your bookshelf."

"Look at you, becoming a detective," I teased. "You do know usually people hide things for a reason, right?"

He smiled bashfully, rubbing a hand against his neck. "Yeah, sorry for snooping. You mad?"

"No, I'm not. I'm touched you cared enough to look." I actually couldn't believe he'd been bothered enough to go to my room, to look through my things. "Did you read it?" He nodded.

"Sorry about that too, but you know my philosophy—better to ask for forgiveness than permission." He shrugged easily.

I laughed. I didn't mind that he'd read it, either. I was glad he cared enough to.

This journal had been mine ever since I was thirteen. I opened the leather flap, and my face melted. These were the pages I spilled my every emotion onto, when writing had become a coping mechanism.

The first entry was from five years ago, the final from last year. In those entries I saw who I used to be, for so long. I ran my fingers gingerly over the words, feeling the valleys the letters had carved into the paper. I thumbed through the pages, thumbed through the months, eyes wide at times with horror, then sadness, then joy, then sadness again.

"It doesn't even feel like I wrote this," I told Ahsen when I was done paging through.

The disparity was alarming, when I compared who I was then and now. My heart fractured in despair at the girl I once was, so anguished and angry and aggravated—then nothing but apathy. I could picture those days so perfectly.

"I can remember the emotions, the words, well enough, but . . . Ahsen, I don't feel them anymore," I said. My heart split open with sunshine. I was a bystander, watching the memories roll without being the actor, seeing through her eyes. Those days, those weeks, those months, how awful they had been.

But they had passed.

"How can so long have passed?" I shook my head and laughed.

"You were just a kid, Z," he said, eyes sad. "Still are."

"Yeah, but at the same time, it feels like yesterday."

I could imagine myself writing these words, remember exactly the day and the circumstances and the emotions surrounding the entries.

"God, if I close my eyes and imagine hard enough, I'm thirteen again," I said. "Isn't that wild?"

Ahsen looked at me, listening, and it gave me strength. I took a deep breath.

"As I skimmed through the journal, I thought that the thirteen-year-old at the beginning of the story would be different from the eighteen-year-old at the end," I told him, fumbling with the journal's leather strap. I couldn't quite meet his gaze. "And while the dates in the upper left-hand corner changed with the seasons and years, the emotions remained stagnant. The expressions varied, but the rage, the frustration, the despair, the hate—it was all there, across the pages and years, across the memories and time."

I knew that beneath it all lay the hopes and dreams and desires of a little girl waiting for the future. A girl waiting to be happy, a girl wanting and wishing. A thirteen-year-old girl yearning for better times, yearning for her pain to end and for her life to become picturesque and for her heart to be content. *For everything to be perfect.*

By the time the journal was through, the thirteen-year-old

girl was still there, but she was simply five years older, five years more bitter and angry and depressed.

It made me sad that I spent all those years trapped in those emotions, not recognizing or understanding them. I always thought I was just sad, but I saw now that I had been depressed, on and off, for years. If I had recognized it earlier, I could have started therapy much sooner.

"I read it, and I—I never knew you felt like this," he said, looking at his hands. "I'm sorry. That I was never around. That I never paid attention."

"I was stuck, Ahsen," I told him. "But I'm not stuck anymore."

He nodded, still listening. Who was he? The old Ahsen was afraid of emotion and vulnerability. But the man in front of me looked me straight in the eyes, unflinching. I would be brave too.

"This is what my life *was*," I told him. "Past tense. But it isn't anymore. I promise, it isn't. Sometimes . . . I feel like it is. I fall back into the mold of all this sadness and hate and disappointment. But then I remember all the good, and it's all right again."

Ahsen was speechless, listening and processing. Again, I was dumbfounded by how patient he was being. In the past, the few times he visited, we could barely get through a minute's conversation.

What had caused this change? What had the past six months looked like for him? His own story, his growth?

"I remember you sometimes," I said, smiling. "How your

eyes close when you laugh too hard. How sometimes you called me Zaz or Baked Ziti or anything else that started with the letter Z. How you used to take me in the summer sometimes to get smoothies and we would just drive around. Little things. I can still remember being a toddler and you tickling me—isn't that so strange? I was probably two and I know they always say kids don't start remembering things until they're five, but I remember, Ahsen. It's vague, but I remember."

I wanted him to hear it, to know that I had thought about him. That I had missed him. I needed him to know that I hadn't wanted to go. That I didn't hate him.

And he knew. I saw his eyes start to glisten and his bottom lip tremble, but he forced a laugh.

"Shit, Z," he said, wiping tears from his eyes. "You're making me fucking cry in public."

"It's okay to cry, you know," I told him seriously. I wanted him to know he didn't have to be the hyper-masculine version of himself he thought he had to be. He was so much more.

"I know," he told me, bumping his knee with mine. "My punk little sister wrote me an entry in her journal about that."

We laughed, and I realized he had read my journal thoroughly. I could distantly remember writing an entry like that. I couldn't remember exactly when, but it was like he had it memorized. Like he had read those words a thousand times.

"I remembered you too, you know," he said, clearing his throat. "How you were the fattest little baby ever, but you were so cute, and I was so glad to have someone to play with. How we'd run through the sprinklers as kids. How you'd sit by the fireplace in the winter, reading your books. How Mama would always badger you to call me Bhai but you never did, and I preferred it that way. That time I took you driving even though you failed your permit test. I remember too, Z. I remember."

This time, it was my turn to get teary-eyed, and I smiled at him, both of us feeling emotional. We were left with everything and nothing to say. So we sat in silence for a while. And it was okay. I tried to tell him with my eyes that I was beyond happy to see him, to see him like this. And it seemed like with his smile, he was telling me he was glad to see me too.

"Are we good?" I finally asked, breaking the silence. "From the way you emailed me back the first night I left, I thought you hated me or something."

"Hated you?" he repeated, confused. He shook his head. "Zahra, I was concerned and scared—I thought something terrible had happened to you. And then you emailed back saying not to look for you, that you loved us ... I thought you were suicidal or something. Hence the swearing and the all-caps."

"*Oooh*. Oops."

"Yeah."

"So ... you looked for me?"

"Obviously. You're my stupid little sister," he said, running a hand through his hair. "And besides, there's only room for one screwup in this family, and that title is already mine, thank you very much."

He bumped my shoulder, trying to make me smile.

"How did you find me, all those months ago?"

I pulled my legs into a crisscross, settling into the seat, ready for a story. He hadn't even told Sadaf how he had found me—he just came and left so quickly.

"It wasn't easy," he started dramatically. His eyes glittered with mischief. "For one, you didn't take your phone with you, so it's not like I could have simply used 'Find My iPhone' or some shit. I had to devise some top-secret, covert way to figure out where you were. So, naturally, I called upon my spy instincts, did a fuckload of snooping, and eventually broke into your email address with my incredible hacking skills. Then I read your bank statement, and BAM knew exactly where you were. You would make a terrible felon, by the way. I found you in like five minutes flat."

I laughed, but I suspected he was lying. It couldn't have been that easy, no way. It seemed simple, but to get there must have taken longer.

"My friend Sadaf told me she saw you," I said. He immediately perked up.

"Oh?" he said. There was something strange happening to his face. I raised a brow. He cleared his throat. "I mean, yeah, I think I met her. We chatted a little because I wanted to know if you were doing okay."

"Yeah, she mentioned something like that."

He scratched his neck, nodding to himself. There was something in his eyes I couldn't quite decipher. Again, I had a sense there was more to that day than I was being told, but it didn't have to do with me.

I would have to ask him *and* Sadaf about it sometime.

"Well," I said, "I'm glad you found me. Even though I wasn't there. I'm glad. I wouldn't have come home if it wasn't for you."

It was true. I didn't know if I would have had the strength. Ahsen shook his head, his eyes tearing again. It made me so happy, in a way, to see him cry so easily. It meant that he cared. It meant that he felt. That he was alive.

"What about you?" he asked me. "What have you been up to?"

I told him about Haya and Sadaf and Nabila Auntie and Lubna Auntie and Yaseen and the friends I'd made and the experiences I'd had. I told him how happy I was. How genuinely content I was, no matter what happened. I had faith, and I had hope, and I had love.

"What about you?" I asked when I was finished. "What are your plans now?"

Ahsen smiled. "I'm looking for jobs before graduation in May, so I might be moving home if I get one close by."

"What!" I said, entirely shocked. "You want to come home?"

"Shocking! I know, right." He laughed.

"Only because you barely visited ever since you went away! And always said you'd never come back to California. That's a direct quote."

"Maybe you're not the only one who ran away from home. Mine was just more acceptable since it was for college. But now, I think I want to come back."

I was proud of him for those words. I had always wanted

him to choose us, to choose his family, to come home. Finally, he was.

"I'm better than I was," he told me. "But I still have a long way to go, I think."

I nodded, agreeing. "Me too, but that's the thing about improvement. It never stops. We are constantly evolving and learning and growing because that is life. That is truly living."

"Am I in a Ted Talk or something?" He snorted. I laughed. "Shut up, you loser."

At that moment, I was excited for the future, for what it would hold for both of us.

We talked some more, but after we'd exhausted the past six months, I felt my tummy turn into knots. It was time.

"We have to go home at some point," I said, fidgeting with the end of my sweater sleeve. Reality came back to us— we were still in an airport terminal, and it was nearly noon. Ahsen winced. Immediately, I began nibbling my bottom lip in anxiety.

"I won't lie, Zahra," Ahsen said solemnly. "Mama's still pretty pissed."

My heart dropped.

"Did you tell her I called today? Or that you came to New York to find me?"

Ahsen shook his head. "Nah, I figured it wasn't my place to tell her, that you'd tell her when you were ready. I'm just warning you, though—it won't be easy."

"I know, but I have to go back," I said, steeling myself. *I have to go back.* "It's like—I'm so happy all the time, but sometimes, *sometimes*, I can still feel this abyss in my heart, like some big empty hole, and I know it's my past. It's you guys and my family and those memories and my life. I can't run from it anymore. I don't want to. You can't run from your past. You have to embrace it and learn from it, or else you can't move on. I want to move on, *with* you guys—not *away* from you guys.

"And Mama deserves an apology. I know that. I know she does, I'm just . . . scared. Ahsen, I'm so scared."

My voice was so small. I looked down at the floor.

"Hey," my brother said, catching my eyes. "Everything is going to be all right, okay? I'll be there. Don't worry. You're gonna be okay."

I looked at him, at this man who was my brother, and all I heard were those words—*I'll be there.* They gave me strength. They gave me courage. I took a deep breath. I stood up.

"Then let's go home," I said.

Chapter 32

$\mathcal{Y}$ears of memories waited for me the moment I entered my childhood town.

One stood by the coffee shop, drinking a cinnamon-apple latte in the fall. One laughed in the park, pumping a swing into the sky. One exited the library, carrying a stack of books. I saw old faces and homes, schoolmates and teachers, years and months and days and hours clearly.

It felt like yesterday; it felt like years ago. I was a different person then; I was the same person now.

We finally made it home. Ahsen parked, and we walked up to the front door. It was Sunday—both my parents would be home.

Ahsen unlocked the door, then waited for me to open it. I took a deep breath then pushed the door.

When I walked through the front door, my house smelled the same—cotton and citrus. It was like Ahsen had just picked me up from a friend's house, and we were coming home now.

It was as if time had frozen in this house, and I was back two years ago or three.

But then—

"As-salaamu Alaikum, beta."

Mama's voice from the top of the stairs, coming down to the foyer where we stood. My heart stopped upon hearing her voice. I knew she hadn't seen me yet because she sounded so happy. For a moment, I considered turning back.

Then I saw her—still round and smiling, the picture of how my features would look with age. The sight of her knifed through me. I froze but my voice was ready.

"Salaam, Mama," I said. For a millisecond, she stood completely still, shocked to her core. Then rage engulfed her features and Ammi was before me in two steps.

She slapped me across the face.

The sensation was familiar, reverberating back through the months, back to a year ago. For a moment, I was that girl again—a broken bird, broken wings.

All the healing of the past five months seemed to disappear, and it was no time at all since January, since June. My entire life was a string of beads, stretched apart, each representing moments such as this, but with that single slap, they all slammed together. I felt all the pain of each moment in that instant, the past and the present blending into one.

"Mama!" Ahsen cried, stepping between us.

I held up my hand to him. I stood before my mother and through my tears, I looked into her dark eyes. There was nothing but a vast coldness there, covering all else.

"What are you looking at?" she spat. "Samaj'ti kya ho? That you would come back and we would forgive everything?" She was shouting. "That we would fall at your feet? I won't forget so easily."

"Ma—" I began, but she cut me off.

"Bas." She held her hand up. "Get out." She pointed to the door. "*Get out!*"

"Mama—" Ahsen tried, but before he entered the blast zone, my father did. He came into the foyer from the kitchen. My eyes cooled at the sight of him—his thin frame, the dark brown of his skin, the glasses upon his face.

"Kya shore mach raha?" he asked. *What is this noise?*

And then he saw me.

His face paled, more aged and weathered than I remembered, but it was softer too. I wanted to cry.

Did Baba hate me, too? Would he want me to leave, as well?

"Salaam, Baba," I croaked. He walked to me, face blank, and raised his hand. Though he had never hit me before, I shrank into myself until . . . his hand rested on my shoulder. He nodded.

"Ghar aate hue itni der kyun lagai? Did you forget your way home?"

I laughed, then began to cry. I tried to hold it in but couldn't. Ammi glared at me. "I said get out," she snapped.

"She isn't going anywhere," Baba said.

Ammi began to protest, but Baba gave her a stern look, and she pressed her lips shut. I knew she wanted to argue, to yell and fight, but the look in Baba's eyes—it was absolute. There would be no quarreling with him, not on this.

"Fine," Ammi said. "Good. Apna hi ghar samjho."

The sarcasm nipped my ears, and she cast one last scornful smile in my direction before going up the stairs to her bedroom. Ahsen cringed.

"Fuck," he muttered, not loud enough for Baba to hear.

"I'll talk to her later," Baba assured me, squeezing my arm.

"No," I said. "I'll talk to her now."

"Are you sure?" Ahsen asked.

There was concern in his eyes. I wished I could have bottled up that love and carried it forever. I took a picture of that memory and stored it alongside Haya's smile and Sadaf's laugh—my arsenal. I nodded.

"I have to do this, but thanks."

I offered my older brother a smile, then headed up the stairs. The creaking boards were so familiar, the railing curving beneath my fingers. How could so much have changed and yet ... so much stayed the same? My feet knew this carpet, knew the steps to her room, the exact space in the hall, and the little dent in the knob of my parents' bedroom door.

I knocked once.

"Khabar daar agar yahan ayee. I don't want to see you."

Her voice was broken. *Is she crying?*

A year ago, I would have obeyed. I was too afraid of her then. I still was, but this was the moment of truth—the moment I would overcome my fear. Were the past five months nothing? Would I slip back into the shadow of the girl I had been? Docile and afraid, voice too small to be heard?

I will not. I opened the door.

"Get out!" she screamed.

I summoned the sound of Ahsen's voice calling my name in the terminal this morning, the sheer joy his voice could not contain.

"Mama—" I started. I crossed the room until I was sitting on the floor by her bed, at her feet. She turned her back to me, wiping angrily at her eyes. I could barely see her face.

"No. Don't." She held a hand up. "I am not your mother. My daughter died six months ago."

"Mama, please." My voice was small.

"Kya tera koi bacha nahi hai?" she asked, finally turning and looking at me. "You don't have a child?"

Her voice was sardonic and cruel. It hurt me to see her so pained, and I didn't understand the accusation at first. But then it dawned upon me.

"I thought that was why you left," she continued. "Khair. I'm sure you spent six months with that bastard anyway."

How could I tell her it wasn't true? She would never believe me, and I knew it too. So I forgave her for those words. I knew she did not care for my forgiveness, but *I* needed to forgive her.

Only after forgiving could I ever hope to forget. I wanted her to forgive me too. I wanted to move forward together.

"Bas," she said. "Enough. Go."

Her voice was eerily level, but the anger beneath it was

evident. A year ago, she had been this angry with me. A year ago, I was a different person. One who stayed quiet and absorbed her words of fire, hoping to put them out within me—but they scorched me, and I was still healing from those burns.

I didn't have it within me to be burned anymore.

"I've made mistakes, Mama, I know I have. I was wrong in my disrespect. You have every right to be angry," I said, the words broken pieces of glass cutting my mouth as I spoke them. It was the truth, what she wanted to hear.

In a way, I had been wrong by running away the way I did. She did have every right to be angry. Instead of vilifying each other, we needed to understand one another, and if I had to take the first step, then I would.

I loved her; I needed to salvage this. I needed to make things right.

"I'm sorry," I said, and I was crying then, too. "I'm so sorry for hurting you when I left."

She gave me a look as if to say, "And?" But that was all she would get from me.

I was sorry to have hurt her, but I was not sorry for leaving.

"Bas?" she spat, finally looking at me. "You're sorry?"

"Yes, Mama," I said, voice clear despite the tightness in my throat. There was nothing else to say. Bringing up the past, all the pain and the mistakes, leading to our estrangement would do no good.

I wasn't the only one who had made mistakes. Ammi did too. She also had things to apologize for. But a part of growing up was knowing you were due an apology but not needing it. She didn't need to apologize to me—I couldn't control her actions. I could only control myself.

And I was doing my best to make things right.

Ammi would not change, but I had.

She would not forgive unless she was ready, unless she wanted to. I had treated her awfully, but there were justifications for my actions, reasons behind why I left.

For her, worse than my abandonment was my disobedience. Worse than my actions was my defiance. And it made sense, from her point of view. She was in charge of me, responsible for me. I had to obey her. She was my mother. She had rights over me—but so did I.

I had rights over myself that I would not sacrifice for her contentment. Not anymore.

I realized then why I had resented her so much—she had taken me away from myself, molded me into the daughter she wanted me to be, and left nothing for me to decide for myself.

But I was a person, not a doll. The six months away from her gave me space to recognize myself. I finally understood my own truth, but only when she was not around to dictate it to me.

I would not let her control me any longer. I owed myself that much.

Still, I knew apologizing was the right thing to do—for her, for me, for us. I would never stop craving her approval or her happiness; it was ingrained within me to yearn for it. Moreover, my happiness was tied to hers. She was my mother.

I could never run from that reality. It was time I stopped trying.

She was my mama, and I wanted her to be happy and happy with me. I loved her. I knew I couldn't live with her hating me, and for as long as it took to break my habits, I knew it would torment me to think about the constant pain my actions caused her. I needed to make this right. I owed her that much after everything I had done.

I inched toward her, heart in my throat, eyes fuzzy with fear. Trepidation pulsed through me, but still I reached for her hand. She didn't turn, but I spoke anyway.

"I'm so, *so* sorry, Mama." My voice was toffee, thick and sticky. "Please, please forgive me." I was crying, but I would not beg. Not again, never again. She must have known.

Ammi took her hand out of mine and turned her cheek.

"*Just go*," she whispered.

"Okay," I said, swallowing. A weight lifted off my chest because I had tied my camel—the rest was up to Allah. "But know that I will always be sorry."

I would be. I always would be.

Then I left.

Chapter 33

Ahsen was waiting for me outside my parents' room. Upon seeing him, I began to cry even more. They weren't sobs, just tears, leaking from my eyes even as I smiled.

"It's okay," I said, before he could ask. He looked so unbearably sad for me. I didn't want him to worry.

"It's not," he told me, frowning. He put his arm across my shoulder. Six months ago, this would never have happened, but now, it felt normal. I leaned into him, and he supported me.

"I'll talk to her soon. She'll come around. Mama never stays mad forever."

But Ahsen didn't know, because Mama was never angry with *him* for more than two hours. He was her precious son, who could do no wrong, and even when he did, she ignored it. I let it go.

"Let's go downstairs," I said instead. I wiped my cheek with a sleeve. "I'm so hungry."

"I'll make you something to eat," he offered. I laughed.

"You?" I said, arching a brow. "When did you learn how to cook?"

"I've always known how to cook," he scoffed, indignant. I snorted.

"Remember that time you tried boiling an egg in the microwave?"

He waved a hand, grinning. "Yeah, yeah," he shushed me. "I was young and naive then. I'm a changed man, Baked Ziti. Just you wait and see."

He started down the stairs, but I paused, needing a moment to myself. "You go on," I told him, hands shaking as the emotions caught up to me. "I'll be down in a second."

He nodded, leaving me alone. I went to the bathroom, closing the door behind me. I felt triggered, being back here—back at the site of so much misery. This was the bathroom I used to hide out in, where I harmed myself. On old instinct, I itched to do something like that again, but I forced my balled fists open.

I focused on my breath in the way Eya taught me to when I felt anxious or close to a dark place. I breathed in, held, then breathed out. My chest hurt, but I kept doing it, until the tightness in my torso had loosened.

"You're okay," I whispered to myself. "You're okay."

Feeling a little better, I went to the sink and splashed cold water on my face, and that helped too. Then I stretched, pulling my arms up over my head and reaching up, up, up, standing on my tiptoes until my whole body was awake and pulsing. Eya always said taking care of our physical being helped facilitate peace for our mental being, and I did feel more tranquil.

I kept focusing on my breaths, narrowing down my life to the next moment, and the next, and the next, until, finally, the fog in my head and heart cleared and I felt okay again. I released a long breath, then met my gaze in the bathroom mirror.

"You're okay," I told myself, nodding. I gave myself a little smile. "You're okay."

And I was.

As I walked downstairs to Ahsen, the longing for all I had missed washed over me as I looked over my home. These wide windows, the view of my backyard, the rose bush. The sofas, the fuzzy blankets, the pillows. Our sunroom. All of it.

I had missed it so, so much.

We went to the kitchen, and I ran my hand across the marble countertops, feeling like a kid again. Ahsen made me lunch, stirring some chicken together in a wok. As he did that, I warmed up some tortillas for both of us. He spread hummus and sour cream on them, then I added the chicken and some chopped onions. Ahsen pulled out chocolate-vanilla cookies, jalapeño chips, and cans of raspberry sparkling soda.

I wondered if he remembered we used to eat stuff like this all the time as kids. I remembered us snacking and watching television when our parents weren't home.

Upon hearing us in the kitchen, Baba entered. Even though I knew he wanted to act like everything was normal, he couldn't.

By force of habit, I immediately became wary of Baba and Ahsen in the same room. They usually couldn't be in the same space for more than five minutes without a fight breaking out.

But Ahsen seemed calm. He took a deep breath and asked Baba if he wanted a wrap to eat as well.

"Sure," Baba said. No sarcasm, no snideness. I was impressed with them, particularly Ahsen as he put together a sandwich for Baba. We all sat down and started eating.

"So, what are you up to these days?" Baba asked, turning to me.

"For now, I have a few jobs, and I love them all, but my favorite is cooking," I said. "We live near the campus where my friend Haya goes to school, so she gives me amazing advertising and I make food to sell to students since the campus food is terrible. It's really fun, and sometimes I cater desserts for parties. One day, I hope I can be a chef somewhere—it would be very cool. Or maybe have my own little restaurant.

"I earn a pretty good amount of money, between everything, and I've saved a bunch of it up, so my friends and I were thinking of going on a road trip in the summer. The community in Long Island is great. They are so kind and welcoming."

I told him more about my life there. About Haya and Sadaf and the masjid girls and the kids and the community I had knit myself into. How I watched the sun rise and drank good coffee. How I spent time gardening and reading and cooking and breathing and living.

Afterward, Baba's eyes turned sad.

"You can't stay here, can you?" Baba asked, voice soft. "You have to go back?"

Yes, I had to, but I wasn't sure when.

"I don't know, Baba," I told him honestly. "I don't know."

I really didn't. I couldn't leave like this. Not with Mama so upset with me. I couldn't leave her again. Last time I had run, but this time I wouldn't—not until things were at least a little okay.

"Let's see how things go," I said. Baba nodded, understanding at least in part. There was still so much to be said, but we didn't say it yet.

Slowly, slowly. We all had to adjust to being around one another again, so we just ate.

"Make for your mama too," Baba told Ahsen. He already had, and I was surprised by the thoughtfulness. He really had changed.

"I'll go give it to her," Ahsen said. He disappeared for a bit but came back down with the plate.

"She won't eat," he told us.

I figured she was mad at him now too, for being an accomplice.

"It's okay," Baba said, waving a hand. "Don't worry. I'll talk to her. You know how she gets when she is angry. You kids go out, have fun. She needs time to be alone."

He was right. Mama probably did need space.

"Okay, Baba," I said, getting up. I put the food and dishes away, and Ahsen came to offer me a hand.

"Look who's being so helpful," I teased.

"Hey, I've changed," he said, waving the sponge at me. The work was done quickly with the two of us at it, so after, we grabbed the keys and went out to get smoothies. I got a strawberry banana smoothie and a snickerdoodle like always, and Ahsen tried some new concoction and a sugar cookie like always.

Some things never change.

California was quiet and peaceful, everything with a golden sheen to it. Ahsen got onto the Pacific Coast Highway, the two-lane road that wound along the coast. I stuck my head out the window, tasting the salt in the air.

My beautiful ocean! And the mountains. Oh, how I had missed them. The landscape felt like a cozy blanket, like home.

We went to the theater to see a movie, too drained to speak anymore. The only interesting thing playing was an animated film that surprisingly made us both cry and laugh. When it was done, Ahsen shook his head in disbelief.

"Pixar needs to stop fucking with my emotions like that," Ahsen said, running a hand through his hair. "Unbelievable. I'm gonna lose all my street cred like this."

I snorted. "What street cred?"

"Ha, ha," he said. "Just you wait until you need me to beat somebody up, then you'll see."

Not wanting to go home yet, we headed to the arcade and played games we hadn't played since we were kids. It was nice, just hanging out and being competitive. Everything was good. We laughed and made jokes and sat in silence, and then finally, we went back home.

We parked in the driveway, but before Ahsen could open his door, I spoke.

"What happened after I left?" I asked, because I had to know. "With the wedding and everything."

Ahsen took a deep breath and shrugged. "Honestly, I'm not exactly sure—I didn't ask. But Baba handled it all."

"Baba did?" I asked. My father, who hated dealing with family matters and propriety. He had weathered the storm I had left behind?

"He dealt with Zayn's family and made calls and canceled everything and told everyone you were in London for some study-abroad program, then university during the fall," my brother told me.

And I realized I had been wrong. About everything I had been so sure of—my views about my brother, my views about my father. They had both proved me wrong.

I had been so focused on my slice of the story that I had neglected how human my family was—how human my mother was. I hadn't heard or seen their sides but had cast them as the enemies and blamed them for not noticing me or loving me enough.

And maybe there were no villains—only humans the whole time.

Chapter 34

When we went inside, Mama was still in her room. Ahsen went to say goodnight, but she refused to talk to him, either.

"She just needs time," he told me.

Maybe that was all any of us ever needed—time. So I gave her space and didn't try to talk to her again for the night. It had been a long day for all of us, and I only realized how tired I was when Ahsen led me to my bedroom.

"I kept it clean for you, you little neat-freak. Dusted off your bookshelves and everything," he said, cracking a grin as we entered. It took me an instant to become reacquainted with my room.

My room.

"Wow," I said, mock-impressed. I clapped my hands, smiling. I audited my room, my things. It was all the same. Exactly as I had left it. The sage-green walls, my white furniture, my bookshelves.

"My room is the same," I said, exhaling, "but everything is so different now."

"Different is good," my brother assured me from the doorway. "I'm different now too, but I'm better. *We're* better now."

I could tell—just by the way he was spending time with me, talking with me, how he interacted with Baba, how his voice was softer. I saw all these little clues. He had a gentler aura, seemed more at peace, whereas before, he was always so angry and wanted nothing to do with us.

"You're right," I told him, turning back to look at him. "Thank you."

"Well, goodnight, then," he said, half-smiling.

"Goodnight, Ahsen." I half-smiled back.

And I closed the door to be enveloped in the room that had seen me through so much. These walls had witnessed euphoria and anxiety and sadness and indifference. These pillows, sheets absorbed buckets of tears and some hidden smiles too. These blankets had always wrapped me warm, safe.

I ran my fingers across the books on my shelves, the titles corresponding to different years of my life. I opened my closet and saw my clothes and remembered the days I wore them. Everything was distinctly mine but someone else's too. And that feeling only amplified when I opened my drawer.

My old phone.

It was dead, of course. I plugged it in and ran my fingers across the floral case. It took a few moments, but then my old phone came alive, buzzing with notifications from six months ago.

There were missed phone calls from Mama and Baba and Ahsen from that night. There were urgent messages from them, telling me to come home, to tell them where I was. And then it all stopped—I supposed by then they had found my car and phone and knew what had happened.

And it was time travel, going back all those months. It felt like another lifetime as I combed through messages from my old family friends, asking me to hang out for summer, inviting me to graduation parties. There were texts from some of my cousins too, and other relatives, asking me how I was liking London. And then silence.

There wasn't much else of importance on the phone. But what caught my eye was the photos app. I knew it would hurt to go through them, to travel back to precise moments, but I wanted to.

At first, there wasn't much. Some pictures of my baby cousins and some from graduation. My entire senior year, I had been too depressed to take any photos, and I hadn't wanted to capture any of those moments. It was almost like I hadn't existed. Like I had been a ghost.

But farther back, Before, there were clear memories embedded in those pictures, moments I had captured so perfectly. There were bright flashes on a friend's smiling face, me and a few girls around a bonfire, us on the swings in the park, drinking lattes, lying in bed, watching a movie, eating crepes, sunsets, snowfall, laughter, life.

And suddenly I missed them all.

I remembered the girls I used to be friends with in school, and how one day I was so angry I simply cut them off. I deleted all their numbers and our messages and all our social media connections. When I saw them in the halls, I looked right through them.

I had been angry at them for not noticing, for not helping, but I was the one who had pushed them away. I had isolated myself.

I felt sorry then. I wished I had their numbers so I could at least apologize for abandoning them. We had been such good friends.

Back then, we had thought it would be forever, but we had hardly lasted even a slice.

Loneliness weighed upon me, heavy around my body. I felt unbelievably melancholy until I remembered the friends I had now.

I dropped my old phone and picked up my current phone. "Zahra! How are you, girl?"

Even across the country, Haya's voice calmed me. I closed my eyes and clutched the phone to my chest for a moment before responding.

"I'm all right," I told her, and it was the truth. Then suddenly something struck me. "Shit—it's late there, right? I completely forgot about the time-zone difference! It's almost ten here."

"No, don't worry! It's almost one, but I'm home for the weekend so Sadaf and I were watching a movie. I'm glad you called, and I'm glad to hear you're okay. Now tell me everything. How did things go? Are you home? Are you safe?"

"Yes," I said. My voice was slow and quiet, but I knew Haya must have been dying for details. "Ahsen and Baba are good," I told her. "It was nice being back with them today."

"And your mom?" Haya asked, voice tentative.

"My mom . . . ," I started, but I didn't know what to say. "She's so angry with me, Haya, and I can understand why. After all, I ran away from her."

"But she loves you, I know she does," Haya said. "She just needs time, like you did, for the love to come back."

"She needs more space."

"Don't give up."

"I won't," I told her. "I'll give her some time before trying to talk with her again."

I could do this. And I would. But she needed time, and so did I.

Now, I also needed a change of conversation.

"How's Wonderboy Carlos?" I asked. It made me smile, just the thought of my best friend and her (Maybe) One True Love. Haya sighed, and it was a sigh of infatuation. She met with him on her own, so I hadn't spent much time with him beyond that initial meeting at the park. But she always filled me in on all the details.

"He's amazing, as usual," she said. "But it's hard for him, you know, not telling his parents. He converted almost a year ago, and his parents have no clue. Even though he doesn't live at home, since he's at nursing school, he can't share this massive portion of his life with his family, which really sucks. I was talking to Mama about it, and she thinks his parents will understand, but I don't know."

"You told Nabila Auntie about him? When?" I asked, surprised. This was new.

"You know I can't keep anything from her," she replied. "It gives me indigestion. And God, what a relief. I couldn't stand not being able to talk to her about it for the past few months. Even though Carlos and I are taking it slow, I still want Mama Dearest looped in."

"How'd she react?"

"Well, I think. You know Mama. As long as he's a decent guy and a good Muslim, she's fine," Haya told me. "Which is great. I can't imagine having to deal with my parents hating him because he isn't Pakistani, you know? Like, it would make things a thousand times harder if *both* of our families were against the idea of us."

"But it's good your mama isn't being absurd like Pakistani aunties can get, saying their kids can only marry into the same ethnicity and looking down upon everyone else," I said.

"Yes, I'm glad Mama isn't a snob like that," she said. "I actually adore how Chilean he is."

Haya had a dreamy quality to her voice, and it made me laugh.

"Okay, lovebird," I said, snickering. "Get a room."

"We're all fools in love," Haya sang. "But don't worry."

I could feel her getting excited. "Carlos has like two dozen cousins, and I'm sure one of them is just as cute as he is, so I'll work on converting one and then we can set you up too!"

"How thoughtful of you."

"I am a very generous person, I'm told."

We both laughed. It was a nice thought, but I didn't need romantic love in my life just yet. I was content with myself, and I needed to work on my other relationships before starting a new one.

I talked with Haya a bit more, until Sadaf took the phone from her sister. She skipped the hello and went straight to the point.

"You'll get through this, that's all I'm going to say," Sadaf told me. "You're one of the strongest people I know. Remember that."

"Thank you, Sadaf," I said with a sigh, and I meant it.

"So, what's new?" I asked. We talked a bit about random things and work and university. But Sadaf was less chatty than usual, so I knew something must have been wrong. It was only when she tried to say goodnight that I asked her.

"Everything good?"

She sighed.

"I'm a little scared," she admitted. "What if I start work, and I hate it? I've always told everyone and myself that this is what I want, but what if when I finally get it, I realize it's wrong?"

"Then you'll find something else to adore," I told her. "You are so full of passion and life, Sadaf. There is absolutely no way in hell that this life will pass you by without you accomplishing something great."

"Are you sure?"

"Positive. Remember when I was telling you about Ahsen? And you said older siblings are tough to deal with because they take a long time to figure things out? I know, without a doubt, that you will figure things out, and no matter what you do, you will excel and do great, great things."

"I love you," she said.

"I love you too."

"How is Ahsen, by the way?" she asked, voice purposefully light. "Is he still a tortured tool?"

"Tortured probably still, but less of a tool," I told her, laughing. "He's actually really nice." I paused, thinking of the strange look on his face today when I mentioned Sadaf. "I think you two would get along well."

"Well, we do have too-wise younger sisters in common, so probably," she said, and there was a giddy quality to her voice. I could see her smiling across the country. We talked some more, then said goodnight.

I nestled into bed, climbing into old pajamas that still fit me.

It felt entirely wrong but also really right to be back here again.

Chapter 35

*W*hen I woke up, there was a moment of time travel.

I had gone back years and was in high school again, waking up on a weekend, sunshine filtering into my bedroom. I was in my bed, the same lavender-scented sheets, the pillow that curved perfectly under my head and neck. My warm comforter, my sage-green walls, my room, my things.

The same view as a thousand other mornings. The same sounds: downstairs, I heard the exhaust running in the kitchen as Mama made breakfast, heard the whisking of eggs and chopping of onions and coriander.

It was strange how easily we forgot and how easily we remembered.

The bathroom was still seven steps away. My toothbrush was still there, along with my toothpaste and face wash—all old and not good for use—but everything was frozen in time, waiting for me. I showered, and I still knew exactly how much to turn each knob to get the perfect amount of hot water. I had missed this familiarity, this comfort.

This is home.

Mama was still ignoring me, so after she made breakfast for herself and Ahsen, she didn't leave her room. She still wouldn't speak to me, but it was not an irate silence or a bitter one—it was merely the silence of thinking.

Since it was Monday, Baba was at work, so it was just Ahsen and me. I told myself I would give Mama three days of space. Then I would talk to her again. In the meanwhile, I would spend time with my brother.

We both got up pretty late. I was famished, so I made myself a big breakfast, falling into the routine of where things were in this kitchen. Again, it was strange, like traveling back in time to a memory. I made myself eggs the way I used to, and I didn't have to think about where the salt or red pepper was, where the bowls or forks or frying pan were. It was all muscle memory.

Which was lovely. While I was used to the kitchen in my apartment back in New York now, we'd only been there for four months, so it was not *this* level of familiarity. I'd had years and years of use and practice in this kitchen. I felt akin to a tennis player hitting the courts after a long hiatus, or a sailor out at sea on their ship again after months.

"Whatcha wanna do today?" Ahsen asked while I was eating, and he was picking Skittles from a bag.

I shrugged. "Let's just hang out."

So we went out and got hot caramel lattes and spent time driving around long, looping roads, taking our time to meander aimlessly. We passed the park where we used to play, and since it was sunny out—not too cold—we hung out there for a bit, sitting on the swings. Then we continued driving, and there was this one road I had forgotten about until I saw it again.

It was on the way to school, and in the summer, there was the most gorgeous canopy of leaves atop the straight, one-lane road. Everything would be tinted green with patches of sunlight peeking through. And in the winter, all the trees were bare, but ice would solidify over the branches, and if the sun was out, everything sparkled like a winter wonderland.

Everything was sparkling now as we drove.

"I forgot how much I missed this," I told Ahsen, pressing a hand against the cool window.

"Me too," he agreed. "Cali has its own charm." He drove slowly, leisurely, with one hand. We had all the time in the world.

We drove around for a while, listening to the radio, to old music and new. We drove until we reached my high school. There were kids running around the track, and the parking lot still had some cars I recognized as my old teachers'. It was all still so perfectly familiar.

Just six months ago, I had attended this school. It felt like a year and a lifetime ago.

"Do you want to go inside?" he asked.

Before I could think, Ahsen was parking, and we were

going. For a moment I was scared—the last time I had been here, I had been a different person. But coming back didn't mean I would become her again. I was strong; I could handle this.

I wasn't afraid of my past catching up to me anymore, because I had caught it first.

Since it was a small school, there wasn't any security or anything, and we walked straight in. We pushed through the doors, and with that first wave of warm air, everything reeked of memories and nostalgia. It was the type of feeling that was both bad and good, hurting and healing.

We walked through the halls. It was strange for both of us. But I was glad I wasn't alone, and I knew he was too. The school day had just ended, so the building was mostly empty, but I saw some students I recognized and some teachers I knew, all staying after for extra help or clubs or sports.

We walked mostly as ghosts until I made eye contact with a pair of green eyes.

"Zahra!" my old-world history teacher, Mrs. O'Connell, called. "I'm so happy to see you!"

"Ohmygod, hi!" I said, excited to see her. She had been one of my favorite people in the entire school, and I had adored her class.

"Ahsen, hi to you too! How are you guys?" she asked. Before I could respond, Ahsen did.

"I'm well, but I'll let you and Zahra catch up. I was going to go see Mr. Baxter," he said, referring to his old math teacher. He said goodbye and left me with my favorite teacher.

"Zahra, you look great," Mrs. O'Connell told me, her hand light on my arm. She looked the same with her short brown hair and the freckles on her nose. Her face was just as kind as it always was. "You are simply glowing."

It made my heart surge. We talked for a while, and it was nice speaking with this older woman about my recent life and experiences. She was immensely enthusiastic about catching up. When I told her about catering and how much I loved cooking, I could tell she was happy for me.

"You seem so happy," she said, smiling wide. "And it makes *me* so happy to see you like this. I'm always rooting for you. I can't wait to see all the amazing things you accomplish! You're extraordinary, truly."

"Thank you so much," I said. "Can I give you a hug?" She nodded, and we hugged. "I'm so happy I ran into you," I told her.

"Well, please, by all means, run into me whenever you want! I'll always be here," she said.

We said goodbye. I realized I had missed her and school and the entire portion of my life that had transpired here. I felt airy inside but angry with myself too, for not relishing the last semester of high school. I had been so focused on the aftermath of that one, fateful decision that I hadn't seen all the good around me.

It was ironic, because just as I was thinking about how I would never let him or any other boy affect me so horrendously again, I saw him. It was on the way home, in the car beside me, both of us stopped at a red light. It was a coincidence and not, him being there. I hadn't seen him in so long that it was strange to see him again but so normal too. This was his town as well.

For an instant, I was afraid he would see me, but then that fear went away too. I realized that whether he saw me or not, it didn't affect me at all.

There was no anger or love or hatred. When the light turned green, we drove straight on, leaving this boy in the past where he belonged.

When we got home, I saw that Baba was sitting alone in the living room. He looked so tired. I went and sat with him. We were alone—Ahsen had gone to meet a friend after dropping me home—so he finally asked me.

"Why did you leave?" he asked, eyes sad. "I know it is something between you and your mama, but I talked to her. She's not listening right now, but she will. I know you could never do anything bad. She overreacts. You have always been good."

It made me want to cry, how highly he still thought of me. I shook my head.

"No," I said. "Don't talk to her. It's okay. We'll work it out."

"Was it the wedding?" he asked. I didn't know what to say, so I nodded. The wedding had been the last piece of the puzzle, but he didn't need to understand the entire picture. The wound was healed—there was no use reopening it now.

"I told your mother it was too soon, you were too young—" he began, but I cut him off.

"No, no, it's okay. Really. Mama and I will figure it out." We needed a topic change. "How's work going?"

He told me, and I noticed that he was softer now, kinder. His temper was not as short, a fuse always being lit. I couldn't understand what it was until he said something about Ahsen.

"These past few months, Ahsen called me from Boston every week," he said. "When I yell at him, he doesn't yell back. I stopped yelling. He's changed a lot. He sounds happy. Even smiles when he is home. This time when he came, he hugged me."

My father's eyes seemed to glaze over, like he was talking to himself. I had never seen my father speak so rawly, so honestly. It bothered something within me, but in a good way. Then he refocused on me.

"Did he see you in August? He said he went to Florida with his friends, but when he came back, he seemed different. More like you. He cared more."

"No, Baba," I told him. "He didn't see me." Baba nodded to himself, and I saw him lost in wonder.

"I think it was you who changed him," he said. "Something about you."

I shook my head. "It wasn't me. I may have been a small part of it, but really, it was all him. He's trying harder to be better, and I don't know if you guys are okay, but please don't fight anymore. He's had a tough time too."

"We don't argue so much anymore," he told me. "This

summer he will graduate and get a job, and I don't want to lose him like we lost you."

He didn't mean to upset me, but fresh tears welled up in my eyes. I quickly blinked them away. I had never wanted to go. I had never wanted to be lost to my family.

"You haven't lost me, Baba," I said, voice scratched. "I came back, didn't I?"

"Not completely. But it's okay. You need time, maybe."

I nodded. Gathering my courage, I took his hand as I used to so many years ago, when I could still fit in his lap and his hair wasn't as gray. Then, I would trace the protruding veins on his hands, the wrinkles they made. I did the same now, and he smiled, remembering.

"There are more wrinkles now," I told him.

"Getting too old."

"Not too old yet."

Things were okay between us.

Chapter 36

The next day, Ahsen and I visited our grandparents at our mamoo's house. He was my mom's brother, and I forgot how much I had missed my extended family too. We knocked on the door, and in the few moments before we entered, fear flashed through me.

What if my little cousins had forgotten me?

"As-salaamu Alaikum!" Mamoo said, opening the door. He was a wide man with a thin beard and warm arms. He pulled me into an embrace. "We've missed you, gudiya."

"I missed you too," I said. Mamoo hugged Ahsen as I hugged my mami, his wife, and then I heard my little cousins running down the stairs to see who was at the door.

"Zahra Aapi!" the seven-year-old, Yashra, called. She bounced down the steps and hugged my legs.

"Hi, how are you?" I asked. I kneeled down to reach her eye level and gave her a big kiss on both cheeks. "I love your dress!"

"Thanks!" she said, twirling. She was adorable, and I hugged her again. My three-year-old cousin, Musa, stood behind her, and while he didn't recognize me entirely, he hadn't forgotten me, either.

"Look, it's Zahra Aapi," my mamoo said. Musa slowly offered his hand to me, and I laughed, shaking it.

"Hey, cutie," I said, pulling him into a hug. "I missed you."

"I miss you too," he said softly. My heart just about broke.

"Well, come in, come in," my mami said before I could get too emotional. "What are we all standing here for? Zahra, you haven't seen the baby yet, have you? I'm sure your mama sent you pictures, but come, see the little munchkin in person."

"The baby?" I repeated to Ahsen under my breath. He nodded and I remembered that my mami had been pregnant, so of course she had her baby while I was gone.

My breath caught, and I followed her into the living room, where my grandparents were sitting on armchairs. They were wrapped in chaddars, and my grandfather was wearing a warm woolen hat over his white hair. Both of their faces lit up when they saw Ahsen and me.

"Nana Abu," I said, hugging my grandfather. His beard scratched against my cheek. I was engulfed in warmth. I hugged my grandmother next, letting her envelop me in the softness of her arms.

"Kaise hain?" I asked them how they were, trying not to cry. I had missed them so much. Nano led me to the rocker where my newest little cousin was asleep. She was a rosy baby, three months old. Simply seeing her, I loved her. She was so squishy.

"What's her name?" I asked.

"Hadiya!" Yashra excitedly told me. "Isn't she so cute?"

I nodded, and sat in front of the rocker, touching her soft cheek. She scrunched her face, and I picked her up, pinching her chubby cheeks. She was so warm and cuddly, cooing and holding onto my finger. She was so small. I wanted to protect this little baby—wanted to be around to see her grow up.

"How have you been?" my mami asked me. "How's life? You have to tell us everything—it's been ages!"

"Everything's good, alhamdulillah. It's amazing," I replied.

We talked, and I played along with the half-truth of Baba's story that I'd gone to London. It was too difficult to explain the history, and besides, not everybody needed to know. It was all right, and nobody asked me anything about the wedding or the radio silence of the past months. They just accepted it and moved on, asking Ahsen about his school and graduation and looking for jobs.

I sat between my grandparents, my grandfather's arm around my shoulder, my grandmother's hand in mine, and we all enjoyed one another's company and warmth. This was family.

But we were missing my mother—these were her parents, her brother. She was the only one not there.

After spending the day with my cousins and grandparents and uncle and aunt, I came home to a silent house. My mother nowhere to be seen. She had made dinner and left it on the counter.

"Is Mama not coming?" I asked Baba when he, Ahsen, and I sat down to eat roti and saalan. Baba shook his head.

"I asked, but she doesn't want," he replied. "Said she's not hungry."

I sighed, and we ate in silence. Despite how full of light and love today had been, this house was still cold. I knew it wasn't all my fault. No single person was completely responsible for the upset in a family. But I had taken part in the fissuring, and I wanted to fix it.

"Ya Allah," I said, alone in my room that night. "Please have things work out with Mama and me. Please mend our relationship. Please."

I talked to Him because I was at peace with the way things were, but there was still one wound that needed to be sealed. I needed to clean the injury before I could be healthy again.

I needed to make things right with my mother.

Chapter 37

On the third night, I gathered my courage.

Give me strength, ya Allah, I prayed, heart beating fast.

I headed to my bedroom door.

Please, give me strength.

When I opened my door, across the hall I saw my mother's bedroom door open as well. I met her eyes, and everything went soft. She looked so sad, but calm too. Normal, almost—not angry.

Deep down, I knew she didn't want to be furious with me anymore because she did love me. So I imagined her holding my face in her hands and telling me she loved me, and the memory buoyed me.

"Will you come sit with me?" she asked, hesitant.

"Yes, Mama," I said. "Yes."

With tears in my eyes, I followed her into her room. *Thank you, Allah*, I whispered.

Relief soothed my curled fists, but anxiety still simmered

in my stomach. I went and sat on the chair across from her bed, thinking about that time I had been in her room, when she had first found out. I had accepted defeat then, retreating and running away, but I refused to let this battle continue any longer.

The war would end today. It would end. We would be okay.

"Tell me from the beginning," she said, hands folded in her lap. "Tell me what happened. The truth."

"From the beginning?" I repeated. From the beginning of when? Looking into her black eyes, the same as mine, I felt all my resolve crumble. All the strength I had reserved inside me vanished.

I had hurt her. My mother. I had hurt her so much. I could see it now. How deep the wound was. And the distance between us was wider than the thousands of miles that had separated us these past months.

Where do I begin?

"Um," I started, voice shaking. I swallowed hard, trying to collect my thoughts. She was waiting, patient, and somehow, I felt like I had lost her. Without the anger, my mother seemed indifferent, almost. At least when she was furious, I knew she had cared.

Now I was scared I had taken myself too far away to be recovered.

"Mama," I said, and I began to cry. I didn't want to, and I didn't want her to think I was trying to make her feel sorry for me, but I couldn't help myself. My throat was clogged. My eyes overflowed with tears. I started to rub my eyes, trying to rub the pain away, but I couldn't. It was too deep inside me.

"I—um—I'm—" I hiccuped. I was a stuttering mess, unable to articulate myself. This was so much harder than I had thought it would be. I didn't know how to move past this, like I had made it somewhere I couldn't go beyond. Like I was stuck behind a gate and no matter how I pushed, it would not open or yield.

But my mama reached me halfway.

"Zahra," she said, voice breaking. "Idhar ao."

The way she said it, it wasn't a command or an order. She was pleading with me to come to her.

I shook my head. *I can't. I can't.*

After all the pain I had caused, I still felt ashamed.

"Zahra," Mama said, this time her voice steady. "Jaan, idhar ao."

Finally, I did.

I was a kid again, sniffling and crawling into my mom's bed. She was on the other end, but she met me in the middle, this time pulling me close to her. Suddenly, we were hugging, limbs crashing into each other, and I couldn't remember the last time I had felt her body against mine. I felt her wet cheek against my neck.

"Talk to me," she cried. "Zahra, talk to me, please."

When I pulled away, her face was as pink and crushed as mine. I took a deep breath.

Where did I begin? With the truth.

"I never wanted to go," I said, wiping my eyes. "But in the end I felt like I had no choice, and I'm sorry for what I put you through when I left."

I bit my lip. The words hurt to release, but I had to speak them. I had to let them out.

"You didn't deserve that. It was cruel of me, and I'm so sorry. But I had to go."

I steadied my breath. Found my strength. I thought of Ahsen and Baba and Haya. I thought of Mama holding my face in her hands when I was a little girl.

"I never wanted to hurt you," I told her. "I never wanted any of this, but I can't complain because I feel like I'm a better person than I was before, Mama. I feel like it was only when everything fell apart that I really realized who I am and how I want to be. And I'm trying my hardest, I promise, to be a good person. To be someone you can be proud of. And I know I did things I shouldn't have, that I did things that were wrong and made you ashamed, and I'm sorry, but I'm better now. I promise. Let me show you. Give me a chance."

"Give you a chance?" she asked, confused. She shook her head. "I don't need to. I know how good you are—I always have. Do you think because of one mistake I would think you were an awful person? That I would forsake you?"

She shook her head, but I didn't understand, either.

"Then why were you so angry?" I asked, voice breaking. "If you didn't hate me for what I did, why did you always seem so cruel? You were always yelling at me, and I felt like you were just waiting for me to screw up again."

"You think I hated you?" she asked, eyes sad. Shock contorted her countenance. "No, bachi, *you* hated *me*."

"What?"

"You were so angry," she explained. She swallowed. "At everything. At everyone. Always snapping at me. I wanted to help, to talk to you. I wanted to be there for you, but it was like I didn't exist to you. You never spoke, never responded."

"No. No, I thought you hated me," I told her, shaking my head, shocked by her words. *Is that really how she felt?* "I thought you were angry with me."

"Just because I'm your mother doesn't mean I don't make mistakes," she said, eyes wide. For the first time, she looked young. "You shut everyone out, and I realized we weren't as close as I thought we were, so I did get angry, at times. Yes, I did snap at you, but it was because I wanted you to talk to me. To ask me for help because I would have given it to you."

Her voice broke, and she paused. Looking down, she fiddled with the gold bracelet on her wrist. She was still looking down when she continued, voice a little quieter. "I'm not proud of how I reacted or what I said, but I didn't know how to deal with it. And I thought maybe I could shake you hard enough to snap out of it because Allah knew giving you space and letting you alone was pushing you further away." She released a breath, looking up to meet my gaze again.

"And about the marriage—I gave you those options because those were the same options given to me. After my ammi caught me talking to the boy in the garden, she told me I could either get married or devote myself to studies, to invest in the future and forget the past. I chose marriage, and it turned out okay. So, I said the same to you because I didn't know what else to do."

I heard the fear in her voice, how scared and lost she had been.

"What could I do but sit there and think how this was all my fault? That I did something wrong in raising you that made you feel you couldn't turn to me when everything was falling apart? I'm your mother. I always wanted to be the first person you turned to, not the last. What could I do when you were hurting, and I couldn't help you?

"What could I have done?"

And I realized I had no idea.

What had I wanted her to do? What would I have done if I had been in her place?

I supposed I had wanted her to listen to my side of the story, to be calm and to understand, not yell at me. Not frighten me. But then I realized, too, that it was culture. It was ingrained in my mother to scare me in order to protect me. It was how her mother and the mothers before her had protected their children, so of course she would do the same.

And hadn't it worked, in some twisted way? Hadn't I learned the hard way to never do anything close to that ever again?

I had never actually told her how I felt or what I wanted or what I needed. I had simply expected her to know—to be everything I wanted her to be as my mother.

When she wasn't, I had gotten angry—just as she had gotten angry when I hadn't been what she expected me to be. Neither of us had ever spoken. We had just wanted and wanted and then been disappointed.

"I guess I understand why you acted the way you did," I admitted. "But . . . I didn't know how to talk to you because I was so ashamed. I didn't know how to act normal because . . . well, I felt so guilty. It was easier to just push everyone away."

We had both been wrong. We had both handled things horribly and hurt each other and behaved badly. It would take too long to go back and forth, to relive each grievance and remember and reanalyze. It didn't matter anymore.

Because the truth was, I forgave her. I forgave her, and I knew she forgave me too.

So what was left?

"I love you, Mama," I told her.

That's what mattered. The past was over; it was gone. What was left was *now*. The future.

"Meri jaan," she said. She tucked a strand of my hair behind my ear. Her lips flickered into a broken smile and in her eyes, I saw tears, which made me want to cry with both happiness and despair. "And you think that I don't love you?"

I lifted my shoulders into a half-shrug, half-shaking my head. I didn't know what to think. I still didn't. But the way she asked made me certain of how absurd the notion even was.

"Of course I love you," she said. "Of course. You're my daughter. You're my girl. My favorite thing in the world is to be your mother. Haven't I always told you I love you as the moon loves the stars?"

"You did," I said through tears. "But it didn't always feel like it."

"I'm sorry I didn't do a good job of showing it, but don't

ever think I don't love you," she said, gripping my shoulders. I met her gaze and saw the truth and ferocity of her words there. "*Never.*"

There wasn't anything left to say. We both leaned back against the headboard. I let my head drop onto her chest, and we both breathed, faces wet and eyes teary. Mama's arm was still around me—we were fused.

It was the start.

Chapter 38

The next morning, I woke up early and headed to the kitchen.

It was what I had always done in the past. The secret to Pakistani mothers' hearts was always in the kitchen—in cleaning and cooking. I washed the dishes, then began Mama's breakfast like I used to on anniversaries or birthdays or Mother's Days. I hoped she still had the same taste as I began assembling the components.

I made her chai with a quarter teaspoon of sugar and a dash of milk—she liked it strong. While I cooked her eggs with loads of vegetables and cheese, I toasted whole wheat bread until it was crispy and spread butter across its browned edges.

Baba was at work, Ahsen was asleep. The house was quiet. It felt strange, at first, like these past six months hadn't even happened, like I had never left. But I pushed the cobwebs of anxiety away from my tummy and breathed.

Things *were* different. I was different, even if this house was the same.

I was just finishing up making coffee for myself when Mama entered the kitchen.

"Making breakfast?" Mama asked. She offered me a small smile—this was just as awkward for her as it was for me.

Seeing my mother standing there tentatively made me realize how young she was. It was interesting how much older Mama had seemed back then, like the distance between us was so many miles apart. But now, it felt like we were almost on the same level, or just a few feet apart.

It wasn't fair of me to put her on a pedestal and forget that she was still finding her way too. She stepped closer. I inhaled the scent of powder and cotton.

"You still like it this way, right?" I asked. She came closer, eyeing what I'd made. She nodded.

"Yes," she said. "But you didn't have to. I was thinking of making you a paratha. You must not have had it in so long."

"Sooo long. I really missed your cooking," I admitted. "You can make it for me tomorrow morning."

I made myself chai, split the omelet, and grabbed some toast for myself. We sat at the counter and ate our food in silence. The air felt delicate, but not entirely in a bad way. When we were done eating, we took our mugs and moved to the living room. We sipped our warm drinks, staring out at the wintry backyard.

The sky was a soft white gray, and the trees were bare, and it was home.

We were both trying to bring things back to normal, whatever that was now. But we had both changed, so the mold of who we were and what our relationship was had shifted. But I knew, with time, we could fit together again.

"What did you usually eat for breakfast over there?" she asked me. "Pancakes?"

"Actually, I got really used to New York bagels," I replied. "I know everyone says they're amazing, so you don't know if you should believe them, but they really are. But sometimes if I'm running late, I'll only have coffee."

"Tch, you know you shouldn't have coffee on an empty stomach," Mama said. "I always tell you."

But she wasn't angry or upset—it was simply the concern of a mother. I smiled.

"I know, I know," I said. "But sometimes I don't have time to make anything! Then I'm starving by lunch, so, yeah, it is a bad idea."

"What do you do to keep yourself busy?" she asked. "School?"

"No, I'm actually working for now," I told her. "I might start school up again, though."

I had been considering it these past few months, though I hadn't applied anywhere yet. Maybe I was ready to go to university next fall.

"You should," Mama told me. "You've always been so smart and hardworking."

She had no idea how much those words meant to me. Knowing that my mama believed in me made all the difference.

"What are you working as?" she asked me.

There was so much learning we had to do, so we talked and

talked. I told her about everything—about my friends and the community and my jobs and how content I was with everything and everyone. It was similar to the way I had caught up with Ahsen—just as I had asked him how his months had been, I asked my mother.

It was strange at first, because I never really talked to my mother before like she was a friend, like she was an equal. But I was starting to learn. And so was she.

"You know Shumaila Auntie?" she asked. "She started doing a Qur'an class every Tuesday at the masjid, so I've been going to that. She's an excellent teacher and inspired me to take classes online. So, I've been busy with being a student again, after so long."

I asked her more, and this time, I listened while she talked. It was awkward in the beginning, but the more we talked, the more comfortable we got. We were getting better, but I knew it would be difficult.

It will take time.

That evening after dinner, I laid down in bed, emotionally exhausted. I wondered how long it would take for Mama and me to fall back into place, and suddenly I was afraid. Being apart for so long had made things awkward between us, but she was my mother, and of course things would be okay in the end.

But what about Haya? And my friends in New York? Would they forget about me and move on? We had really only known each other for a few months.

Just the thought made me inconsolably upset, but then, by the grace of Allah, my phone rang.

I answered and immediately my best friend sprang into dramatics.

"ZAHRA! I'm going to die," Haya proclaimed. "*Die!*"

She was breathing in short little bursts, and I could imagine her sitting on her bed, flustered, and fanning herself. It was around midnight there, so around nine in California. I sat up on my bed.

"Salaam to you too." I laughed. "What happened? What's wrong?"

Just hearing her voice centered me, reminding me that I had a life and people who loved me across the country too. People who wouldn't forget about me.

"Wonderboy," she said, exasperated. "I can't deal with his stupid curly hair."

"I'm sure the dimples don't help," I added.

"Nor does the fact that he wants to marry me," she said flippantly. I screamed.

"WHAT. MARRY? YOU'RE, LIKE, TWELVE?" It had only been a couple of days since we last saw each other, but so much had suddenly changed.

"I KNOW," she replied, equally shaken. "Remember when we told each other we liked each other and wanted to see where it would go? Well apparently, now he's so certain he likes me—and he knows that I don't date, and he doesn't want to, either—that he said he wants to *marry* me one day. Emphasis on *one day*. If I could ever feel so strongly for him."

I squealed. "What did you say?"

"I said I had to think about it and get back to him," she

responded. I could imagine her biting her lips. "But . . . gah. This is so much. Like, I am a child! I'm an eighteen-year-old child! And so is he! I don't know if this will last. I want it to, but I don't know how to feel."

"Okay, first, take a deep breath." She did as I said. "Now, let's talk this through," I said. "Do you like him and like being around him?"

"Definitely. A lot. Obviously."

"How does he make you feel when you're around him?"

"Like I can do anything in the world. Like I'm a good person. I feel like the best version of myself, a version that I only feel like around people like you and Sadaf and Mama and Baba."

"Are you guys compatible?"

"I think so."

"Do you think he makes you a better person?" I asked.

She didn't even need to consider the question. "Absolutely," she replied. "Like, at first, it was all him asking me technical questions about Islam. And I have the knowledge because of everything Mama and Baba taught us through the years, but, Zahra—he has the heart and soul. Genuinely. I feel like he's been Muslim all his life because he's embodied the core characteristics all along."

"Ooh, really? In what way?"

"He's so open-minded and kind and forgiving. And I feel like he's always reminding me of things. Like, if I'm ever annoyed at anyone for anything, he makes up a thousand excuses for them until I'm not annoyed anymore. And he's always reminding me to make sure I pray and to talk to Allah and, I can't explain it, but he's so *good*. Asking about my parents and you and finding ways to be more active at the masjid. He makes me want to be good too."

"You should tell him how you feel," I told her.

"Yeah, I probably should," she agreed. "Just to be clear . . . how *do* I feel again?"

"You tell me, and I'll let you know if it sounds right," I said, laughing. For someone so smart, she really could be stupid. But it was like she said—we're all fools in love.

"I feel—" she paused, taking a deep breath. I could feel her thinking and almost sense the moment things fell into place. "I feel like in a few years, when we're both sorted and ready for it, I would want to marry him." She paused, then squealed. "Ah, that's wild!"

"It is!"

"And until then," she continued, "we could check in on each other, and be distant-friends-with-feelings? Because I don't want to date, and I think the more time we spend together, the harder it'll be to stay halal, you know?"

"Well, what are you waiting for!" I said, smiling. "Tell him. Because to me, that sounds right."

"Ugh, thank you, as always. You're the best."

"Of course, what else am I here for?"

"But, Zahra, wait. I want to say something else," Haya said, dead serious. "I want you to know—you were, and still are, the answer to my prayers."

My heart sang to hear her say that. "What?"

"You're my best friend in the whole world," she told me, sniffling. "And I never told you this, but about six months before I met you, my then-best friend and I had a parting of ways. It was an unhealthy relationship, and I felt like I was investing so much love while getting nothing back. And so for a while, I felt like I had nobody. I mean, of course, I had Sadaf, but she's my sister, you know? I didn't have that main person.

"And I kept wishing I wasn't so alone. It felt like everyone I loved was so far away—my best friend/cousin Mina all the way in Pakistan, my family friends at different colleges. Mina told me to pray. She said Allah sends people our way when we least expect them, that He had sent someone her way, and it just clicked.

"Then one day I was in the masjid and I saw you enter, and you looked so sad, but so alive beneath it all too. And I felt like I just had to say hello, so I did, and now I can't imagine what my life would be like without you in it."

"Haya, you're making me ugly cry right now," I told her, half-laughing, half-crying into the phone. I could hear she was doing the same. "You can't begin to understand what that means to me. I love you so much, and truly, *you* saved *me*. I didn't even know what to pray for back then, but Allah must have known I needed you, so He crossed our paths. And I'm so happy He did. And I'm sorry that in the beginning I was selfish at times and acted so awfully."

"No, don't apologize!" she told me fiercely. "You were sick. And anyway, I think you made me a better person because I knew I had to be gentle with you, so I learned to be kind with others and myself too. If that makes sense. Like, if you were hurting, I tried to help you, which taught me to help myself when I was hurting too—instead of telling myself I was being dramatic or overly emotional. Because I would never have said that to you, so I shouldn't have said it to myself either."

"Aw."

We both sighed.

"I miss you so much," I told her.

"I miss you too," she said. "Do you know when you might be coming home?"

"It's hard to tell, but I don't think for at least a couple of weeks," I said, releasing a long breath. I fell back onto the pillows. "I'm looking for someone to sublet my room to, and Lubna Auntie said they'll cover for me at the restaurant. And I already talked to the tutoring clients for a more extended leave, which thankfully, they were all cool with."

"Aw, okay," Haya said. "I'm glad things are covered, but please come home soon! We all miss you! My parents keep asking about you, and Sadaf too, and all the girls at Youth Group."

"I miss you all too!" I replied. "Tell Auntie and Uncle I miss them. And what's the update on the girls? What am I missing?"

"Everyone is making big moves—Naadia got into medical school! Imaan is applying to some journalism conference, and she and Madiha are scheming to go to Ireland for spring break, can you believe that? I told them they better bring me back a nice woolen sweater or a scarf at least and told them to bring you something too. Oh, and Sadaf's graduation is in May, and we really want you there! So come home! Immediately!"

I hoped I would.

But Mama and I still needed time. We had all the time in the world, in a sense, because I was ready to stay in California until things were okay again, but I missed New York too. The routine and the people and the work that I had there. It was another life. And I wished I could be here and there at the same time, somehow fusing my two lives together.

I wondered if I would spend my whole life torn between two lives, living in one while yearning and aching for the other.

Chapter 39

About a week later, Ahsen went back to college in Boston for his last semester. The house felt emptier without him.

We had never been phone people, even Before, and despite being closer now than ever, it felt strange to call him. We usually just hung out in person, not really talking about much unless it came up naturally. But Allah was listening, knowing exactly what I needed, because some time later, Ahsen called me.

"I got a job!" he said, beyond ecstatic. "In the Bay Area!"

"You're lying! You're coming home for real?" I asked. My heart surged. It was so nice to hear his voice.

"Yup, after graduation, so a little far off, but still," he said. "You can't get rid of me."

"I'm so excited," I told him. "I can't believe you're moving back."

"Well, don't tell Mama or Baba yet. I want to tell them in person when I come home. I'm planning on visiting the first weekend I have time."

"Don't worry," I told him. "I won't say anything. But come home quick! It's weird without you here."

"It was weird without you there too, last summer," he told me. "But I'm glad we both found our way back."

I was glad too.

"How are things?" he asked. "With you and Mama?"

"Things are getting better," I told him. "We just need time, I think. I can't believe how wrong I've been."

"Join the club." My brother laughed. "You think you've got everything and everyone figured out, but turns out you were wrong the whole time."

"Honestly," I replied, shaking my head. "And I was wrong about pretty much everything. You and Baba, but especially Mama. I made her out to be such a villain, but I guess it was because it was easier to blame her for all the shit going wrong."

"What caused the change of heart?"

"I don't know," I said. "I've just been paying better attention. Thinking about things from her perspective. Being more open-minded, like I always wished she would be."

"You get what you give," he told me. "So keep giving. It'll be hard, but insha'Allah things will keep getting better. You got this."

I followed Ahsen's advice, even though he had once been the last person in the world I would have expected to be helpful. He warned me it would be tough, but I had no idea just how difficult healing would be. How long it would take.

With Baba at work and Ahsen in Boston, it was only Mama and me at home. We talked a lot, learning about each other, spending time together. I tried to do things that would make her happy, like cook for her or wash the dishes or tidy up. I knew she appreciated it. We sat together too, watching Pakistani dramas, or talking about world news. Or she would show me funny Facebook posts, and I would show her pictures of New York.

And while at times we got along perfectly, it was easy to remember why I had gotten so frustrated with her, and her with me.

Sometimes we would be cruel again, but we were both trying not to be.

In those difficult moments, I wanted to revert to being angry and upset, then anxious and depressed. But in those times, I called upon everything Eya had taught me in therapy—the breathing exercises and stretches and soothing words. I didn't think back to every past grievance or imagine a bleak future filled with cruel or frustrating instances. I stayed in the moment, until the darkness passed and I was okay again.

Love was a choice. You had to keep choosing love. Over and over again, you had to choose to forgive and move forward and heal.

I forgave my mother for anything and everything, making sure to sleep with no hard feelings. Making sure to never let little grievances build up into an explosion ever again. I forgave her for Allah's sake and for her sake and for my own sake. I video-chatted with Eya once every other week for therapy.

I kept choosing love.

Ahsen was right—the more I gave, the more I got. Almost like every ounce of love that flowed from me returned to me tenfold. I didn't notice at first, but slowly, we both softened. I couldn't remember exactly when it happened, but the love within me for my mother grew and grew.

Time passed—January into February, February into March—and we healed.

Everything was good. I wanted to stay here, but I also wanted to go home.

I wanted to go back to New York. I had gotten accepted to culinary school there. I had also applied to some universities in California and gotten in, and while I could stay here, what I really wanted was to go back to New York and start this new chapter of my life, studying there.

But I couldn't bring myself to ask. Couldn't bring myself to leave again, not when things were finally getting better.

If I left, I didn't know what would happen to everything behind me. Back then, when I had run away, I hadn't cared. I had thought it was best . . . but now? I couldn't leave my mama or my baba. Not again.

So I stayed.

It was March now. The winter was starting to thaw, greenery peeking back into the landscape with the rebirth of spring. Flowers were beginning to bud in the bushes, and the world wasn't as cold anymore. It rained a lot, the earth being revived with water to soon give way to the gorgeous blooming of summer. The sun shone a little brighter, a little longer.

Everything was glittering. We were lucky enough to

witness a June day in March, on which the sun shone through the pouring rain. The rain itself was beautiful, streaming down like waterfalls, the sky a soft blue. And right afterward, when everything was wet, the sun spread across the greenery, making everything glisten so bright you almost had to look away.

It was my favorite weather.

It felt like a gift as I pulled into the driveway. Ahsen was home for spring break, and I wanted to get him to drive us all to a park nearby so we could properly enjoy the day. I intended to tell him once I got inside, but when I unlocked the door to my house, I was struck by the silence. Wondering why everything was so dark, I reached for the lights and—

"Surprise!"

I gasped.

It was my family.

But not only Mama and Baba and Ahsen. My grandparents and uncles and aunts and cousins were there too. The house was full of people and faces, old and young, all familiar.

"Happy birthday!" they all shouted. A laugh burst out of me, and I covered my mouth with my hand, crying a little and laughing too. I was emotional in the best way.

"Oh my *God*," I blubbered. "Who did this?"

And my mama, the most beautiful person in the world, came forward and wrapped me in her arms.

"Happy birthday, jaan," she whispered, squeezing me into her. She kissed my cheek. "I know your birthday is tomorrow but we wanted to give you a surprise."

"Well, it worked!" I cried, laughing into her arms. I was handed along to my relatives, getting hugs and kisses from everyone, and it was a massive party. So many people brought together after so long, and it was all for me. I felt beyond loved.

Everyone was so happy to see me—I could feel it in the air. We spent the evening eating and playing games and lounging around in the living room. Mama made Black Forest cake, and I blew out nineteen candles while looking out at the faces of all these people who loved me.

After eating, we adjourned to the living room, and there wasn't enough space for everyone, but somehow, we all fit—kids on laps and people on the floor and bodies squished on sofas, no one wanting to be apart from the gathering.

These people, their lives, their histories, their stories—they intertwined with me and the people I loved most.

I could have stayed there forever, sipping warm chai and laughing.

The next day, I woke up to breakfast in bed. It was over the top and too special, but it warmed me all the way to my toes. I looked at Mama and Baba, piling onto the bed with me, passing one another plates and juice and fruit, and I couldn't stop the grin spreading across my face.

It felt like a dream, everything rosy and sunny.

"I made the french toast," Ahsen told me proudly.

"After burning two batches," my mother added.

"Well, *I* made the coffee," Baba said. "Like you always make mine."

"Everything is perfect!"

I spent my nineteenth birthday drenched in love, surrounded by my family.

It was so vastly different from my last, when I had been at my worst. Just one year had changed everything. My last birthday felt like a year and a war and a lifetime ago.

I felt one hundred years old. I felt six years old. Both too old and too young, but really, I was just right. And I was excited for the long stretch of life I had ahead of me. Excited for the people I would meet and the places I would go and the love I would feel.

I felt divine. God-loved and God-blessed.

I had so much love within me, it was incredible, and I knew it was all from Allah. He was inside me; He always had been. All the good and all the light within me was from Him. And I was done letting the light be drowned by the darkness.

I would love and love and love.

That night, after a day of activities and food and laughter, Mama, Baba, Ahsen, and I all sat at the dinner table, eating together.

As I looked around the table at their faces, I knew that no matter how much I had ever hated them, I loved them too. Loved them more.

I couldn't fathom my own peace and faith and hope and love. Couldn't fathom how I hadn't had any of this last year.

Now, I had everything.

Well, almost everything. But even that Mama gave to me.

Late at night, Mama came and sat on my bed with me. It was almost time to sleep, but I was accustomed to her seeking my company now. We had both gotten used to each other. I put my phone to the side and smiled at her.

"Today was the best birthday I've ever had," I told her, leaning against a pillow. "Thank you."

"Pagal ladki, your birthday isn't over," she said, smiling. "I haven't even given you your gift yet."

"Ooh, what did you get me?" I asked, sitting up. "Personally, I think we should all go on vacation."

"I agree," she said, responding seriously to my joke. I cocked my head to the side.

"Seriously? Then, I'm thinking Egypt. You've always wanted to go see the Pyramids."

"How about New York?" she said, handing me an envelope. I paused, understanding her meaning.

I didn't even open it. I simply gave it back.

"No, Mama," I said, voice thick. I shook my head. "No, I can't go."

"Tch, kyu nahi?" she asked, eyes warm. "It's from all of us."

"I don't want to leave you all." I didn't want to ruin anything. Mama smiled and put her hand on my cheek.

"Don't worry, jaan," she said. "I saw the email open on your desktop—culinary school?" She paused, eyes tearing. "Zahra, I am so proud of you. I want you to go, to learn, to enjoy your life."

"But I don't want to leave you." My voice shook.

"It's okay," she told me. She took my hands in hers. "We'll be okay."

I wanted both. Here and there. But I couldn't have both.

"No matter how far you go," she told me, "this will never change. You will always be my daughter, and I will always be your mother." She was infinitely gentle. "Go to the life you worked so hard to make for yourself. There isn't much left for you here."

"But *you're* here," I said. "My family is here."

"And we aren't going anywhere," she said, voice sure. "You visit, and so will we. I want to try all the new dishes you'll learn how to make. Maybe you can teach me a thing or two as well."

I didn't know what to say.

"I know you miss your friends," Mama said sadly. "I know you miss your work and everything you built for yourself. I know, meri jaan. I know." She smiled, eyes teary. "And I'm sorry we couldn't be enough for you here, but all I want is for you to be happy."

"No, Mama," I said. "Don't think that. I was just . . . greedy. I was lost. You are enough. You're more than enough."

Mama smiled.

"Still. Go," she said, pushing the envelope into my hands. "With your mother's blessings, go."

Here Ahsen and Baba and Mama were sending me off, and there I had Haya and Sadaf and my life waiting for me when I landed. The past and the present, and together they would fuse to create the future.

On the plane, suspended between here and there, I was both happy and sad. But I knew I would make the most of it. I would be okay. I was content, and everything was good and happy and pure. I would stay in touch. We would visit. I was going to my friends, to another perfect life.

And I was the luckiest person in the world to have two homes.

Acknowledgments

Alhamdulillah, all praise is for Allah; everything that I have and am is because of Him. I am so grateful I've been given the opportunity to publish another book, especially this one, and it is my sincere hope that my works are a source of goodness in this world, now and long after I am gone.

Thank you to my wonderful agent, Emily Keyes, who juggles the chaos of my career with such grace; I appreciate you so much. Thank you to my editor, Stacy Whitman, for your tireless work. Thank you to my other editor, Elise McMullen-Ciotti, who believed in this story from the start and gave me crucial editing guidance that made this book shine. Thank you to copyeditors Sheeba Arib, Melissa Kavonic, and Jill Amack for your fine-toothed combing.

Thank you to my family: Mama, Baba, Sameer, Zaineb, and Ibraheem. Thank you to Papa and Mimi, to Khala and all the kids, and my best-friend cousins, Hamnah, Umaymah, Noor, and Mahum. You guys are my support and add such vibrancy to my life. I don't know where I would be without you. I am so glad Allah chose us to be bound in this life, and I hope we are together in the Next.

Thank you to the best friends in the whole world: Arusa, Isra, Sara, and Justine. Thank you to Sadaf; I wrote book-Sadaf before I met you, and I'm just as lucky as Zahra to have you. Thank you to Uroosa, who influenced so much of the Youth Group scenes from our own time at Selden Masjid; you inspired a generation. Thank you to Biha, for reading a messy draft of this back in 2016 and for always supporting me.

Thank you to my wonderful bookish friends and early readers: Ifrah, Fatima, Silke, Famke, Narjis, Alaa, Kashvi, Humnah, Amani, Umamah, Iqra, and Sahar. Thank you to Saydah and Ammarah, for using this book as a comp title; that was an author goal of mine you checked off, and it made me so happy.

Thank you to the wonderful authors who blurbed this book and showed support: Karuna Riazi, Adiba Jaigirdar, Jesmeen Kaur Deo, Racquel Marie, and Christina Li. Thank you to Sheila Smallwood for the beautiful cover and interior design. Thank you to Kate Forrester for the gorgeous cover illustration. Thank you to Jenny Choy, Shaughnessy Miller, and Jen Khawam in Marketing and Publicity for your excellent work promoting my book.

Thank you to the book bloggers and fans on social media who have been hyping this book and building excitement. Thank you to everyone who has spread the word about me and my books. Thank you to everyone who has bought a copy or requested it at their library. The love and support of perfect strangers never fails to astound me.

I hope this book is a source of healing and joy for all those who read it. I hope, also, that it gives people a glimpse into my wonderful religion of Islam, which is the sole reason for which I am here today. And if you can, I ask that you forgive, be kind, and spread love in this world.

Please pray for me.